THE
PRIVATE
RESERVE

THE PRIVATE RESERVE

JASON HUEBINGER

NEW YORK   LOS ANGELES

Jacket design by Rejenne Pavon
Jacket Copyright © 2025 by Winding Road Stories
Interior Design by A Raven Design
ISBN#: 978-1-960724-40-3 (pbk)
ISBN#: 978-1-960724-41-0 (ebook)

Published by Winding Road Stories
www.windingroadstories.com

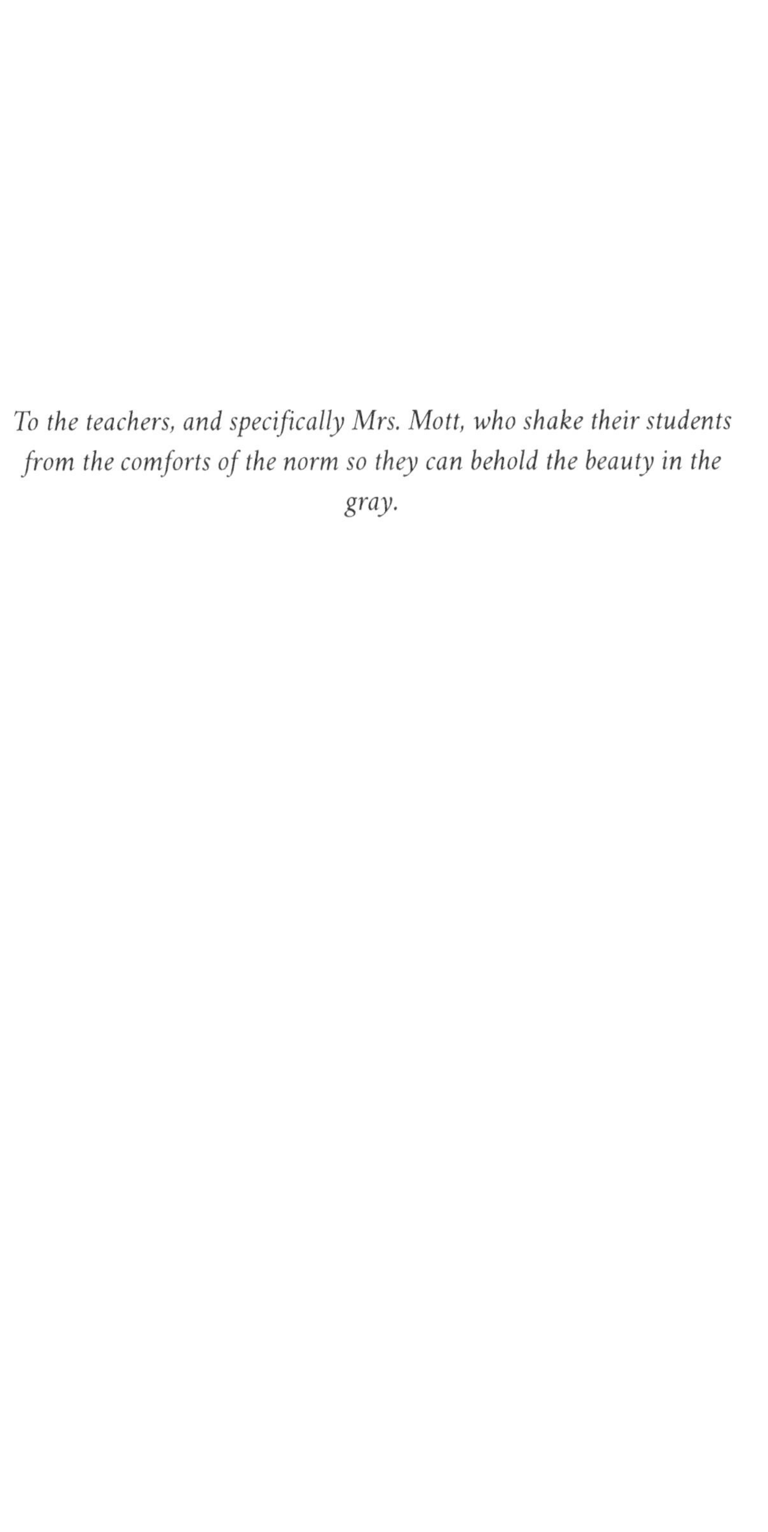

To the teachers, and specifically Mrs. Mott, who shake their students from the comforts of the norm so they can behold the beauty in the gray.

1

———

Jacob flicked on the flashlight. The beam cut through the night, revealing his masterpiece. The sudden brightness startled him, and he scanned the scene to ensure he was alone. Satisfied, he returned to examining his work, each detail a seed that would grow into his envisioned vineyard.

"Perfect," he muttered. His mother would have chastised him for such declarations of overconfidence, but humility is best reserved for lesser accomplishments.

He clicked off the flashlight and slid it into his pocket. The sweet, icy air tickled his arms, delivering a pleasant chill down his spine. He shut his eyes to better appreciate the stillness. His heart began to decelerate. His breathing slowed, and his racing thoughts unified into a single, coherent vision so clear he could taste it.

Now, he concluded, *time to get my hands dirty.*

He turned away from his creation and headed back to the truck. Before entering, he kicked the tires to knock the grit from his shoes. Unlike outside, the interior of the truck was not at all peaceful. As he still had time to kill, he took a moment for himself, closing his eyes and blocking everything out. He had planned for this moment for so long, and his careful planning, so far, bore delicious fruit.

A soft buzz shattered his trance. He blinked and searched for the source of the buzzing. His iPhone in the cupholder was lit. As he read the message, his pulse raced.

After rereading the text, he again opened the truck's door, stepped outside, and stood motionless, the phone hanging in his arm, rage building within his chest. Unable to contain himself, he screamed, "Shit!"

His voice echoed, mocking him and his arrogance. His mother, as always, was right: *You haven't finished a race until you are looking back at the finish line.*

Jacob slammed his foot again into the truck's tire. He wanted to tear something apart, rip something to shreds, yet he understood his plan relied on creation, not destruction. He could ill afford to succumb to his primal desires. There would be ample time for that later.

Only a hitch, he concluded. *Only a hitch in the plan.*

His anger tempered; he slid back into the driver's seat. He shifted calmly to gaze into the backseat. A body thrashed like a wounded animal caught in a bear trap. The body tried to lunge forward, but the ropes prevented it.

Jacob grinned as he watched Ethan thrash. But Jacob knew he dealt with dangerous prey. Unlike others, Ethan would not so willingly submit. If Jacob wasn't careful, Ethan could and would seize any advantage afforded. This was part of what made Ethan desirable. What good was a dull hunt?

Jacob leaned in and said, "I want you to know something."

Ethan did not react to Jacob's words and instead continued to resist. Frustrated, Jacob flung his open right palm forward and across Ethan's face, stunning him.

"Sorry," Jacob said. "I need your undivided attention."

Ethan's shock lasted but a moment before he returned to struggling.

"Listen up, asshole," Jacob yelled, grabbing both of Ethan's shoulders, shaking him as he spoke. "I was going to take you to see Jenna, but you screwed that up. Screwed that up royally. A royal-fucking-flush screwup. I have no clue how the hell you got a message out, but I'm gonna have to change plans now."

Ethan's resistance slowed, and he shifted his blindfolded eyes towards Jacob.

"Don't worry," Jacob continued, now tenderly rubbing Ethan's shoulders. "I know a quiet place where we can chat."

2

____

A buzz awoke Debra from her restless slumber at her desk. She cursed under her breath and prayed Bill had not noticed her slip away from the bed.

Her phone screen informed her of three missed calls, all from "Officer McCarthy." She returned his call, worried that he would resort to calling the "emergency" landline, which would wake her entire family.

After two rings, a gruff voice answered: "Deb?"

"Hey James," Debra said.

"I wake you?"

"No, I was just jogging on the treadmill." This lie skirted McCarthy's wrath about the truth. "So, what's up?"

"What's up? I'll tell ya. We got a murder-kidnap situation. A little girl taken."

Debra stood and grabbed her notepad. "Another girl?"

"What?"

Debra shook away fatigue and said, "Where?"

"Off of Sage. I'll text you the address. On my way there. Not many details to report."

She shifted the phone in her hand to select the speaker audio option but, in her haste, it slipped from her fingers and dropped to the floor. "Shit," she whispered under her breath as she grabbed it from the ground. She placed the phone on her desk and hit the speaker button.

"The hell was that?" McCarthy asked.

"Nothing. Don't worry about it. Give me what you have."

"Got a call a little before four from a woman in San Francisco named Sarah Meyers, 31-year-old Caucasian. Said her boyfriend, Ethan Paxton, fifty-four-year-old white male, got a strange text from his ex-wife, Beverly Paxton, 50-year-old Caucasian."

Debra scribbled notes and asked, "Yeah? What did the text say?"

"Here's the thing. The girl talked a thousand words a second. Gettin' all the details was damned hard. Something about his daughter, Jenna Paxton, nine. Don't know exactly. So, Ms. Meyers said Ethan leaves and drives to his former vacation home in Sonoma. About an hour later, Ms. Meyers gets a text from Ethan that says, 'call the police.'"

"Call the police? That's it? That's all she said?"

"Yeah, but I haven't seen the text. She reports the situation, the morning beat officer does a welfare check, and he finds Beverly's body. No sign of Jenna."

"Cause of death?"

"Stab wound. Knife near the body. Also, two cell phones in a pitcher of water. Huge house, Deb. I swear I'm in the wrong business."

"Issue an AMBER yet?"

"Yeah. You didn't get it?"

This question caught Debra by surprise. She swiped away from the call and checked her notification history. Sure enough, she did get the alert. The buzz from the message just had not been enough to wake her up.

"Debra, you alive?" McCarthy asked.

"Yeah, yeah. Sorry. I got it. Looks good. Tell me more about the scene."

"Havin' officers check the house top-to-bottom to make sure she isn't hiding. But I know what you're gonna say. That's not stoppin' me from settin' the parameter. I'm not countin' on finding this girl under her bed."

"Good." Debra considered a question, hesitating for a beat before asking, "Think it has anything to do with the Jodi Johnston case?"

McCarthy paused before intoning, "Debra—"

"I know," she interrupted. "I get it. Not supposed to touch it."

"Well, don't matter even if you could touch. Don't think it would be worth it. The cases are different. I mean, I get it. Two missing girls. But one bolted, and one's kidnapped."

Debra nodded, agreeing in principle. "Get moving. Every second counts with a missing child."

"Yes, ma'am."

"Let's see." She checked her watch and considered the distance to the scene. "I'll be there in like thirty. Don't touch anything until I get there."

"No promises."

She ended the call and sat for a few seconds in silence.

Why would he have Sarah call the cops? she wondered.

In her periphery, she spotted the outline of a folder. This folder contained important information about the Jodi Johnston case, and it rarely left her desk. She wasn't supposed to possess this folder, but she had read its contents obsessively the night prior before passing out on her hard wooden desk.

Jodi Johnston, a female in her early twenties, disappeared about six months earlier. After an extensive investigation, the working conclusion from the department was Johnston left voluntarily. Debra disagreed and pressed on until she was told, forcefully, to stop.

She shook her head, thinking about her last conversation

about the case with her Chief. Her ass would be cooked if he learned she still stayed up at night pouring her soul into that file.

She could not shake the Johnston case from her mind. Even if Jodi ran, what were the odds of two girls going missing in such a short period? It's not a big town.

Debra reached for the folder but pulled back. The cases were too different. She could not afford to waste time worrying about Jodi when Jenna was certainly kidnapped. She figured her fatigued mind drew connections that did not exist.

She stood and walked out the door. As she passed by the nearest bedroom, she heard a meek voice call, "Mom."

Though adrenaline surged through her veins, Debra could not resist the voice of her child. She cracked open the door and stuck her head in. "Everything okay, baby?" Debra asked.

"Yeah. I just heard you on the phone."

"You did?" She made a mental note to talk softer when discussing police business in her office. It also was a mistake to put McCarthy on speaker. "What did you hear?"

"Not a lot. Just something about a kid being missing. That man talks loud. He woke me up."

"We don't know if she's missing yet, baby. We're just not sure where she is right now. I'm sure we'll find her." She wanted to step into the room and cuddle with her beloved, but there was no time.

"I guess." Charlotte did not sound convinced.

"We can talk about it later," Debra continued, "But I have to get to it. Love you, baby, more than the moon and all the stars."

"Love you too, Momma."

Debra blew a kiss to Charlotte before shutting the door. She rested her head a moment on the wooden frame, collecting her frazzled thoughts.

In their bed lay her husband, Bill, fast asleep. If he had it his way, she guessed he would sleep until his afternoon classes.

Debra tiptoed to the bathroom, hoping not to wake Bill from his beauty rest. No time to shower, she dressed and applied makeup, adding more eyeshadow than usual to conceal her baggy eyes. She slipped out of the bathroom and headed to the door, but before she reached it, Bill said, "No matter how quiet you try to be, you always wake me up."

Debra chuckled and replied, "Sorry, gotta go. Pretty serious situation. You good to take Charlotte to school?"

"Yeah, yeah." He replied with a dismissive hand wave, his face still buried in the pillow. "I'll take care of everything. Go handle your business, Detective."

"I always do."

"Hey," Bill called out before Debra could exit, and she noticed timidity in his voice.

"Yeah?"

"I—" he paused, then continued. "I missed you in bed last night."

She sighed. "Sorry." She bowed her head and tried to think of an excuse. "I just couldn't sleep, I guess."

"You guess?"

"Alright," she shrugged. "I fell off the wagon." Her use of this cliché surprised her since she rarely drank. She knew better than to touch alcohol.

"It's alright, babe," he replied with a gentle tone. "Go take care of your business. We can talk about it later if you want."

She nodded, her eyes welled, and she wondered what she did in a past life to deserve such a patient husband. She guided the door shut and her eyes drifted to Charlotte's room. One of Debra's great joys was taking Charlotte to school each morning. Debra's heart always ached a little when work got in the way of their morning routine.

Charlotte on her mind, Debra gave in to her desires and headed back to her office. Picking up the Johnston file, she noticed she had placed it in front of her favorite picture of Charlotte.

Do I always put it there? Debra wondered, but only momentarily.

She lifted the folder and opened it. A picture of Jodi was taped on the top-right corner of the first page. Debra lingered on Jodi's wide smile and small dimples. Jodi's eyes, clear and unconcerned. Debra had handled many runaway cases in her career, and most runaway files contained a picture of a child with a dark expression or hollow eyes.

Under Jodi's file lay another, thinner file. This folder's cover was blank aside from two words: "Peter Sullivan." She'd be in hot water if the Department discovered she possessed a copy of its Johnston file; the Sullivan file would end with a one-way ticket out of the force. She grabbed the Sullivan file as well.

Folders in hand, she walked through the kitchen and the mud room into the garage. In her periphery, she noticed the second refrigerator, which was home to Bill's drink stash. Knowing she would not be able to make coffee, and with exhaust lines dancing within her vision, she opened the refrigerator, pushed aside a few of Bill's disgusting IPAs, and grabbed a single bottle of his pre-workout energy drinks. She had never consumed one before, but she had no choice this morning. She needed caffeine to excite her waning alertness.

She slid into her unmarked civilian vehicle and checked her phone. A notification displayed a new text from McCarthy: "1231 Sage. Get your ass here ASAP."

She put the address into her Google Maps, tossed the folders into the back seat, and pulled out of the garage. As she drove, her headlights cut through the fog-filled roads. Her eyes drifted towards her rear-view mirror and its reflection of the Johnston file, sitting there quietly, not hurting anyone.

No downside to being over-prepared, Debra concluded.

Lost in her thoughts, she barely noticed when the radio

played the Rubber Duckie Song. Charlotte's love of *Moana* and *Frozen* had destroyed Debra's curated internet radio stations, often causing them to play juvenile songs that even Charlotte now rejected. Debra reached to shut off the music but pulled back and instead drifted away to the tune which ushered memories of her singing the song with Charlotte in the bath as she splashed and giggled. Charlotte used to refuse to take a bath without copious amounts of bubbles. Her favorite game was rubbing the bubbles on her face to create an imaginary beard. "Just like Daddy's!" she would shout, her wide grin distorting the bubble beard.

The missing girl, Jenna, was close to Charlotte's age. In Debra's experience, one had to have a screw loose to harm a child. She gripped the steering wheel as if she held a screwdriver.

3

"Damnit," Jacob cursed under his breath. "Damnit, damnit, damnit." He repressed the desire to slam his fist into one of the wine barrels that encircled him. A single text shattered his immaculate plan.

How did the cops find Bev? Jacob wondered. He knew they would discover her body eventually, but not so soon. Nothing about the situation made any sense. The plan was going off without a hitch, and then his phone buzzed, providing the biggest fucking hitch imaginable.

Jacob collected himself. His plan wasn't ruined. It just required a little adjustment. In fact, if he played his cards right, the pot he took home could be even larger. First, though, he needed to think clearly, an act which seemed impossible under the circumstances.

He stood and walked to a cabinet; in it sat a small, locked refrigerator. He pulled out keys, found the gnarly gold one, and placed it in the keyhole. After opening, a nice chill hit his hand, tingling the tips of his fingers and slowing his heart. He reached in and located the right bottle: dark and unlabeled.

Pavlovian drool filled his mouth. One glass? Two? The whole shebang? God, he wanted it all.

Relax, he reminded himself. *Only a taste.*

He inserted the corkscrew, twisted, and opened the bottle; in it, his escape awaited.

Slowly, he poured. The liquid flowed like a calm stream and coated the bottom of the glass in beautiful crimson. He filled half the glass, considered pouring more, and refrained. From a nearby drawer, he retrieved a Vacu Vin; after sliding the rubber stopper into the bottle, he pumped furiously. The stopper clicked, signaling he had successfully pumped all the air possible from the bottle, and thus preserving it for later.

If this day goes to plan, he thought, *I'll be in the mood to celebrate.*

He placed the air-tight bottle back in the refrigerator, made his way to the counter, and admired the half-glass. He lifted and swirled, the legs smearing residue that refracted the light like a Pollock painting, instigating a dance within the crystal, with Jacob as the waltz partner. The residue clung to the glass, refusing to drip to the bottom, staining the glass with fat blots of scarlet. Jacob surveyed them as a child may clouds in the sky, searching for hidden meanings within the shapes.

The wine, he concluded, while beautiful, was too thick, a shade too light. Perfection evaded. Not that it mattered. A step below perfection remained pretty damn good.

He brought the glass to his lips, lifted slowly, and dripped ounces into his mouth, coating his tongue in a thin deluge of delight. Blackberries. Strawberries. Spices. Rhubarb.

My God, he thought. *It has everything.* A universe of pleasures flooding his pallet, intense and divine. The experience made him crave the future more, for if this was the imperfect batch, the perfected method may well suffocate him with joy.

He normally allowed the flavors to settle before taking another swig, but he couldn't resist the wonderment. He took a second, extended swig, and the experience forced him to take a seat, his knees still trembling as he sat.

Too much, he concluded.

He reviewed the empty glass. Rage tickled his chest. He had not intended to drink the entire glass in one fell swoop, but the power of the wine overtook him; it was much more potent than he could ever control.

Though his thirst endured, gnawing at his belly and throat, he refused a second glass. Another half a glass would lead to a third full glass. Soon, there would be no going back; instead of calmed nerves, the wine would imprison his entire body. Later, such release would be appropriate; now, he could not afford it.

As a substitute, Jacob fetched a 1970 Chateau Palmer from a nearby secret stash and poured a large glass. Though it paled in comparison to his own creation, in a pinch, it fared well. The silky notes of tobacco and cedar helped blunt his racing thoughts. He sat and enjoyed his wine while revising his plan.

There was an unanswered question Jacob needed answered: What had Ethan done before Jacob captured him? Who had he told, and what had he said? Jacob needed this intel or making any alternative plans would be pointless.

Yes, he thought. *I need to have a chat with Ethan.* For this chat, he would need to retrieve a few tools to better facilitate the conversation. But that could wait. He had plenty of time to enjoy his wine.

4

Debra turned onto Sage. Red and blue lights colored the pre-dawn sky like a secluded carnival. Illuminated in her headlights were the silhouettes of expensive homes, each unique and worth more than she could earn in twenty years on the force. Debra couldn't help but gawk.

James was right, she thought. *I'm in the wrong business.*

She abutted 1231 Sage's curb and parked. Before her spanned expansive oaks within a freshly shorn lawn in front of a massive yet quaint home with painted white bricks encircled by a wrap-around balcony and porch. There was even a small vineyard near the front yard, and though she doubted the vines produced commercial-quality fruit, she suspected for this vineyard's owner, results were not the point.

Per her personal protocol, she scoped the scene before exiting her vehicle. She observed about half a dozen uniformed officers on site, all of whom she recognized. And in the middle of the chaos stood Officer McCarthy, barking orders.

Before stepping out, she slurped down the last drops of Bill's energy drink. She repressed a gag at drink's overt artificial sweetness and synthetic fruitiness.

After killing the engine, she got out of the car and headed towards the madness. With each step, she inspected her surroundings. No blood. No kicked-up dirt. No personal objects or notes. Nothing appeared out of place.

When she approached McCarthy, he was screaming at a rook to quit "lollygagging," his gut jiggling in synch with his animated hand gestures. It was one of his favorites, a go-to complex word to emphasize his seriousness.

She sidled up to him and asked, "Any sign of Jenna?"

McCarthy shook his head, jiggling his jowls. "Nope, nada."

"What's the status of the search? Make any progress?"

"Haven't been sitting on my ass, Deb." He ticked off each of his tasks with an extended finger. "We've scoped the scene, set up a 10-mile search perimeter. I'll have a few boys knock on doors. Hopin' something shakes from all that."

"Good. You keep handling this mess. I'm gonna talk to the neighbors, see if I can get some details about Beverly and Ethan's relationship. Maybe we can figure out some possible hiding spots."

"Sounds good."

She shifted from one foot to the other and asked, "So what's your working theory?"

"The dad did it. Ethan." He ceased observing the other officers and focused squarely on her. "You got some other thought?"

She shook her head. "Nope. Makes sense. Let's stick with that unless something different shakes out." She assessed the scene, her eyes blurry, and asked, "But what's your bead on that weird text? Why would he have his girlfriend call the cops? Something about that just seems off, you know?"

McCarthy shrugged his large shoulders and replied, "Not sure. Crazy people do weird shit."

"Yeah?" She repressed a giggle. Her exhaustion almost caused a lapse in her professionalism.

"I'm guessing he came over after gettin' that text from his ex. Who knows what that was 'bout. When he got here, the two fought, and he ended it with a knife." He mimicked a stabbing motion.

She waved her hands dismissively. "I get the picture. Don't need the demonstration."

He grinned and continued: "Then he panicked and texted Sarah Meyers, tellin' her to call us. These guys usually can't face the music. Goddamn cowards, all of 'em. He freaked out again and bailed with Jenna."

Debra nodded. She did not agree yet, but she needed McCarthy to remain focused. "You talk to Sarah since you got here?"

"Tried to," he replied, his tone dripping with frustration. "She's talkin' at a million miles a minute. Hard to follow."

"Mind if I have a go at her?"

"Be my guest," he said as he half-bowed and motioned towards the door in a grandiose fashion. "She's all yours."

"Thanks. Keep working the scene out there."

"Will do."

She sidestepped McCarthy and put on rubber gloves. She also slipped on shoe covers before she stepped into the house. Unlike the pristine outer shell, the interior was in disarray. For a moment, she worried her officers had caused the mess, turning over furniture in the pursuit of evidence. But upon closer inspection of the crust-plastered plates and grit-caked floors, she concluded someone created the mess before any officer arrived, providing her some relief that her guys hadn't contaminated the scene.

In her periphery, she spotted a group of officers huddled in a semi-circle around the lifeless body of Beverly Paxton, her eyes still open and gazing heavenward as if questioning, *What the hell happened*? She reviewed each officer to confirm they donned the correct hazmat attire to ensure proper evidence collection. As

McCarthy described, the cause of death was obvious: a single stab wound to the chest. On a cursory glance, she saw no other obvious injuries. The knife, however, was not in the wound or near the body.

The sea of officers parted as she kneeled before the victim. The first things she noticed were Beverly's clothes and makeup: AG skinny jeans and a Gucci top. Light-red blush kissed her cheeks, and heavy foundation pooled with the blood. Her appearance gave the impression of someone who had looked forward to the night, a striking departure from the evening's eventuality.

Why would she dress like this for her ex-husband? she wondered. Perhaps she hoped to lure Ethan to the house with the Jenna text, then seduce him back into her arms. Yet, the logical gap in that conclusion was obvious: He wouldn't be too thrilled with his ex-wife feigning an emergency for his attention, no matter how good she looked.

"Hey," she said and pointed at a rookie named Kurt Robinson, "where's the knife?"

The rook snapped to, his body stiffening at her tone. She stifled a laugh. She needed to get her shit together. The fatigue was unsettling her composure.

"It was over by the thing there," he said, pointing with a trembling finger. "Near that, what's it called… sofa, yeah. It was by the sofa, ma'am. It's been bagged and forensics has it for dusting."

"Got it. Do you have a picture of it?"

"Yes, ma'am." He grabbed a camera from another officer, jogged over, and handed it to her. She clicked into the photos and scrolled as she reviewed various angles of the serrated knife. She had seen similar knives for sale at Sur La Table, perhaps even this exact model.

"Thanks, rook," she said as she handed him the camera.

"My, my pleasure, ma'am," he replied.

"Hey, get Sarah Meyers on the phone again so I can talk to her. ASAP."

"Will do!"

She nodded as he scurried away. She explored the kitchen, which was much cleaner than the living room. Stunningly clean, in fact. She noticed no dirty dishes, the faucets were spotless, and the island's marble countertop sparkled as if it had never been used. As she scanned the area, she discovered a row of drawers where she assumed the family stored kitchen utensils. She selected a drawer at random, which contained the typical array of forks, spoons, and knives, all neatly organized and pristine. At the right of the drawer lay five steak knives matching the one displayed on Robinson's phone.

A larger drawer at her side caught her attention. It held a trashcan, which was filled almost to the brim with rubbish. She focused on the contents in the bag, and her eyes fixed on a wine bottle that rested at the top. Her pulse accelerated as she read the bottle's label: "HOLLAND VINEYARDS." She focused on the bottle's lip, which appeared, to her eyes, to be a little wet with residue wine, as if the bottle had been recently finished.

"Ma'am," a voice said from behind, startling her. She turned and saw Robinson holding out a phone with a trembling hand. "Sarah Meyers is on the line."

She took the phone and said, "Thanks, officer." She covered the phone's receiver and nodded her head towards the trash. "Make sure forensics bags that trash, got it? And tag the wine bottle separately. *Separately*," she emphasized. "I don't want cross-contamination."

"Will do!"

"Thanks." She shot him a look that said, *Now please leave*. It took him a couple of seconds before he comprehended her meaning and darted away.

"Hello?" Debra asked.

"Yes, hello?" a panicked female voice said. "Who's this?"

"My name is Detective Debra Foley, ma'am. I'm running this scene."

"Good. I hope you are more competent than that last jerk I talked to. He kept saying Bev was murdered. Bev wasn't murdered!" Sarah yelled, forcing Debra to pull the phone away from her ear.

"You talked to McCarthy, right?" Debra asked. "What did he tell you?"

"Jerk claimed that Ethan stabbed Bev and ran off with Jenna. I don't believe it. Ethan would never do something like that."

Debra flushed hot with frustration. She had chastised McCarthy on many occasions about revealing too much about an investigation to witnesses. Seemed like another dressing-down was in order. But that could wait. The good news was that Debra no longer needed to beat around the bush. Debra put on her best *it's going to be okay* voice and replied, "We're not saying Ethan did it. But Beverly is dead. You get that, right?"

"Oh, stop with your bullshit!" Sarah's voice cracked and she emphasized each word as if speaking to someone whose second language was English. "This is all bullshit. Bullshit! Ethan texted me to call you. Why the hell would he do that if he was a killer? Does that happen a lot in your world, Detective? Do the criminals usually call the cops right after they kill someone? Of course not, makes no dammed sense. I told that other idiot the same thing, and he didn't get it, either."

Debra allowed the rant to finish before saying, "Sarah, listen. The best thing you can do for Ethan is talk to me so we can find the person who did it. Believe it or not, I'm on your side."

"How?" Sarah asked curtly. "How are you on my side if you're investigating Ethan for something he didn't do, couldn't do?"

"I'm not investigating Ethan, Sarah. I care about Beverly. I care about Jenna. That's all. Ethan is a person of interest. Take a step back. Pretend he was a stranger to you. Can you blame me?"

Sarah paused before muttering, "I don't know."

"Yeah, you do," Debra replied. "Listen. If Ethan didn't do it, if he's innocent, then I want to find the real criminal. But the more time we waste, the harder that becomes. Now, please, calm down. Let's discuss this like grownups."

Sarah loudly inhaled. "Okay, okay."

"It'll be fine, I promise. If Ethan didn't do this, I'll catch the bastard who did. Now, how long have you known Ethan?"

"A few years now. I was a paralegal at his firm."

"Okay, paralegal. So, Ethan is an attorney?"

"Was. He retired after his divorce from Bev."

A few pieces clicked into place. "Was it a forced retirement?"

"What? Forced retirement?" Her tone shifted from sorrow to ire. "What does that have to do with anything?"

Debra tried to rebut Sarah's antagonism with evenness. "It may not make sense to you, but I need to understand everything. Everything about Ethan, you two, his relationship with his ex-wife. I need to understand his mindset so I can figure out if he did this, and if he didn't, who might have. Does that make sense?"

Silence for a while, to the point where Beverly wondered if Sarah hung up. Then Sarah admitted, "A little, yeah."

"Okay. Okay, good. I'm not here to judge."

"There's nothing to judge," she replied. "No, it wasn't a forced retirement. We didn't start dating until after he filed for divorce. He retired because he got sick of the grind."

"Okay, okay. That's helpful. Has Ethan ever displayed any signs of anger?"

"Anger? What do you mean, anger?"

Debra considered the question for a bit before answering. "I mean, did he ever yell at you? Did you ever hear him yell at

Jenna or Beverly? Anything like that. Divorce can take a toll on a person."

"Listen. If anyone was angry, it was me." She exhaled a regretful sigh. "I'm the emotional one in the relationship. Ethan is pretty even. That's why he was such a great litigator. I never saw him lose his cool."

"Alright. So, tell me about tonight. Why did Ethan rush over here at such an early hour?"

"I already told the other guy this!"

"I want to hear it straight from you, though, in case I have questions."

Sarah moaned loud enough that it had to be intentionally flippant. "Okay, fine. Ethan got a text from Beverly at like two in the morning."

"Okay. What did the text say?"

"Something like, 'I need you to come over because of Jenna.' Words to that effect. Ethan tried calling her a bunch of times after getting that text, but Beverly wasn't picking up. So he rushed over there just to make sure everything was okay." She paused before continuing: "Ethan loves Jenna more than anything. There's nothing he wouldn't do for her. She's his world."

Debra reflected on Sarah's comments about Ethan's love for Jenna. Did that love make his guilt more or less likely? Ethan didn't sound like a murderer, but love can make people do strange things. Especially love for a child.

"Okay," Debra said. "And then you got a text from Ethan around 3:30 a.m. telling you to call the police?"

"Yeah, and I haven't heard from him since."

"Did you try calling him after he texted?"

"Yes. I called and called, but I kept going straight to voicemail."

Debra glanced at the pitcher of water. "Okay, got it. Anything else you can think of that might help us?"

"I don't believe so. Ethan would never do this. I already told you that, but it's true. He gave up so much money in the divorce just to keep it amicable. Bev kept demanding more and more, and Ethan kept giving in just to shield Jenna from all this shit. Why would he do all that just to end up killing Bev? Makes no sense."

Debra nodded at this conclusion. She agreed with Sarah, in part. In Debra's experience, random violence from an otherwise nonviolent person was rare. Not impossible, but unusual. And often there was an instigating factor—she recalled one case where an abused wife snapped and stabbed her husband fifteen times before smoking three cigarettes and calling the cops. But here, evidence showed a perfectly placed stab wound, as if the attacker had ample time to pinpoint the strike. Yet, a fight with an ex who was keeping a child away from Ethan may have been just the flicker he needed to light a repressed flame.

"You there, Detective?" Sarah asked.

"Sorry," Debra responded. "Got lost in my thoughts." She normally did not drift like that when speaking to a witness, but Bill's energy drink was doing little to compensate for three measly hours of sleep. "I may have to contact you again if I have any other questions."

"That's fine. Just please don't hurt Ethan. I swear to you he didn't kill Beverly. He's a very kind person."

"I won't hurt Ethan, Sarah, unless he tries to hurt me or someone else. I can promise you that."

"Okay, okay," Sarah said, her relief evident.

"Please call if you remember any more information that may help us. Anything at all. The smallest thing may be very important."

"Small? How small?" Sarah asked tentatively, as if ashamed of the inquiry.

"Nothing is too small." Debra remembered one case that

broke because the maid noticed a broom placed on the wrong hook.

"Well, it's a super small thing, but kinda weird. Ethan rarely texts, and when he does, he's very precise. No abbreviations, grammatically correct. He's old school."

"Yeah, I know a few people like that." Debra's husband was maddeningly proper in his texts and emails.

"Well, the text I got from him to 'call the police' didn't have punctuation. No period or exclamation point." She paused, sighed, and continued: "That sounds stupid, but I don't think he's ever sent a text without punctuation."

"That's interesting. I'll definitely keep that in mind."

"I hope it helps. Call me if you have any other questions. I'll be glued to my cell phone until I hear something about Ethan."

"Thanks." Debra hung up the phone and stood still as she went over the conversation in her mind. Her stomach stirred as if filled with spoiled milk. Ethan's actions exhibited a blend of chaotic coolness that deviated from the personality described by Sarah. Perhaps sense would follow additional evidence.

She tossed the phone back to Robinson. "Thanks."

"Yes ma'am," he replied.

Debra nodded and departed through the front door. Outside, the lights from the patrol cars flashed through the pitch-black night, momentarily blinding her. When her vision adjusted, she scanned the yard searching for the vineyard and spotted it to her right. It was small, with only four rows of vines.

Even with the red and blue beams, the area was too dark to conduct any true investigation. She stepped into the front door and yelled, "Hey, any way to get some light out here?"

"The panel by the door," Robinson yelled. "One of the switches turns on the front lights."

Debra nodded and hit all the switches. A few lights in the

house turned off; the lights outside flicked on. "Thanks, officer," she yelled back before heading outside.

With the illumination, she better witnessed the house's splendor. The white paint of the wrap-around porch glimmered in the light as if coated with glitter. Two large fans hung above the porch, creating a gentle breeze that complemented the natural gusts. Beautifully crafted brick accents highlighted the understated woodwork and French doors. Though the house was worth well into the seven figures, its subtle design disguised that fact. She figured this was not the house of an ostentatious sort; rather, this was Mr. Paxton's private hideaway, an escape from the hustle and bustle of San Francisco city life.

She walked over to the vineyard and noticed a small shovel, bucket, and fake plastic clippers on the ground; Jenna's playthings she supposed.

Poor, sweet girl, Debra thought, her heart accelerating.

Her eye caught an unusual shape near the road; she pulled out her flashlight and shined it towards the object. In the beam appeared a cork for a wine bottle. After readjusting her gloves, she carefully picked the cork up and reviewed it: typical shape and size. There was one striking difference about this cork: It bore no branding, unlike corks used by the large producers in the area.

"McCarthy," she yelled. "Come take a look at this."

Soon, McCarthy arrived next to her, huffing as if he had finished a marathon. "What's up?" he asked.

She held up the cork to McCarthy and swiped away his hands when he tried to grab it. "Not without gloves."

"Sorry, sorry boss."

"Think this could have something to do with Jenna?" she asked and presented the cork. "No markings on the cork, so it's not just a leftover."

Reviewing the cork, he said, "Could be. Or could be just the guy's own cork. He might be one of these 'amateur' winemakers." He used finger quotes when saying "amateur." "I mean, the guy's got his own little vineyard here. Probably tried makin' his own product."

"Yeah," she concurred. "You might have a point. I still want it bagged and dusted, okay?"

"Sure thing."

She placed the cork into a Ziploc bag, zipped, and handed it to McCarthy. "I just don't know," she said, her voice soft. "There's just something off here."

"Yeah?"

"Yeah. Can't put my finger on it." She pulled out her phone and checked the time. "Look, here's the plan. First, I'm going to talk to the next-door neighbors, see if they knew the family well. Here's to hoping they give us something, anything. If nothing pans out from that, and we're not finding any more evidence, I may talk to some of the surrounding businesses, see if they picked up anything on a security cam. But let's keep focused on the here and now. Find Ethan ASAP, got it?"

McCarthy nodded. "You're speakin' my language."

"Just so I know, any idea when the wineries open around here?"

McCarthy shrugged. "I mean, they're all different. Landmark and Ledson open at like 10:30."

She nodded. "And Holland?" She saw his face twist, and she braced for the lashing.

"Debra," McCarthy bellowed. "I don't wanna hear that shit."

"I'm just doing my job."

"You ain't gonna have a damn job if you go down that road again. You know how many times I had to cover your ass for that mess?"

Debra nodded, but she really did not know. She tried to avoid the hallway whispers.

"And," he continued with a step towards her, "I'm not doing it again. I'm not. Stay away from Jacob Holland, Debra."

Debra fought the urge to flinch when he mentioned Jacob. "I will."

"I'm not kiddin', Deb."

Debra met his sternness with softness. "Look, I've gotten past all that crap. I'm not interested in Jacob. Swear. I just need to talk to winery employees to see if they have any videos of the road."

McCarthy paused before saying, "Okay." He opened his mouth to speak, but she interrupted him.

"Now," Debra said, "Sarah told me about your little chat. Apparently, you told her every detail about the investigation. About the scene. Damnit, McCarthy," she tapped her finger in the middle of his wide chest. "How many times do we have to go over this?"

"I—" he started before pausing. "I couldn't get anything outta her. I needed to tell her something."

"No, you didn't. That's my call. Not yours. Got it? Now, hop to." She tapped his chest a second time. "I want Ethan now. Find him. Every second is a second Jenna doesn't have."

McCarthy opened his mouth again, paused, and stayed silent as he spun and headed back with his head low to run his operation. Debra watched him disappear into the house, and she stood a while in contemplation, considering how much weight she should give to the cork. Likely little to none, but something about it troubled her.

Unlike the house's living room, its exterior was immaculate. A stray cork seemed out of place.

Alone, she wondered if she should have come down so hard on McCarthy. He was just doing his job, and, in general, he was doing his job well. But her weary mind and fear over the seconds ticking without any leads caused her to act more on emotion than usual. McCarthy bringing up Jacob didn't help matters, either.

Alone and frustrated, she gazed towards the dark road, the road likely used by Jenna's kidnapper, now a ghost on the run.

5

Tools in hand, Jacob headed back to his office; there, Ethan fought against the ropes binding his arms, rubbing incessantly, pulling with all his might. Jacob observed for almost a minute with admiration and repressed laughter.

Soon bored, Jacob slammed the door; startled, Ethan jumped backwards and winced as the ropes tethering him to the wine barrel pulled his arms forward.

"Awe, Ethan," Jacob intoned. "Such a fighter. That's exactly why I wanted you so badly. But it won't help you here, trust me." He walked over to and leaned near Ethan. "You can't fight the inevitable." He yanked off the blindfold shielding Ethan's vision and allowed him a moment for his eyes to adjust. "Care to explain this?" Jacob asked as he shoved a bright screen in Ethan's face, which read:

AMBER ALERT
Sonoma, CA. AMBER Alert: check local media. LIC/0JHD536 (CA)
2019 Mercedes SLK 2 door

"Well?" Jacob's tone deepened and darkened. "That

description sounds a lot like your fancy pants lawyer car." In one quick motion, Jacob tore off the duct tape from Ethan's mouth and a few pieces of his face went with it. Ethan groaned with pain, but otherwise remained silent.

Jacob winced and said, "Sorry man, really am. That shit's gotta sting. A guy did that to me once in high school. I'm not kiddin'. The sonofabitch put tape on me and then ripped it off. Fuckin' hurt like hell, I swear to God. But I still need you to answer me. Why." Jacob tapped the phone against Ethan's head, almost playfully. "Is there." Jacob smacked Ethan's head again, harder and with no playfulness. "An AMBER alert." Jacob reared back and struck Ethan across the face. "On my fucking phone?"

Ethan blinked rapidly and said, "I, I really don't know. I swear."

Ethan was obviously lying. Even accounting for the stress he suffered, he exhibited all the signs of a bullshitter. He blinked rapidly. His gaze never centered on Jacob. Ethan fidgeted with every word, and he uttered each syllable with an unusual cadence, as if his ability to determine a story dictated the beat as opposed to the truth of his statements.

Jacob noticed Ethan's eyes shift to the surroundings. At first, Ethan's eyes narrowed, as if trying to focus on something. Then Jacob saw the moment that realization clicked. His eyes widened and trembled, and pools of sweat beaded on his forehead.

Jacob glanced around the room with a large, toothy grin and said, "Like the decorations? I designed this room with you in mind. Oh, and little Jenna, of course."

To regain Ethan's focus, Jacob slid a Taser from his pocket and displayed it in front of Ethan's face. Ethan's eyes focused first on the Taser, then on Jacob, anger replacing any confusion.

"Ethan, Ethan," Jacob whispered. "Let's get back to the matter at hand. You are lying, which I get. I do. But here's the thing. You'll soon discover that, with me, honesty is always the best policy." Jacob cocked his head as he looked down with a furrowed brow. "Honesty is the best policy. Didn't Franklin say that? Or am I making that up?" He laughed and said, "I do that. Talk out of my ass."

"Fuck you," Ethan shot back as he started fighting again with the restraints.

"So, you don't know? Eh, doesn't matter. It's a good saying either way. And, unfortunately for you, I have certain, other policies for lying."

Jacob slammed the Taser against Ethan's leg and pressed the activation button. A crackling sound rang out, and Jacob watched as every one of Ethan's muscles tensed up in unison. With glee, Jacob observed Ethan try to fight against an unbeatable opponent, try to gasp air through a throat that would not relax. Ethan's shaking caused Jacob to tremble, as if they drove along a bumpy road.

Satisfied he had demonstrated his point, Jacob pulled back the Taser, and Ethan's body crumpled forward onto the wine barrel like a dead fish off a hook.

"See what I mean," Jacob said, his voice again joyful. "I'd much rather continue having fun with you. Just be straight with me and there'll be no need for anymore, well, fireworks, I guess." He lifted the Taser near Ethan's face and pressed the trigger; the hot sparks flashed and crackled.

"Please," Ethan pleaded. "No more. I won't lie again."

"Atta boy," Jacob replied and lowered the Taser. "Now, let's try again. Did you call the cops before you got to the house?"

Ethan shook his head.

"Then why the AMBER Alert?"

Silence.

"Wanna stay the strong, silent type, eh?" Jacob stated, breaking the silence. "Fine."

Jacob stood, strode to a nearby cabinet, and pulled out a

Ruger revolver. The steel felt meaningful in Jacob's palm, like Thor holding his hammer. The power, the control, all earned.

"Now," Jacob said, "I need you to tell me how the cops found Bev so fast."

Ethan glared at him with a stare that could burn through the ropes binding his wrists.

"Ha!" Jacob laughed. "I've seen that look before. That glare. My Dad gave me that look a bunch as a kid. Didn't change what happened to him, and it won't change what's about to happen to you."

Ethan said nothing; his stare endured.

Jacob continued, his tone tempered: "Ethan, Ethan. I've been in a lot of relationships. The silent treatment isn't going to phase me. Especially not right now, I've got too much on my mind." Jacob sat, shoulders slumped, bracing himself against the ground with his free hand. Once seated, he used the barrel of the gun to play with Ethan's hair. "See, this morning, I planned to take you straight to see Jenna. I told you that in the backseat. I wasn't lying then. But whatever you did, you made it too 'hot,' as they say."

Ethan's face softened, the wrinkles around his watering eyes and cheeks relaxed. But he remained quiet.

Jacob slowly glided the barrel along the crown of Ethan's head. "I'm sorry, I really am." Jacob kissed Ethan on the head and whispered, "I wish things were different. But we gotta play the hand we're dealt, you know? You can't complain. You wanted to be the dealer. Don't worry, I'll get us through this. I'm a great bluffer. It'll just take longer than I hoped." Jacob stood, sizing Ethan up and down as he did. "Hey, by the way, how much do you weigh? About 220? 230?"

Puzzlement replaced Ethan's glare.

"I need you to do me a quick favor." Jacob walked towards a nearby wine rack, the gun still aimed at Ethan. From the rack, he selected a label-less bottle and a stemless glass. A Vacu Vin stuck out of the top of the bottle. He squeezed the rubber and air rushed from the cork, allowing him to remove it and pour the liquid into the glass. "Just FYI, this isn't my best batch. Not nearly ready. But it should do for these purposes."

Once liquid coated the bottom of the glass, Jacob stopped pouring and placed the rubber stopper back onto the bottle and used the pump to vacuum out much of the air. He slid the bottle back onto the rack, pulled out two pills from his jacket pocket, and walked over to Ethan while balancing the glass and pills in one hand, a wine opener in the other.

He positioned the wine and pills on the ground like a waiter delivering food.

"Fuck you, you psycho." Ethan's attempts to free himself amplified, like a runner experiencing a second wind. While watching him, Jacob considered the circumstances. Perhaps ropes weren't enough. For a little insurance, he grabbed the handcuffs that lay nearby and cuffed Ethan's arms to his legs.

"There," Jacob said. "That won't be as comfortable, but you left me little choice."

"Let me out!" Ethan screamed. "Help! Help!"

"Open your mouth," Jacob said as he placed the gun's barrel against Ethan's temple, massaging it with the cold steel to drive the point home.

Ethan stared up at Jacob, his eyes fixed, his brow furrowed. "No," Ethan said flatly.

Jacob slammed the gun into Ethan's head, snapping it backwards. It was a hard hit, but soft enough to avoid knocking him out. Ethan's body began to quiver again, and crimson spittle dripped down the sides of his lips. He coughed, spraying blood droplets over Jacob's nice wine barrel. Jacob took a moment to admire Ethan's body art splattered on the barrel.

"Now," Jacob said, "let's try this again. Maybe I didn't ask the right way. Open your mouth, pretty please."

Ethan again looked up at Jacob. His eyes trembled in their

sockets, obviously trying to focus through a blur. But his tone did not change when he replied, "No."

Calmly, Jacob placed the gun on the ground and gripped the wine opener with his right hand. He reached towards Ethan and glided the metal protrusion down Ethan's face, rotating the corkscrew as it descended. Jacob began near Ethan's scalp, then slid the opener down towards his forehead. Jacob placed the tip against Ethan's temple and spun it, smiling as Ethan obviously tried to slow his shaking to avoid any cuts. Slowly, Jacob navigated the corkscrew from Ethan's temple towards his left eye. Ethan's entire body stiffened. Jacob could taste Ethan's fear, and it tasted good. Like a beautiful port with a decadent slice of chocolate cake.

With his free hand, Jacob lifted Ethan's head. Jacob placed the corkscrew against Ethan's Adam's apple and pressed. Ethan recoiled in instinct, but he had little room to move. Jacob pushed it deeper, so deep that beads of crimson formed around the corkscrew's tip.

"Now," Jacob said as he rotated. Ethan started to scream but then withheld as any projection pushed against the tip of the corkscrew. "Open your fucking mouth. I won't ask again."

Tears streamed down Ethan's face, but he did not submit.

"Fine, have it your way." Jacob pulled back the wine opener and studied it. Slowly, he licked the bloodied tip while eyeing Ethan. Ethan's eyes widened in disbelief, much to Jacob's enjoyment.

"By the way, do you like movies?" Jacob asked.

Ethan spit at Jacob, the loogie barely missing Jacob's face. "Go to hell, you psycho."

Unfazed, Jacob continued: "I love movies. That and books are the best escapes on this Mother Earth. All the modern special effects, man. I don't know how they do any of that stuff. But, what's weird is sometimes I like the complete opposite kind of movies more. You know, those grainy, found-footage flicks? There's something about those movies that really strike a chord with me. Love those movies when done right." Jacob grabbed a remote on a nearby workbench, placed the glass and pills where the remote once lay, and clicked on the 46-inch television that hung in the corner of the room, angled in a way that Ethan could see it from behind the barrel.

The screen was black at first, only reading "Select Input." From his pocket, Jacob pulled out his iPhone and clicked the Chrome Cast app; a few seconds later, the background of his iPhone appeared on the television. He opened the Nestcam app, selected the "VIC 7" zone, and, after a short delay, a blurry image appeared.

Jacob watched Ethan with joy as realization set in. The grainy image displayed a young girl's face and little else aside from a few dolphins at the top of stained pajamas. Her eyes were closed, but her small chest rose and fell.

Ethan inhaled, his jaw clenched, and screamed, "Jenna!"

"See!" Jacob pointed at the screen. "I'm not a director, but that's impactful, no? Moves the spirit."

"Jenna!"

"Wail all you want. I spent a fortune soundproofing this office." He pointed to a guitar and amp resting against a wall. "Told the guys it was because I was learning how to play the guitar and didn't want to annoy anyone. Part of that's true. It's amazing what people will believe when blinded by enough green."

"Let me go, damn you. Let me go now!"

"Sure, I'll do just that." Jacob put down the remote and shook his head as if he addressed an untrained puppy who had pissed on the carpet. He retrieved the pills, wine, and gun, then approached Ethan. "Ethan, Ethan. There's no way out of this. You really have two options. One, you can answer one question and take these pills like a good boy," Jacob lifted the hand holding the pills and glass and shook them. "And I'll take you to

Jenna. Or, there's option two," Jacob shook the gun. "Here's how number two will go down. If you won't take the pills, or if you won't answer my question, I'll leave this TV on, take a quick trip down to see little Jenna, and shoot her in the head. I'll also cut off your eyelids so you won't miss a minute." Jacob described each option matter-of-factly, like an insurance agent explaining the limits of various policy options. "So, what's it going to be?"

Ethan maintained his strong demeanor for a few moments, but it cracked as he studied his helpless daughter.

"I'll take the pills and answer anything," Ethan replied. "Please don't hurt Jenna."

"She doesn't interest me, Ethan. You do. Once everything is in motion, she'll just be a liability to keep around." Jacob turned and faced Ethan. "Ready, my friend?"

Ethan nodded. His eyes were unlike any Jacob had witnessed. He had seen eyes the moment before death, quietly screaming for escape, for salvation. But the torture in Ethan's eyes eclipsed all.

Love of a father, Jacob concluded.

"Okay," Jacob said. "Like I said, one question. How did the cops learn about Jenna so fast?"

Ethan's shoulders slumped. "I was able to get out a text."

"When?"

"Right before I dropped the phone in the water."

Jacob nodded. "Did the text include my name?"

Ethan shook his head. "All it said was, 'call the police.'"

Jacob smiled. He believed Ethan, and what he said made sense. Jacob figured that had been what happened, but he was happy to receive confirmation.

Jacob stepped towards Ethan and stood above him, the gun resting at Jacob's side, his finger on the trigger. "Open your mouth."

Ethan complied, and Jacob did not waste any time; he tossed the pills into Ethan's throat and chased them with the glass of wine, some of the liquid spilling onto Ethan's clothes. He choked and gurgled for a few seconds, his body attempting to reject the unwanted items, but soon his throat relaxed. Jacob scanned Ethan's mouth and saw that it was empty.

Jacob stepped back with a pang of pity and reviewed Ethan, who sat with his head lowered and eyes closed. He imagined Ethan's days in court, the killer litigator no one could bully. Jacob heard a story that an opposing attorney once got so frustrated he threw a notebook at Ethan during trial, which he dodged without missing a beat of his examination.

Nonsense or not, stories like that bloom from a seed of truth. Ethan still cast the shadow of that once great courtroom warrior, but it was also hard to picture such stories about the defeated man at Jacob's knees.

Jacob returned the glass and clicked off the television, then he re-wrapped Ethan's mouth with duct tape; Ethan no longer put up a fight. His eyes remained closed, his head bowed.

"It's okay," Jacob whispered. "It should only take a few minutes, then you'll have several hours of rest." Jacob sat on a nearby stool and watched. First, Ethan's shoulder muscles unclenched, his chest lowering as his arms gave way. He laid his head against the barrel as his breathing labored. Jacob waited a few more minutes before walking over and checking; Ethan was out like a light.

"Goodnight, sweet prince," Jacob whispered. "May flights of angels sing thee to thy rest."

6

Debra didn't like the neighbor's house, a traditional monstrosity outlined by hedges that eclipsed her height, supported by wide ivy-covered columns, and guarded by marble statues of naked children. She approached the massive oak front door with intricately detailed windows and a metal iron knocker.

She slammed the knocker against the thick wood, and a deep thump echoed in the night and vibrated her hand. As she waited, she swallowed back the rancid, lingering taste of Bill's energy drink. Its effects were starting to wane. A slight pang of a headache bloomed in the back of her skull, which often happened when she ran on fumes.

The silence and darkness remained for almost a minute before a distant light switched on. Another minute passed before a second light shone in the entryway. A female face stared out the door window, her frown unnaturally elongated by the distortion of the glass carvings. When the door creaked open, a weary, annoyed face appeared first, the resident's body tucked behind the door for protection. Much of her face appeared unnaturally young, but certain wrinkles and untended strands of grey hair hinted at her true age.

"May I help you?" the lady asked with an eloquent yet sharp tone, a voice Debra thought perfected by many years of luxury living.

"Yes, hi ma'am. I am Detective Debra Foley." She extended her badge and allowed the woman to review it. The lady opened the door and stepped one foot out to better appraise the identification. "I am investigating a scene at your neighbor's house. 1231 Sage."

"Bev's house?" The woman's tone and body language shifted from exasperation to concern. "Is Bev okay?"

"I can't discuss the specifics, ma'am. I can tell you it's a serious situation. Very serious. Understand?"

The lady nodded, her eyes wide and fixated on the badge as if it were the newly discovered Eighth Wonder.

"Good," Debra continued. "What's your name?"

"Heather. Heather Harrison." She extended her arm but pulled back, confused about proper etiquette. Noticing the awkward moment, Debra reached out and took Heather's clammy hand, shaking twice before releasing.

Debra scribbled the named into her notebook under the category "NEIGHBORS." "Got it. How long have you lived here?"

"Oh, a long time. Twenty-one years, thereabout. Moved in before Beverly." Heather turned her head towards the Paxtons' house as she finished her sentence.

"How well do you know Ms. Paxton?"

She turned back to Debra and said, "Well, we're more than just neighbors. We're friends."

"What's she like? Beverly."

"Oh, I mean, that's kind of a vague question." She twirled her hair and continued, "She's a sweetheart. Loving mother and, when married, wife. She worshiped Jenna and Ethan and loved their life together, when they were together at least."

"Was she friends with any of the other neighbors?"

"Not really. We all know each other around here, but I would say she was closest with me. She talked to the Sheltons down the way a little," she pointed south, "but mostly small talk. I'm not sure she would consider them friends."

"How long have you two been friendly?"

"We hit it off immediately. A lot in common. Both grew up in the Bay area. Both married to distant workaholics." She stared down at her feet as she said, "Lots to talk about."

Debra noted the reference to Ethan's work schedule and asked, "Distant workaholic. Is that what caused the divorce?"

"Well, that and that bitch Sarah Meyers."

Debra had no desire to rehash ground covered by other witnesses, so she asked, "How has Beverly been handling the divorce?"

Heather shrugged and said, "As well as can be expected, I guess. She was a mess for a while, but lately she's been doing much better. She's been coy, but I think she may be dating someone."

"Oh?"

"Yeah, she never told me his name, but I know she meets a man at least once a week at the little bookstore and coffee shop in Kenwood, The Grapes of Write. Isn't that a cute pun?" Heather's grin widened and Debra detected a hint of jealousy. "Ever been to it?"

"No, but I've heard good things."

"Yup. Anyway, Bev said this mystery man assigns a 'book' for the week. Then they meet there and discuss it. Just adorable. She's actually been smiling again since all that."

"And you don't know this mystery man's name?"

"Nope. Bev kept her trap shut. But he's young. Maybe even early 20s young."

"Interesting, thank you. That is helpful information. How would you describe Ethan?"

Heather looked taken aback, as if she didn't understand the question. "What do you mean, describe Ethan?"

"Well, what is the first word that pops into your head when I say his name?"

The corners of her eyes wrinkled. She seemed somewhat confused, but also interested. "I mean, that's tough. I guess *father?*"

Debra scribbled that onto her notepad. "Father, why father?"

"Well, Ethan and Beverly always had issues. But the one constant was Jenna. They both love her so much. Whenever I was around him, all he would talk about was Jenna. 'Jenna said this today. Jenna's grown so much. Jenna's so smart.' Stuff like that. It was sweet, he loved being a dad. He just wasn't the best husband."

Debra wrote 'not the best husband.' "Why wasn't he the best husband?"

"Like I said earlier, distant." She tugged at an earlobe and said, "Distant, yes. Even when we would go out to dinner on double dates, he would check his phone a lot, mind always somewhere else. Beverly figured having a kid might help, and it got his mind off of work. But his attention switched to Jenna, not Beverly, if that makes any sense. I've always figured their problems were deeper than just work, but I never had the heart to tell her. Wasn't my place, anyway."

"Thanks." Debra considered pushing forward but figured she could not get any more intel from this witness without giving up details about the case. Instead, she handed Heather a card and said, "Call me if anything else comes to you. Especially about that mystery man in Beverely's life."

Heather analyzed the card and said, "Okay, I guess." She opened her mouth as if to add more, but then closed it before receding into her mansion and shutting the door. Debra expected Heather would probably try to call Beverely and would soon learn her call would never be returned.

Debra's phone vibrated in her pocket. She reached for it and saw that McCarthy texted, "Call me ASAP."

Debra complied, and McCarthy answered on the second ring saying, "McCarthy."

"Hey, was interviewing witnesses. Got some interesting stuff. What's up?"

"Just talked to Beverly's parents. They got a text from Jenna that said, 'Gonna go play ball with Dad.' Got it right after the AMBER Alert went out. When they couldn't reach Ms. Paxton or Ethan, they called the station, who transferred them to me."

"Gonna go play ball? What's weird. What the hell does that mean?"

"No idea. They said Jenna isn't really into sports. Yeah, and when I had to tell them what's going on, it got ugly Deb. Real ugly. Like, I don't wanna do this shit anymore ugly."

"Been there." The faces of Jodi Johnston's parents flashed in her mind.

"Anyway, they're so messed up I'm guessin' we ain't getting nothing more out of them. I got teams going out to different fields. Ball fields, her school gym. Can you think of any place else we should go?"

Debra considered for a few moments before saying, "No, that works. I'll keep asking questions around here, see if I can get any more intel."

"Got it."

"Call me if you find anything," she said before ending the call. She could hear McCarthy's words in her head, arguing that Ethan became obsessed with losing Jenna after the divorce.

But she disliked this neat narrative. Nothing about Ethan struck her as the type who would commit such terrible acts, and

Heather didn't mention anything about custody disputes. The tickle in Debra's gut remained, a nagging sensation that everyone, including her, missed something.

Also, Beverely's mystery man presented another wrinkle. Perhaps Ethan learned about Beverly's new lover, and that discovery was the source of his rage. But why would he care about Jodi's new partner while he dated Sarah?

In sum, McCarthy's story that a rich retiree who loves his daughter beyond measure and dated a much younger woman decided to break bad and kill his ex-wife simply did not add up. She didn't buy it, at least not in its current form.

Her phone buzzed again, sending her heart racing, but it was just an update text from Bill. She stared at it and thought about her exit from their bed the prior night and her rushed morning away from it. All she wanted to do was crawl back into bed with Bill and Charlotte at her sides and sleep for days.

Neither Bill nor Charlotte deserved her recent inattention, and she resolved to pull her family close once Jenna was safe and sound. Debra would later have ample opportunities to reevaluate her priorities.

For now, Jenna was Debra's first and only priority. Perhaps finding Jenna would give Debra the closure she so desperately desired.

7

As Jacob stepped into the nursing home, the frumpy lady manning the desk stared at him over large glasses, her stained scrubs seemingly an extension of her blotchy skin. He figured she was new as he did not recognize her.

"May I help you?" Her eyes returned to the files in her hands.

"Yes," Jacob replied while balling his fists, his fingernails digging deep into his palms. "I'm here to see my mother."

"Name?"

"Gretchen. Gretchen Holland."

At that name, the lady's entire demeanor shifted; her eyebrows rose, lips pursed, and shoulders tightened.

"Yes, yes sir," she replied. "You must be Jacob."

"That's the name she gave me," Jacob said with a smile. "What name did your momma give you?"

"Excuse me?"

"Your name," he said as he leaned in, eyes fixed on hers. "What's your name?"

"Edith Groundling, sir."

"Edith, that's a pretty name. We haven't formally met." He offered his right hand. "I'm Jacob. Pleasure to meet you."

She extended a trembling hand, which he took and shook. And shook again. Her hand wiggled in his grip, trying to escape his grasp. He increased his grip's pressure and said, "Edith Groundling. I'll remember that."

Eyes wide, she mumbled, "Yes sir."

"Wonderful!" he exclaimed and released the shake; she stumbled back a step, fear still outlined on her face. "Is she still in her normal room?"

"Yes, yes sir. The Holland Suite."

"How fitting!" he said with a wink. "I'm going to make my way over there. I don't need an escort or badge or anything, do I?"

"Um," she began, but noticed his stern stare and said, "no sir. You are always welcome."

"Always welcome, how accommodating. We may just grow to be good friends, right Edith?"

"Maybe, sir."

"I hope so. My favorite thing in life is meeting new friends. Have a good one, Edith!"

"You too, sir."

He beamed her a grin and sauntered through the nursing room turnstile after Edith hit the "buzz" button. He turned right towards the "nice" wing of the facility and held his breath to combat the smell, a combination of urine, mothballs, and death. Anywhere else in the world would have been preferable to his current location. Death's certainty caused him goosebumps and curdled his stomach. He longed to be in his vineyard with a glass of wine warming his body and reaffirming his love of life. At this thought, his mouth watered, and he swallowed back the saliva, knowing he needed to press forward. Later he would numb the memories of this hellhole.

He arrived at Room 201. He opened the door and stared into a lavish suite, adorned with expensive original paintings, a seventy-inch flat-screen television, Italian leather furniture, and, among this misplaced luxury, a King bed covered by 1,000 thread-count Egyptian cotton sheets, in the middle of which a tiny, motionless figure lay clothed by a robe so bulky it may have well been a blanket.

"Hello, mother." Jacob took off his coat and placed it on a hook. He tiptoed over to her, pulled up a chair, and sat; he barely recognized the woman before him. Gray, thin hair replaced the jet-black Bob hairdo she sported well into her fifties. The body's limp, ashen skin outlined by varicose veins in no way resembled Jacob's mother's prior tan and toned figure. Her small chest rose and fell slowly, mechanically.

"Ma, you there?" Jacob whispered, not expecting an answer but asking in case a nosy nurse peeped in. Unsurprisingly, she remained lifeless, so he took her icy hand into his, leaned back in the chair, and waited. He considered how long he should wait. Twenty, twenty-five minutes seemed ample.

Lost in his thoughts, he barely noticed the pressure of his mother's grip intensify, warmth exploding in her palm. Startled, he released her hand, which fell limp and struck the side of the bed with a *thump* that echoed.

"Mom?" he asked with a gulp. "Are you there?"

Slowly, she opened her eyelids and gazed at the ceiling and the ceiling alone. For several seconds, she lay motionless, her body rigid and limbs limp. Then, she turned to stare at him, her eyes rheumy and irises silver.

Breathless, she muttered, "Da…"

"Momma," Jacob replied as he stroked her emaciated biceps. "It's Jacob. Remember?"

"Da…"

He barely heard her utterances as the noises from outside the room—carts wheeling, equipment banging, patients screaming—rang in the background. He shut the suite door and returned to his seat, the silence suddenly deafening.

"Mom, what are you trying to say?" he asked as he slid her hand into his. "Tell me, Momma, it's okay. I'm here."

"Da…" Her eyes widened and sharpened, their spark blazing for a moment. "Demon."

"What?"

"Demon," she repeated, her voice stronger and deeper. "Demon."

Jacob freed her hand and chuckled. "Well, it's always nice to see a mother's unconditional love. Nothing more beautiful."

"Demon."

"But for now," Jacob said as he glanced at the closed suite door. "I think you need to rest."

He rose to feet, stood at her side, smiled, and slammed his right palm onto her mouth, forcing it shut. With his left hand, he pinched her nose shut, careful not to leave any evident marks. She struggled, but at her weakened state, she could do little to resist. It would soon be over.

"Fuck you, and your demons," Jacob whispered as he pressed harder and harder, his rage building. His sensible side, however, soon took hold, and he released her, stepping back as her shallow chest lifted with each gasp of air.

No, he considered. *Not yet.* A dead mother would give him the ultimate "Get Out of Jail Free" card, but he needed to save that. He needed to collect some rent before passing Go, and he knew another way to keep her quiet for a while.

He grabbed his jacket, pulled out a small plastic bag from its interior pocket, and selected a small, white pill. Carefully, he snapped the pill in half. After returning the larger half to the bag, he filled a glass with chilly water at a nearby sink, softly whistling Rock-a-bye Baby.

"Demon," she said with great effort. "Demon."

"My, my." He strolled back to her. "Feeling frisky today, aren't we?" He forced open her mouth with the hand holding the pill, dropped it in, and poured a little water to chase. He observed as she swallowed, perhaps involuntarily. With his free hand, he closed her mouth and pressed against her jaw to prevent regurgitation.

"Now," he said, "no more talking, mother dearest. The medicine should not take long to kick in, so until then, what's that game we used to play?" He leaned in and whispered, "Oh, yes. The quiet game. One of my favorites."

"Mmmmm," she replied, her voice muffled by her shut jaw.

"You better believe it," he replied.

A minute later, the medicine took hold, rendering her again peaceful and harmless. He hated wasting his medicine, even if only half a pill, but desperate times call for desperate measures. There was no point in risking his mother regaining more consciousness, slight risk as that may be.

He took his mother's hand in his, kissed it, and said, "I do enjoy our little visits, but I must take off. Got things to see and people to do. You understand, right?"

He released her hand and exited the room. Taking a moment to gather his bearings, he reviewed the hallway to ensure no employees were in sight. Turning right, he ambled down the corridor, his pace steady, eyes drifting. After passing a dozen rooms and several nurses, he spotted his next target: Justin Rogel.

Justin analyzed little clear cups with red labels and placed varying amounts and types of pills into each one. When he finished a cup, he would tug at his light green scrubs that sagged over his thin frame. When Jacob stepped towards Justin, he placed a cup down and stepped back an inch.

"Hey Jacob," Justin said with feigned nonchalance.

"Well, hey there, Justin!" Jacob replied. "Looking sharp there, sport." Jacob pulled at Justin's scrubs and continued, "Still can't find scrubs that fit? Did they run out of the baby sizes?"

"Stop it," Justin said and adjusted his bulky eyeglasses which magnified his shit-brown eyes. "What do you want, man? I'm working."

Jacob propped onto the desk, causing Justin's cup to rattle. "You know what I want. I need my medication. You got it?"

"*Shhh!*" Justin motioned towards an empty patient room. The men stepped in, Jacob closed the door behind them, and Justin said, "What are you doing? Are you trying to get me fired? Don't talk about that crap out there."

"Out where? There?" Jacob pointed to the shut door and rotated his hand in a large, circular motion. "There, being the hallways of the building my family owns? Or there, being the job my family got you?"

Justin's cheeks blushed as he gazed at the floor. "Both, I guess. I just don't want to get into trouble. Get either of us in trouble, you know?"

"My, my," Jacob said as he patted Justin's lean arm. "How sweet of you. Don't worry about me. I'm a big boy. The only thing that will get us into trouble is you crying like a baby." Jacob grabbed Justin's triceps, pulled him close. "And if you cry, I will have to spank you. Hard. Understand?"

"Yes, sir." Justin's voice trembled. "Yes, I understand."

"Good boy!" Jacob released Justin's arm, rubbed his hands together. "Now, how much medicine did you get for Daddy?"

"A lot. More than we discussed."

Jacob smiled. "Good. Good job. And you put it in our normal place?"

"Yeah, like always."

"Atta boy."

"Why didn't you just go check?" Justin asked, his voice cracking on the "you" and "check." "Why did you have to come here?"

"Oh, I have a small request. I'll need more medicine going forward. As much as you can get."

Justin waved his skinny hands in front of his face, shook his mop of brunette curls, and said, "Whoa now. I already get you everything I can. I've told you most of it is the leftovers from the vials that docs use, so there's a limited supply."

"Well, then get more suppliers. Or find another way. I don't give a damn, get it done."

Justin's eyes squinted and the color of his face changed from pale to blushed to bright red. "No!" he yelled. "I told you I can't get anymore. It's just not possible."

"As my mom always said," Jacob replied calmly, "nothing is impossible, *if* you set your mind to it." Jacob tapped on Justin's temple while saying this. "You ever read The Secret?"

Justin shook his head.

"It's a decent book. Lots of fluff, but the main point is a good one. It's all about the law of attraction, positive thinking. It's all about focusing on this." Jacob raised his right hand. "The fact that I'm paying you a shit-ton of money. Or you can focus on this," he raised his left hand, "the fact that, if you stop giving me my medicine, I will end you."

Justin nodded his head. The paleness returned.

"Besides," Jacob continued. "You wouldn't want that little lady you're seeing to find out what you really do, do you?"

Justin shook his head.

"Here's the thing, buddy." Jacob took out his wallet as a demonstrative and shook it. "If you need more money to make this happen, that's fine. I'm a businessman and we can work out terms. But what you can't do is deny me. I don't handle rejection well, never have. And you wouldn't want to hurt my feelings, would you?"

"No. No, not at all."

"Good, because I'm sensitive." Jacob slapped the wallet against Justin's chest and said, "Now go talk to your people and give me a price by next Monday. This will be good for both of us. I get what I need, and you don't get exposed. Keep feeding my medicine so I'm strong enough to keep your skeletons at bay. Understood?"

Justin nodded.

"Good stuff!" Jacob exclaimed as he slipped the wallet back into his pants. "Have a good one, J-man. Talk soon."

Justin stood motionless and silent, watching Jacob's every move as he left. Jacob backtracked through the nursing home's halls and gave Edith a grin as he exited.

Outside, Jacob took a moment to revel, the chilly morning air brushing against his neck, the hums of unknowing pedestrians filling his ears.

8

Debra drove to the scene, frustrated by the lack of progress. But one conversation lingered in her mind. The first, with Mrs. Harrison, the only one who mentioned Beverly's mysterious coffee date. Other interviewees floated rumors, but none were so concrete.

In her fatigue, the road before her appeared hazy and never-ending. She shook her head, which did little to clear the exhaustion. The caffeine from Bill's drink was now gone, and she needed to replace it somehow.

Her phone rang, snapping her out of a daze. "Deb," she answered.

"Hey, it's McCarthy. Big news."

"Yeah?" Debra's pulse quickened. "What's the news?"

"We found the dad's car. Ethan." She heard his distant voice yell at an officer before continuing: "Found it with items that belong to the girl."

"Where?"

"You know the little Adobe Canyon Road by Landmark Winery?"

"Sure."

"About a mile or two down there's a turnoff for an entrance into Sugarloaf Regional Park. Found the car parked there."

"Great work. I know exactly where that is. I'll see you at the scene."

"Get your ass here ASAP. We have a chance to help that girl."

The line clicked dead as Debra slowed to a stop at a red light. With the engine's hum providing white noise, her mind wandered.

A single word jostled in her mind: *father*, the word Mrs. Harrison used to describe Ethan. Why would he put his daughter in danger? He's a former prosecutor, he knows the possible consequences of his actions on both him and Jenna. He's well aware of how this might go down.

She still couldn't think of a good reason why Ethan, assuming he snapped, would inform the police of his crime. The oddity of the text message also stood out, as did Beverly's attire. From talking to the neighbors, nothing gave the impression that Beverly was longing for a reunion with Ethan. In fact, it sounded like she was satisfied with her occasional rendezvous with an unnamed young love interest. So why would she dress so well in anticipation of a late-night visit from Ethan after an alarming text message about their daughter? There was a piece to the puzzle that Debra missed, and a puzzle nearly complete was still not completed.

A loud honk rang out, echoing in the still morning. The driver of the red Mustang behind her flailed his arms like an idiot because she had the audacity to be half a second late at the green light. She sat unmoving until the driver looked like a conductor directing an intense segment. Debra flipped on her hidden lights and the man's hands dropped to his steering wheel. He passed her and continued on his way, his head turning to see if she followed.

She did not follow the angry driver. She turned right and headed towards the scene, her mind racing as she drove. A few minutes later, she turned onto Adobe Road. The lights from the police cars already on the scene danced into the early morning sky, flickering in the orange hue of the rising sun. The light show intermingled serene beauty and harsh reality, emphasizing both.

Though neither Landmark nor Chateau St. Jean—the two large wineries bordering Adobe Road—were among her favorites, she had visited both with her husband. Both were beautiful in their own unique ways: St. Jean a sprawling masterpiece with a mansion-like tasting area, and Landmark a more boutique operation with impeccably landscaped grounds. The Sugarloaf mountains overlooked both vineyards, the proverbial divider between Napa and Sonoma.

After an officer waved her into the area, she parked near multiple police cars arranged snuggly into a small crescent dirt entrance into Sugarloaf State Park. The only non-police car in the area was a sports coupe which matched the description of Ethan's fancy car.

Taking a moment to survey the area, she watched young, uniformed officers jogging about, purpose etched on their baby faces. She remembered those days when each case was the most important of her career. The Jodi Johnston case lit a flicker of that same fire, and Jenna sent it ablaze.

Deb spotted McCarthy in the distance near the entrance's map, arms crossed, his large back to her as he patrolled his herd. Hints of sun lit the area, creating flickering halos highlighting the full trees. In the subdued light, the small concave entry appeared all-encompassing. She hopped out of her car and jogged towards McCarthy. She tapped him on the shoulder, causing him to jump.

"Jesus, Deb," he said shaking his bulbous head and squinting as he focused on her. "Cut out that crap. I don't think workers' comp will cover a heart attack."

"Sorry. What's up?"

"Just working up this scene." He dramatically cast his hand over the area before pointing to the Mercedes. "Found what looked like young girl clothes in the car. Pink toothbrush, also. Guessing in a panic he grabbed some of Jenna's stuff."

"Got it. What else?"

McCarthy nodded and said, "His law school sweater. Berkeley. Covered in blood."

This new evidence brought fresh questions. "His sweatshirt? It's a chilly day for this time of the year. Why would he take his sweatshirt off and just throw it on the ground for us to find?"

"Two reasons." McCarthy lifted up a balled-up fist and one chunky index finger. "One, he knows everyone will think he did this, so he don't care about nonsense like hiding evidence. Two," he raised an equally thick middle finger, "initial forensics show he was running."

"Running?"

"Yup. Running like a chicken without a head. They found tracks everywhere, long strides between each. Guessin' our boy panicked and started running, no destination. It's cold, but the body warms after running for a while. At least so I've heard."

"Wait a sec," Debra said as she raised her hand to her temples. "You've got Ethan's car. His sweatshirt. A bunch of tracks. But no Ethan? No Jenna?"

"Deb, relax. We just got here. There are a bunch of places to hide out there. Probably why he came here."

"That, and a couple of the neighbors told me he took her here often when he was married. Jenna and Ethan would hang out at Landmark before hiking here." She skimmed the area, its tranquility destroyed by their presence. Soon, there would be lookie-loos, which might complicate matters. "Keep surveying. There are some houses near here, right?"

"Yeah, a few, I think. Not many."

"Okay. If asked, I'm interviewing neighbors."

McCarthy's eyes opened and his face tensed. For a moment, he looked ready to question, but backtracked. "Roger."

"Thanks. Shouldn't take too long. I'll circle back up here when finished. Keep the boots on the ground and don't touch anything without asking."

"Yes, Mommy. Do I get a cookie if I'm a good boy?"

"Always." Debra nodded and McCarthy rejoined the younger officers, attacking them like a feckless bulldog.

She pulled out her cell phone and googled, "Grapes of Write hours." A few seconds later, the information she needed popped up: "Weekend Hours: 6 a.m. to 8 p.m." The directions tab showed it was less than ten minutes away.

Perfect. She was little help to the officers already on scene, particularly when distracted by such a deep mental itch.

Debra slid into her car and waved at a couple of officers while driving off. In the corner of her eye, she noticed McCarthy, who watched her intently. She understood what he was thinking: *She's driving away from the houses.* Thankfully, she trusted McCarthy enough to not spill the beans.

As she navigated the vacant highway, she contemplated all the awkward pieces to McCarthy's puzzle. Ethan's lack of a criminal past. No obvious motive. Heather Harrison's comment that he was a good father. The nonsensical decision to grab Jenna, ditch his car near a park, and just run, Jenna in tow, leaving his bloodied sweatshirt as a postcard.

She could accept one unshapely piece. Maybe two. But this many irregular pieces required further probing to make sure they used the correct guiding picture.

The polite GPS lady broke the silence: "Right turn in a thousand feet." Debra complied and parked in front of the Grapes of Write. The exterior and interior lights were lit, but only three cars were parked near the building, and the adjacent businesses appeared vacant. A girlfriend once mentioned this place, a quaint coffee shop and bookstore that also sold decent wine, the type of business that relied on a steady stream of local regulars and curious tourists attracted to its 4.9 stars on Yelp.

The exterior was cute: red brick façade surrounded by old-timey light posts. One window displayed newly released books, the other empty wine bottles, each window flanked by cork Adirondack chairs. Above the blue and white striped awning, a sign read: "GRAPES OF WRITE: BOOKS AND WINE ARE LIFE."

When she stepped in, she noted the interior matched the outside. A granite bar lined with high-back barstools ran near the right wall. Overhead the bar hung a blackboard with the various wine specials etched in chalk which announced today was "CHARDONNAY SATURDAY." Bookshelves, circular tables with wine corks, colorful knickknacks, and two-seat leather couches filled the rest of the interior. In the back, a wooden staircase near a "NONFICTION ABOVE" sign led to a second story jam-packed with more rows of books. Debra took a moment to appreciate the shop's charms and figured she would return on her personal time.

"May I help you?" asked a female voice, breaking Debra's concentration. She turned and saw a girl who looked in her early twenties with blonde, unkempt hair and a coordinated flannel outfit that Debra concluded intentionally looked uncoordinated. The girl's smile, however, seemed genuine, until Debra flashed her badge.

"Hi, my name is Debra Foley. I'm a detective with the Sonoma Sheriff's office." She allowed the girl to review the badge. "Don't worry. You're not in trouble."

The girl's hazel eyes widened as she said, "Oh yeah. I bet I know. Yeah. I got the ding on my phone. It's the first AMBER warning I actually read." She looked embarrassed as she said, "I'm sorry, I probably shouldn't admit that."

Debra shook her head with a smile. "That's fine. But maybe you can help me anyway."

"Anything. Anything at all."

"What's your name?"

The girl pointed to her badge, which read, "Amber Edwards."

Fitting, Debra thought as she took out her notepad and jotted down the name along with a few notes.

"Thank you," Debra said. "I promise I won't take up too much of your time."

"No, please. No sweat. Take up all of my time." Amber flinched, ashamed of her comment.

"Don't be nervous," Debra said as she patted Amber's arm. "I'm just here to ask a few questions. First, are you familiar with a gentleman named Ethan Paxton?"

"Ethan Paxton? It sounds kinda familiar, but I can't really place it. Yeah, not sure. Sorry."

"That's okay. What about Beverly Paxton?"

"Oh sure." Amber nodded with a grin. "Of course I know Bev. She's a regular around here." Amber paused for a moment before continuing, "Oh, Ethan! Her ex-husband. I think I've seen him once or twice. I only started working here, like, three years ago. Not sure, but I think he used to come here more before, you know. They separated I guess."

"By they, you mean Beverly and Ethan Paxton, right?"

"Yeah. I didn't know him too good, but she's a super customer. Even when things weren't going good in her personal life, she always said hi to me with a smile and tipped a lot."

"Got it. Anything else?"

"Not really. She drinks black coffee in the morning and pinot noir at night."

Debra chuckled and replied, "Thanks. What about Ethan? What can you tell me about him?"

She ran her hand through her hair. "Like I said, I don't really know him. I've said maybe ten words to him. What do you call them? Pleasantries?"

"Okay. You exchanged pleasantries with him. Anything else?"

"No, not really. He was quiet, but also tipped well, I remember that."

This is a waste of time, Debra thought.

"Okay," Debra said, "That's helpful. Thank you. Now, are you sure there is nothing else you can tell me about Beverly Paxton or Ethan Paxton? Anything unusual you noticed about them in the last few months, or heard about? Please tell me anything that comes to mind. You'd be amazed what ends up helping us."

"Well," Amber replied after a few seconds of thought. "I guess there's one thing. Nothing big, but kinda interesting."

"Interesting? What?"

"Okay, so, for the first year, two, or whatever that I worked here, Bev usually came alone. She's a big reader. Lots of romance. Steel, Roberts, that kind of stuff, you know?"

Debra shrugged.

"Anyway, so for most of the time I've worked here, Bev came alone, no entourage. Sometimes she had a girlfriend, but not a lot. Just her most times, and she sat over there." Amber pointed to a small nook with two leather chairs next to a bookcase. "That's our romance section. For our regulars, we give them bookmarks, see," Amber pulled a bright-red bookmark from under the counter that read "GRAPES OF WRITE." "If a customer has this bookmark, they can pick out any book, put this in it when they're finished for the day, and we'll hold the book behind the counter for up to a week. Cool program, huh?"

"Yeah."

Where is this going? Debra wondered.

"Anyway," Amber continued, "like I said, she was mostly solo for a long time. Then, one afternoon during my shift, she shows up with a younger-looking guy. Handsome. Blonde hair, well built."

Debra jotted down some notes, now interested. "How often did you see Ms. Paxton and this younger man together?"

"Like twenty or more times over the last few months. Sometimes in the afternoon for coffee, but for the last month it's been during my night shifts. They order a nice bottle of wine, and he always pays, which is kinda crazy since she's worth so much."

"Do you recall this younger guy's name?"

"No. I mean, he looked super familiar. But he never really said anything to me and always paid in cash. I've seen him before somewhere, just not sure where."

A screechy voice chimed in, "The hell do you mean, you don't know where you've seen him." Debra turned and saw a woman in her fifties with bleach blonde hair and too much makeup for such an early hour. The lady sat on an adjacent stool. Debra hadn't noticed her before. She must have inched closer to eavesdrop on the conversation. The woman pointed a bony finger towards a window. "He's from right the hell over there. Holland Vineyards. He's Jacob Holland. And I don't care what this *Ms. Paxton* is worth, she ain't got nothing on him."

"Jacob Holland?" Her pulse quickened. "You're sure Ms. Paxton was meeting Jacob Holland here?"

"Sure. I've seen them a bunch of times."

Debra glanced at Amber for confirmation, who nodded but also rolled her eyes a little.

The woman continued: "Everyone in this town knows the Holland family. They're legendary."

"Hi." Debra reached out her hand. "I'm Detective Debra Foley with the Sonoma Sheriff's office." With her free hand, Debra flashed her badge.

A skinny hand grabbed Debra's and wide eyes gawked at the badge. "Christina Collins at your service, though everyone calls me Tina."

"Nice to meet you, Ms. Collins."

"Tina, damn you. Not Ms. Collins."

"Sorry, Tina."

"I saw you flashing your badge earlier and heard your story about the AMBER Alert. So why are you asking questions about Jacob Holland?"

"I can't speak to that, or anything about the investigation. I'm just asking questions."

"Eh, figures. Well, ask me whatever. I'm an open book."

Notepad at the ready, Debra asked, "Tell me about this Jacob Holland."

"Well, obviously you know Holland wine. He's the heir. The only remaining Holland child. Other than him, all that's left is the mother, and she's sickly. Lord knows how much he'll inherit, or already has. But all the money in the world can't make up for the crap that family has had to go through. Too much to bear, really, no matter the, say, financial stability. That's a term all those highfalutin types use, no? Financial stability?"

"Wouldn't know," Debra replied, though her mind was elsewhere.

"Me either. My ex left me enough to get by, but definitely not enough to run with those folks."

"You said they, the Holland family, has gone through a lot. What did you mean by that?"

"Well, where to start? When Jacob was little, his father offed himself. Story has it the Holland senior shot himself with a shotgun on a camping trip with Jacob. Blew his head clean off. Not sure how old Jacob was then, but he couldn't have been more than ten, eleven."

Eleven years and three months old, Debra thought.

"Yeah," Tina said, "Ten or eleven, something like that. Can't remember exactly. Worst thing is that, rumor has it, Jacob saw him do it. Could you imagine the impact that would have on a little tike? I mean, Lord in Heaven."

"I can't imagine," Debra replied, dishonestly. "But you're certain Ms. Paxton was meeting Mr. Holland here?"

"Oh, one-thousand percent sure. You can't forget that boy's face. Too damned pretty to forget. I may be getting up there in years, but a few things I never forget, like a cute face."

"Okay. What, if anything, can you tell me about their meetings?"

"Tell you?"

"Yeah. Did they seem professional, or romantic?"

"Professional? Ha!" Tina slapped her small knee covered by thin gabardine. "That's a laugh. No, nothing professional about it. Not that they were making out or anything like that. Might as well have been, though, with the way she looked at him. Never got a man to look at me like that, let me tell you."

"How did she look at him?"

"Like they talk about in them books over there." She nodded towards the romance section. "I've never been too good with descriptions, but it was, I don't know, transcendental. Is that the right word?"

Debra smiled. "I get the gist."

"Doesn't take a rocket surgeon to figure it all out. They acted all secretive like, always looking around to see who's lookin' back."

"Were they ever physical?" Debra asked, leaning in, pen at the ready. "Like, did they ever hold hands? Kiss? Anything like that?"

"Not that I saw. But, sometimes a look is, I don't know, deeper I guess? Let's go with that."

"Let's," Debra replied, finalizing her notes about this interaction. Ms. Paxton had a young suitor. And Jacob Holland at that.

"Did any of that help?" Tina asked.

"Not sure," Debra replied. "But maybe. Thank you so much.

Do you have a number I can reach you at if I have follow-up questions?"

"Oh sure, honey." Tina riffled through her oversized Gucci bag for several seconds before pulling out a thick business card, which described her profession as a "stylist."

"Thank you, Ms. Col… I mean, Tina. I'll call if I need anything further."

"Call me anytime, sweetie. I'm not much of a sleeper. Anything I can do to help, you let me know."

"Will do." Debra shook her hand and smiled at Amber.

"Sure you don't need anything?" Amber asked. "Maybe a coffee to go?"

Debra seriously considered the offer, mulling the benefits that caffeine may provide. But she knew she did not have time.

With a smile, Debra replied, "No, that's fine. Thanks, though." She rushed out of the Grapes of Write and headed towards and hopped into her car.

Debra reached into the backseat and pulled out the Jodi Johnston file, flipping through pages to find a particular section. Before her disappearance, Ms. Johnston was a twenty-two-year-old female who had recently graduated from college, double majoring in business and horticulture. It was her dream to get into the wine industry, and it was through that pursuit that she met Jacob Holland, whose family-owned Holland Vineyard, the largest and most profitable vineyard in the Kenwood area. Many viewed the match as almost too perfect. One interviewee referred to Jacob and Jodi as the "Ken and Barbie of Sonoma," an analogy that stuck with Debra.

Debra flipped through a few pages before finding what she sought: the notes from her multiple conversations with Jacob Holland, Jodi Johnston's boyfriend, and the last person to see her before she disappeared.

Their contentious interviews flashed through her mind, as

did her dislike of him. She never had enough to charge him, but his arrogant smugness and evasiveness kept him at the forefront of her personal people-of-interest list before the case went cold. After the third interview, Jacob's lawyer walled her off from any further interviews. Her subsequent, and futile, attempts to obtain a warrant or charge him fell on deaf ears. She had pushed so hard her Chief had come down on her, lecturing her on keeping her "eyes on the prize," whatever the hell that meant. The case officially closed a few months ago, the department concluding that Jodi ran away, meaning it was no longer a police matter.

And yet, that stark conclusion never helped her sleep better at night. Often, as she drifted away into rest, Jacob's face appeared in her view, his smug smile taunting her.

Their last conversation especially haunted her. After a two-hour grilling session, Jacob raised his hands and said, "You know what, Detective? That's about enough." After that, he waved towards his attorney, who entered and shut down that and any future interview. Before leaving, he winked and said, "I'll need a stiff drink after all this crap."

A thought struck her. She flipped to the front of the file, searching for a specific notation. She found it on page two. She read the note, then read it again to confirm.

Before disappearing, Jodi Johnston sent a text to her parents that said, "Gonna take a long vacation. You won't hear from me for a while. I love you." Debra then focused on the text Jenna had sent to her grandparents.

Gonna play ball with Dad, Debra considered. *Gonna take a long vacation.*

Neither sounded like a text a 10-year-old or early-twenties girl would send. Both sounded like a text someone trying to imitate a female would send.

Then there was Sarah Meyers's comment that Ethan's text lacked proper punctuation. A small, likely meaningless point alone. But when combined with the odd text from Jenna and similarly odd text from Jodi, perhaps a pattern emerged?

Also, there was Beverly. Sonoma was a quiet town, and yet in the last six months, one girl goes missing, another is murdered, and Jacob dated both? The coincidences were piling up so high that she could no longer ignore their shape.

The wine cork they found on the scene also resonated in her mind. That, alone, didn't amount to much, but given she now had reason to believe that Jacob Holland, heir to one of the largest Wine Country fortunes, may have dated both Jodi and Beverly, how could she ignore it? Along with an empty bottle of Holland wine in the trash? There was no way she could dance around it: there was the possibility, however slight, that Jacob was involved with both Jenna and Jodi's disappearances.

"Jacob Holland," Debra whispered with a sigh. "Jesus Christ."

As she flipped through the pages, she realized the file did not contain the notes from her first interview with Jacob. She checked the file twice and reaffirmed their absence. He made a few comments during that interview which caused her neck hairs to stand, and she wanted to review the specifics of those comments.

For a moment, she considered what to do. She really wanted to see those notes to jolt her memory, but asking for them might put her back on the Department's radar.

Jenna's face flashed in Debra's mind, cementing her decision. She dialed her office and pressed the phone to her face. Two rings later, a chipper voice answered by saying, "Hey there, Debra. You okay?"

"Yeah, Elizabeth. I'm working this Jenna Paxton matter."

"Yeah," she replied, her voice hushed. "The whole department's buzzing about it. Any good news?"

"Not much yet. But hey, I need you to do me a favor."

"Anything."

"I need to look at the Jodi Johnston file. Could you email me a few things from it?"

Debra waited for a response, but none came.

"Elizabeth?" Debra asked. "You there?"

"I'm sorry, Deb," Elizabeth finally replied. "I really can't do that. The Chief would have my head. Not after everything that happened."

Debra opened her mouth to protest but decided she may be putting the cart before the horse. She needed a stronger connection between Jenna and Jacob, then she could take her suspicions straight to the Chief.

"That's fine," Debra replied. "Could you do me another favor instead?"

"What's that?" Elizabeth asked hesitantly.

"Let's keep this call between us, okay?"

"That, I can do," Elizabeth replied, her chipper tone returning.

"Well, I gotta get back to it. I'll let you know if I need anything else."

"Good luck!"

Debra broke the connection and sat in the car. With an incomplete file, she needed to focus, so she closed her eyes and concentrated on her memories. She recalled how Jacob sat across her desk three times, each time with that smug smile, his attorney within earshot. Each time, his responses made perfect sense, and yet she ended up not buying a single excuse. And after their last interview, when Jacob slipped, she never wavered from her belief that the son-of-a-bitch had something to do with Jodi's disappearance.

Perhaps she had taken it too far in that case. Most cops would agree that the Chief was correct in barring her from the case after Jacob's attorney filed a long, well-researched formal complaint. Debra had been lucky to keep her job. But that luck hadn't stopped her from pursuing the matter outside the confines of her job.

For her, the complaint changed nothing. In her gut, she never budged from her beliefs about Jacob. And this time, if her gut told her Jacob had something to do with Jenna's disappearance, she was determined to push all concerns aside. Her job paled in comparison to Jenna's life.

That memory in mind, Debra lifted the Peter Sullivan file and paused before opening it, instinctively looking out the window to ensure she was alone in the parking lot. She slid out the first picture in the file. She gazed at it, as confused as she was the first day she saw it.

In the picture, Jacob sat in a specific spot on the Holland Vineyard property, staring longingly at the dirt. More disturbing, Peter Sullivan provided five other images of Jacob doing the same thing on five separate occasions.

What the hell are you looking at, Debra wondered.

She replaced the photo, closed the file, and sat back into her seat. Jacob met Beverly for drinks in public. How did Peter miss that?

She lifted her phone and dialed Peter's number. After a few rings, her call went to voicemail, just like all her calls over the last couple of months. Peter no longer returned her calls or texts, and he never provided a reason for suddenly ending their professional relationship. He never even cashed her last check.

Debra considered redialing but figured it was futile. Instead, she lowered the phone, closed her eyes, and put herself into the memory of her last conversation with Jacob, the conversation that sparked her obsession and almost ended her career.

9

FIVE MONTHS PRIOR

Debra sat and tapped her fingernails against the table, a nervous habit she thought she had snubbed out years ago. In her periphery, she glanced at the overhead clock, which showed that Jacob was twenty-three minutes late.

Twenty-three minutes, she considered. Jacob arrived fifteen minutes late for the first interview; for the second, twenty minutes late. Would he really arrive twenty-five minutes late for the third? Debra noted how even Jacob's randomness appeared calculated.

Debra watched the door as the clock clicked. She did not enjoy these interviews. While he said the right things, Jacob unnerved her. Interviewing him was like having a delightful meal with an ingredient that tasted undercooked, though she could never put her finger on exactly which ingredient.

Debra glanced back at the clock, which clicked over to a new minute, meaning Jacob was twenty-five minutes late. As if on cue, Debra heard shuffling from outside the door, which swung open a moment later, Jacob stepping in first, his attorney, Joe Webster, in tow.

"Jacob," Debra said as she stood and extended her hand. "Thanks for meeting with me again."

"Anything, anytime," he said as he took her hand. "Sorry, am I late?"

"Yes." She released his grip, which lingered a beat too long for her comfort. "Twenty-five minutes late."

Jacob put his hands up near his shoulders. "And here I thought I was five minutes early! I've never been great with time."

"Seems that way. Please have a seat."

She gestured, and Jacob took a seat, fixing his rolled-up sleeves as he did so. He wore a turquoise shirt that appeared custom fitted, and the florescent bulbs caused his gold Rolex to blast bursts of light. During their first meeting, Jacob at least put up a façade of a worried boyfriend concerned about his missing girlfriend. Now, he sat across from her with his trademark shit-eating grin, knowing he maintained the upper-hand unless she somehow took it from him.

"As I mentioned in our prior meetings," Debra said, breaking the silence, "you are not under arrest. You don't need an attorney here."

"Au contraire," Jacob replied with a waggle of his finger. "I need him to make sure I don't need him. Besides look at him." Jacob gestured towards Joe. "He's too pretty to leave at home."

After reviewing the small, bespectacled man, she focused on Jacob. "That is your right. Ready to go?"

Jacob nodded. "Always. But why are we here, again? Is there a break in the case?"

Debra shook her head. "No. I'd just like to go over your story."

"My story?" Jacob tilted his head. "And you wonder why I want my attorney here."

"Fine, Jacob. Call it whatever you want. I want to go back and make sure I didn't miss anything."

"Fine, fine."

"I mean, you do want us to find her, right?"

This question obviously caught Jacob off-guard, who repositioned himself and replied, "Of course. That's why I'm here."

"Let's get started, then. Tell me exactly what happened the night Jodi disappeared."

"For the third time, this is what happened. We had dinner in a little house on the Holland Vineyard property we call the butler's house."

Debra reviewed her notes as Jacob spoke. "And this is the same house you won't let us search, right?"

"Of course, I will, when you have a warrant."

Debra rolled her eyes but didn't reply.

"Like I was saying," Jacob continued. "We had dinner in the butler's house. I cooked fish. From the moment she arrived, she looked sad. I kept asking her why, but she didn't tell me. At the end of dinner, she said she needed a break."

"Did she say why?"

Jacob shook his head. "I tried to fish for a reason, pardon the pun, but she didn't give any. Just said she needed a vacation."

Debra blinked twice and took a moment to process Jacob's words. "She said she needed a vacation? That's what she told you?"

Jacob shifted again, more pronounced this time, and replied, "No, sorry. Break. I said break."

"No," Debra shot back. "You said vacation. And," she flipped through her notes, "you said break the two other times we met." She closed the notebook and let her hand linger on the file's cover. "This time, you used the word 'vacation.'"

Jacob inhaled and said, "Sorry, not sure why I used that word. Got confused. I think Jodi's parents used it once—"

"Funny," Debra interrupted. "Because I spoke to them last week. They said they haven't talked to you in a while. And I'm pretty sure they would have told me about any conversation with you." She leaned in and whispered, "You may not want to hear it, but they don't like you."

He narrowed his sights on her and replied, "That so?"

She leaned back and said, "Yeah, but that's not really what matters here. Really, they don't trust you. And neither do I."

Jacob slammed both of his hands onto the table, startling Debra so much she nearly fell out of her chair. "Trust?" Jacob repeated in mocking fashion. "You wanna talk about trust? How am I supposed to trust that you're going to figure out what's happened to Jodi when you've been so fucking incompetent?"

Debra collected herself enough to ask, "Excuse me?"

"Do I really need to spell it out? Fine. Jodi's been gone for a month now. Have you found her car?"

Debra didn't reply, but instead stared hotly at Jacob.

"It's hard to miss," Jacob continued. "2012 yellow Mini Cooper with black stripes. I mean, come on. There aren't a bunch of those on the streets."

"I know there aren't, Jacob."

"And her phone?" Jacob yelled so loudly that spittle ran down his bottom lip, which he wiped away with his forearm. "You never told me what it said, but she sent a final text, I know that. I know it. You can track it. You can get the info from the cell towers or whatever. Where is her phone?"

Debra inhaled, waited a beat, and replied, "We don't know, Jacob. We searched all of Santa Rosa for it."

"Well, why the hell didn't you find it? Santa Rosa isn't a big place." Jacob pounded the table again with less force, an apparent attempt to display his waning energy. His charade had run its course and was having the opposite of its intended effect on Debra, especially with this unintended Santa Rosa admission.

Debra glared at Jacob as she would her fussy daughter and said, "Yeah, I'm not buying it."

Jacob squinted. "Buy what?"

"Your little performance here. I've seen kids do better in school plays."

Jacob's shoulders tensed as if he was about to pounce. "Why you—"

"Hey, now," Joe interjected, with a much deeper voice than suggested by his build. "Let's lower the temperature a bit."

Jacob glanced at Joe, and Debra saw Jacob's shoulders relax. "You know what, Detective?" Jacob said. "That's about enough. This is getting us nowhere."

"I disagree," Debra replied, prompting a confused expression from Jacob. "This got me to exactly where I needed to be."

"That so?" The anger returned to Jacob's face.

Debra smiled and nodded. "Yup. I know what I need to do now."

Jacob's anger drained at this, and a haunting smile crept across his face. "We'll just see about that." He gestured at Joe, who jumped out of his seat. Jacob then winked at Debra and said, "I'll need a stiff drink after all this crap." He then turned and headed out the door, with Joe following, leaving Debra in silence.

Alone, Debra leaned back into her chair and stared at the shut door. In the quiet, she considered his unintentional admissions. First, he used the word "vacation" when describing his final conversation with Jodi. He had never used the word "vacation" before, and that specific word appeared in Jodi's final, non-public text message to her parents. But what really sealed the deal for Debra was his nonchalant reaction to her Santa Rosa reference. The public did not know that Jodi's cell phone last dinged in Santa Rosa.

Under her breath, she whispered, "He did it."

10

FOUR MONTHS PRIOR

Debra stared at the email from her Chief, written in a cold, professional tone. She doubted the Chief wrote many, if any, of the lines in the email. It sounded straight from internal affairs rather than the hothead who had employed her for so many years.

Debra focused on the last two lines: "You are immediately removed from the Jodi Johnston case. Please return all case materials to Human Resources by the close of business today."

Immediately removed, Debra considered. The email instructed her as an instruction manual may, assuming the person reading could "immediately" switch off the part of her brain that had focused on Jodi for the past few months.

Debra glanced at the clock and saw she only had a couple hours to discreetly copy the materials she needed to copy. But first, she needed to place a call.

She lifted her phone and dialed a number she had never placed from her personal cellphone. Three rings later, a gruff voice answered, "Peter Sullivan."

"Hey Peter," Debra said.

"Deb?" Peter asked. "That you?"

"It is."

"Sorry, didn't recognize this number."

"You wouldn't. It's my personal cell."

Peter paused before replying, "Okay. Why are you calling from this number?"

Debra leaned into the phone and said, "Listen, Peter. You and I go way back. I think I'm the only one who didn't give you shit when you left the Department."

"That might be true. You calling for career advice? I can tell you I'm already making more money as a private detective."

Debra smiled. "No, no. That's not it. How do I put this?" She considered before saying, "I need to hire you."

Silence again before he replied, "Hire me? Like, personally?"

"Sure, personally. That's a good way to put it."

"I don't—" he stuttered. "I don't understand."

"You will when we meet. You free for lunch today?"

"I mean, sure. I'm always free for lunch with an old friend."

Debra nodded. "Let's go with that. Lunch with an old friend."

"Be straight with me, Deb. Will I get into some shit for this?"

"What, you're afraid of getting your hands dirty? That's not the Peter I know."

"Trust me. I'm still the same guy."

Debra grinned. "I'll be the judge of that. So, wanna grab a burger? Say meet at Benjamin's at noon?"

The line remained quiet for several seconds. "I don't know, Deb. I don't know. This sounds crazy. We go way back, but this is a big ask."

Debra gripped the phone tight. "Yeah? A big ask? How big was the ask when you asked me to take it easy on your son's DUI?"

"Deb."

"Or when I covered for your ass after you almost screwed up the Buchanan investigation. Remember how you cried in my office? I figure that was a pretty big ask, no?"

Peter sighed. "Fine, okay. But I better get some referrals for this crap."

She smiled. "Absolutely."

"Forget some. A bunch."

"Fine. A bunch. Cross my heart."

"Alright. See you then, Deb."

"Yeah, see you then."

The line disconnected, and Debra let the phone linger on her cheek for a couple seconds, the reality of what she had just done sinking in. Her guts turned, and sweat beads blotted her forehead. If anyone found out that she hired a private detective to look into Jacob, she would be fired in a heartbeat. But finding out what happened to Jodi's heartbeat took far greater priority.

11

THREE MONTHS PRIOR

In a fatigue fog, Debra barely noticed her phone vibrate in the car's cupholder. She lifted it and saw that had missed Bill's call. But more than that, she had apparently missed five calls from him.

"Shit," she said as she shot up and looked at the clock, which read "12:04."

How is it that late? she wondered, but the answer was clear—she had fallen asleep while on an off-the-books stakeout. She called Bill back, who answered before the first ring ended.

"Where the hell are you?"

"I, uh—" Debra wished she had thought of a good excuse before calling him back. "I'm working. I'm sorry."

"What the hell do you mean?" Debra had never heard him so mad. While understandable, an angry Bill was off-putting, like hearing Mr. Rogers curse. "You're working late, and you didn't think to call me and let me know?"

Debra considered his question. How was she supposed to answer? Was she supposed to tell him that Peter Sullivan had learned about Jacob's late-night trips to San Francisco? Was she supposed to tell him that she ran a rogue investigation that would surely get her fired if the Department ever got wind of it?

"Debra," Bill continued, but with a softer tone. "Are you really working?"

"Yes. Wait, what?" The implication hit her like a truck. She pressed the phone against her face and said, "Are you really asking what I think you're asking?"

"Can you blame me? This is the second time this week you've disappeared at night without letting us know, fourth time this month."

Debra sighed. "Here, listen." She flicked on her lights, which flickered with the siren's unmistakable wail. She let the siren run for a couple of seconds before clicking it off. "There, happy?"

Bill paused before replying. "No, Debra. I'm not happy. I'm not happy at all. And neither is Charlotte."

She collapsed into her seat. "I know."

"No, you don't. Do you know I spoke to her school counselor today?"

"No." Debra shot back up. "Wait, what?"

"That's right. I had a special meeting today at the school. I tried to call you about it, but you didn't pick up. They think Charlotte's depressed. And when I asked why, all they said was that she 'missed her mom.'"

"I," Debra started, but stopped to force back tears. "I don't know what to say."

"Say you're going to come home and stay home."

"I will. I promise." Debra meant it.

"Good." Bill hung up without a further word.

Debra didn't even hesitate. She put the car into gear and hit the gas.

12

THREE MONTHS PRIOR

In the candlelight's glow, Jacob watched Debra drive off through a small screen. She was a helluva detective, but she possessed one fatal flaw: predictability. It was easy to find Debra's hiding spot, just off the road and far enough from the vineyard's gates to avoid easy detection, but close enough for her to keep a watchful eye over his operations. Thankfully, her absence the night before allowed him to go on a successful hunting trip.

Jacob placed the monitor on the table and sipped on his wine, which was good, but not great. He had improved as a winemaker, but even the greatest winemaker is limited by the quality of his grapes.

Jacob rested his glass on the table and watched as its shadow danced under the flicking candle, its penumbra causing it to look far bigger, much like his ambitions. He had made great progress, but even greater progress awaited him.

He closed his eyes and considered Debra. In particular, he thought of that brief flick of her sirens. Was she trying to send him a message? Perhaps it was time to get focused. With Debra on his ass, he needed to concentrate on laying the groundwork for his ultimate plan. This may cause him temporary discomfort, but the long-term payoff will be immeasurable.

Lost in his thoughts, he barely noticed the nearby movement. He blinked his eyes and focused on the blob of shadow that lay at his feet, moaning.

"Hey," Jacob said as he kicked the blob, which reacted with a startled jump. "Welcome back to the land of the living." Jacob stood, grabbed the candle, and walked to the top of the blob. He kneeled and shone the light on the man's face. A matted, disgusting beard obstructed his face. Soot covered the crevasses of his haggard face, and his long, white hair resembled that of Einstein. The man's hazel eyes quivered with fear, and he tried to speak, but the fatigue of the medicine and duct tape prevented it.

Jacob stepped back in revulsion and said, "There's no reason to fight anymore. It'll do you no good." Jacob could barely get the words out as the man's stench overpowered Jacob. "First things first," Jacob side, covering his nose. "We need to give you a bath."

Jacob placed the candle on the edge of the table so that it provided him enough light. He then grabbed the nearby bucket filled with a solution of water and soap, lifted it over the man, and poured it over him. The water awoke the man's senses, and he started the fight the restraints with far more vigor.

Jacob placed the bucket to the side and grabbed the second one, repeating the process. The man continued to struggle, but he also uncontrollably shivered. It started as a few minor trembles, but soon his whole body quivered. This made sense as Jacob did not warm the water, and the room was temperature controlled to around 50 degrees.

Jacob reviewed his work with contentment. He would return with more buckets in a day or so. It was important to keep the body as cold as possible without causing hypothermia. Jacob knew through his research that the man's wet clothes robbed his body of internal heat, artificially lowering his body temperature.

The man soon lay flat, no longer fighting. However, Jacob detected a strange noise. At first, Jacob thought the man moaned, but the moan's repetition was too clear and consistent. Jacob soon realized that the man tried to speak.

"Are you trying to tell me something?" Jacob said with a raised eyebrow. He leaned down and towards the man's mouth, focusing on the noises he made. Soon, Jacob realized the man softly chanted, "Please, God," over and over, though through the duct tape the words sounded like, "Pws, gaw."

Jacob couldn't resist laughing at this. Looking at the wreck at his feet, he wondered how anyone dealt this man's card in life could believe in a higher power. He recalled a quote he heard once from Neil deGrasse Tyson: "God is either not all powerful, or not all good." This man's tortuous existence supported this conclusion.

Jacob playfully slapped the man and said, "Look at me." The man complied, ceasing his chanting and focusing his shaky eyes on Jacob. "That's good."

Jacob stroked the man's filthy hair and said, "I need you to understand one thing. It'll help you get through what's about to happen." Jacob moved his hand from the man's hair and onto his face, squeezing his cheeks as a mother would to a cute child. "For the rest of your miserable existence, you will have only one God." Jacob pulled the man's face close to him, and he whispered into his ear, "Me."

13

———

NOW

Jacob parked near the curb of a white cottage in an upper-middle class neighborhood. As he approached the cottage, he studied the exterior and realized that Sherri had done a nice job with the place. The lawn was freshly mowed. He noticed no stray newspapers. A green rocking chair swayed in the breeze before a lively row of red and white flowers. The railing appeared recently painted, and a new rug that announced "WELCOME" lay at his feet.

Amazing what she can do when she has nothing to do, he concluded.

Jacob collected his thoughts for a moment before knocking on the front door. As he waited, he wondered whether involving Sherri was a good idea. He had little choice, though. He needed an alibi, and she was his best option.

A blurry eyeball appeared in the peephole, and a high-pitched voice followed.

"Hey hunny!" Sherri yelled as she attempted to open the door, though it got caught, as it always did, by the safety chain. "Oh, silly me," she sighed and fiddled with the lock.

"Hey there, baby," he replied. "Just take your time."

"I'm telling you, the damn thing won't..." She almost fell over pulling the latch out of the hole. Once composed, she ran into his arms yelling, "What are you doing here, hunny? Wasn't expectin' ya until tonight." She noticed the flowers, a bright, bold bouquet, and said, "Now, now, who are those pretty things for?"

Jacob fought hard to resist flinching at her grating Texas twang. "They are for my pretty little thing."

"Goodness, baby. Thank you so much!" She grabbed and tilted them to her nose, giving them a great whiff. "They are beautiful! Smell amazing, too."

"Only the best for you."

"What did I do to deserve this? Flowers and an unexpected visit?" She twirled her golden locks demurely. "Do you have something to apologize for, Mr. Holland?" she asked with a coy grin.

"No way. Just wanted to see my best girl before heading in and wanted to bring her something nice. Got any coffee brewed?"

"Always!" She kissed him several times, stepped back while still holding his hand, and pulled at his arm. "Come on in."

"Thanks, hot stuff." He smacked her backside as he strolled in, putting on his best love-sick manners and voice. "The place looks good," he commented, and it did. The cottage was not large, but when he bought it, it looked much bigger without furniture. Now, it appeared straight out of a Pottery Barn catalog. She painted the walls a light gray which complemented the tweed furniture and teal-dominant artwork. The kitchen counters appeared remodeled as well, with bright subway tile sparkling in the well-lit room. He calculated the monetary damage, and the total wasn't pretty.

"Don't it?" she replied. "It'll look even better with these beauties." She disappeared into the kitchen, and when she reappeared, she held the flowers in one hand and a crystal vase in the other. She placed the vase in the middle of the table and put the flowers in it. The vase had no water in it, but he didn't tell her.

"Been working my hiney off gettin' it all pretty for ya. But don't sweat now, dear. I made sure I got good deals on all of it. Promise I ain't takin' advantage of your kindness."

I need to review her credit card bills closer, he thought.

"I'm sure you're not, baby," he said. "Besides, once things are all figured out and you move in with me, this furniture will help the place sell way faster. You did good."

"Really?" she asked with a crooked smile.

"Yup. Real good." He often caught himself mirroring her speech patterns; his sentences became short and trite when he spoke to Sherri. This infuriated him, but she also had an odd way of making him forget about himself. These lapses incensed him even more than the altered speech. Today, however, he remained focused. The job was too big. He could not permit unconscious drifting.

"So, what brings you around here? Wasn't figurin' I'd see you until tonight. Call next time. I'm a mess." She looked far from it: a red sundress that matched her lipstick. For an instant, he wanted to reach out and pull her close, escape into that dress and what it hid. He had time, didn't he?

Snap out of it, he thought. *You've got a job to do.*

"Well, I kinda got a weird request. It might not make much sense, but you have to trust me on this."

"Of course, babe. I'd trust you with anything."

"All right, so here it is. I think my mom has hired someone to follow me."

Her face crunched in anger and confusion. "What do you mean, follow you?"

"Like a private detective. She may be even paying off a cop."

"What makes you think that?"

"I saw someone tailing me yesterday."

"What?" Her eyes were wide with shock. "That's crazy."

"Yeah. You know this town and its gossip. It's like a knitting circle."

"I guess." She shrugged.

"Anyway, I'm worried she's going to try to push you away from me or make up something about me to justify dissolving my trusts and cutting me out of the will." He stepped towards her. "She may have lost a few marbles, but the last ones she's got are clear. She knows exactly what's she's doing." His composure returned as he spoke, lying always brought the best out of him.

"Golly babe. Does she really hate me that much?" Her voice quivered with genuine pain.

"I mean, not you, babe. Us." He extended his index finger at her, then back at himself. "She's got it in her head that us being together would ruin the family name. I don't give a shit, though. It's me and you. I just need to hang on until she's, well, gone."

"I get it." She gently grasped his arm.

"Then, it'll just be us. We'll move in together, get married. Have a couple of kids. We can do whatever you want."

"Oh, even move somewhere else? Like, open another vineyard and start new? We could move somewhere like Washington." She clapped three annoying little claps. "I heard they make great wine there. Just get away from all this, you know?"

He hated her in that moment, to a degree that was difficult to conceal. "Wow, that's a terrific idea!" Jacob exclaimed, his voice a pitch too high. "A clean start sounds good. But we'll discuss that later."

"Yeah, I may be putting the ol' cart before the horse," she said, head hung. "So, what's the favor?"

"All right, this may seem weird, but you have to go with me. If someone, anyone, asks you where I was on a random night, tell them I was with you."

"What?" Her eyes focused on his. "I don't understand."

"Like I said, my mom is either trying to pin something on me or break us up. Either way, it wouldn't surprise me if she hired someone, even a cop, to pretend like I was somewhere or did something wrong. So, if someone asks, just say I was with you. Like, last night, or the night before. If we weren't together, say we were. It'll cut them off and they won't know what to do. Does that make sense?"

"No," she smiled and shook her head. "Not at all. But I trust you're doin' the best thing for us."

"Oh, and one more thing. If that happens, if someone asks you something about me, call me ASAP. The second they leave. Got it?"

"I get it, baby, no need to stress." She rubbed his shoulders as she softly spoke. "I'll take care of it. Speaking of, you wanna go into the bedroom so I can take care of you? You seem all wound up and need a little unwinding."

She wasn't wrong, and he was tempted. But he instead kissed her and said, "Not right now, baby. I really need to get to work. But I promise, soon, we'll unwind together. Okay?"

"Pinky swear?" She presented a thin finger and an innocent expression.

"Pinky swear," he replied as he locked his pinky with hers. "Later. Right now I really have to head out. I'll call you later today, okay?"

"You better," she said and smacked his butt as he passed. "Don't call too late though. I need my beauty rest."

"No, you don't," he whispered before walking out the door. "You couldn't get more beautiful." He gave her one last kiss, exited the cottage, and waved before hopping into the truck. Once she stopped waving in return and closed the door, he revisited the issue of her involvement. On one hand, she was a nice alibi, but on the other, she may crack under even moderate pressure. Either way, he did not intend to stick around once the ground trembled.

After turning the ignition, he pulled onto the street and drove towards his next errand. He was doing okay on time. It wouldn't matter if he was late, but he couldn't arrive *too* late. That could lead to suspicion, or at least curiosity.

As he drove, he considered the plan, as he had countless times before. It seemed so flawless, so intricate, so coordinated. But, perhaps, that was its biggest drawback. Like an aligned domino set, one off-center domino can stop the entire momentum of the fall. So, he may have to improvise, step in to keep the pieces falling into place. Sherri was one such piece. He had ideas for a few others.

Distracted, he almost missed his destination. He turned right, drove up to the gate, and pressed in the code. The gate lifted, and after navigating a few turns, he pulled into the parking spot closest to his storage unit.

As he stepped into the hallway, he enjoyed the briskness of the air seeping through the doors of the units, each nurturing a wonderful range of different varietals. He enjoyed speculating about what the units stored, particularly after meeting his storage neighbors. For instance, the owner of unit 613 was a stodgy, pudgy guy with a formal demeanor and clothes that never fit. Jacob imagined pretentious French varietals occupied Unit 613, chosen by arbitrary ratings rather than experience or collection fit.

His unit was 641, the largest available. He plugged in the code 8 – 3 – 4 – 5 – 1. The storage unit was even colder than the hallway. It contained several wine racks and additional coolers for white wines. Large boxes also covered one wall, in which he kept his least expensive wines and most important possession.

Jacob shifted two boxes to the side, relocated the third box to the middle of the room, and opened it. An unmarked cooler rested inside. After lifting the cooler's lid and enjoying its bath of brisk air, he concluded Justin was true to his word.

Vials and bottles of Propofol lined the cooler, each containing varying amounts of the substance. He would later verify the exact amounts and confirm that Justin had indeed supplied "more than discussed" as promised, not that Jacob was overly concerned. An eyeball evaluation suggested he possessed enough Propofol to drug a small infantry.

Jacob slid the cooler back in the box, closed it, and rearranged the other boxes. He then strolled out of the storage unit, the box containing the cooler under his arm, a whistle accompanying his steps. There was no rush. The cooler would chill the medicine until he had a chance to load it into the private reserve.

In the car, the cooler loaded in back, Jacob considered whether he should wait to deliver the other bouquet. He decided to press forward, for he had someone to visit, someone to thank, someone with whom he needed to confide. Besides, he often showed up late. Timeliness might raise more eyebrows.

Soon, he was before the gates to Holland Vineyard. In the distance, he noticed the outlines of early patrons and employees scurrying to welcome the incoming crowd. He drove past the main tasting room and up a hill until he reached the butler's house.

He stepped out of the truck, grabbed the other bouquet—the subtle one—and finalized his decision. A clear head was critical. He smiled and gestured towards a few vineyard workers in the distance. He extended his arms and allowed the immaculate August air to tickle his skin. The air smelled saccharine, like sugar cookies baking in the oven. Fat grapes lined the thick vines, awaiting upcoming harvest. Future faces of those popping corks flashed in his mind. It was his favorite time of year, for it was the harvest, the fulfillment of his family's purpose.

Before long, he arrived at the spot. He sat and gazed at the ground before placing down the bouquet.

"Hey babe," he said. "It's me. I know I haven't been around for a couple weeks, and I'm sorry about that."

He gripped a handful of dirt, caressing it in his palm, the grains slithering between his fingers. Dirt had been such a large part of his life. His first memories involved his father explaining the importance of dirt, how it played a critical role in making excellent wine. He would speak in metaphors, pontificating that the earth spoke to wine makers, and no great wine maker tuned out the dirt. Jacob was raised from dirt, it was no less a part of him than his blood and guts.

"I've been busy," Jacob continued. "Well, that's partly true. I was distracted for a long time after you left, did some stupid things. I wouldn't have done these things in my right state of mind. But you messed me up." He contemplated that statement and clarified, "No, sorry babe. You didn't mess me up. I messed me up. I was the one who made the mistakes. But no longer." He leaned closer to the ground, whispering now. "I've perfected it. I think I've got the formula down. Well, at least the ratio. I've worked hard so I won't repeat the same mistakes I made with you. And now, I'm on the verge of landing the perfect grapes, can you believe it? I almost can't." He kissed the hand that held the dirt and sprinkled it over the ground. "But I promise you, I will not fail this time. I won't let excitement get the best of me. I am going to take my time, enjoy it, like I should have with you."

With a sigh, he stood and brushed the dust from his jeans. "You are still my world," he said. "Without you, I wouldn't be here. I owe everything to you. I am going to finish this for you. Wherever you are, I hope you're proud of me."

Where the hell did that come from? he thought. He gave no credence to the notion of an afterlife. Maybe his mother seized his brain for a moment? Either way, a slip of the tongue meant nothing. His convictions persisted, undaunted and undoubted.

"But Momma always said," he murmured with a smile. "Greatness is earned, not given. I have so much more left to go, and so much can go wrong. But it won't. I feel it. I feel it deep within me. Not sure what that means, but I can't explain it much better."

The tasting room to his back, he stared at his surroundings, gawking at the rolling green hills shimmering in the early-morning shine like massive diamonds, the sun's rays tinting the area with a bright-orange glow. Rows of vines surrounded him for as far as he could see. To his right, the clear water of the vineyard's pond quivered in the gentle breeze, making the reflected trees dance.

"I've been surrounded by beauty my entire life," he whispered with rediscovered awe. "Beauty I could never top. I have worked in a field perfected by others. So now," he cast a glance towards the ground, "it's time to leave my mark. To sign a Holland signature on something new. Different. Better."

He closed his eyes and practiced the breathing he learned in the yoga lessons Jodi used to drag him to. He filled his lungs, the elasticity pressing against his ribs and chest, cloying morning air recharging his essence. Was he ready? Would the plan work? Were the pieces in place? Had he missed something?

The words of his mother rang through his mind. *Doubt is worthless,* she would say. *Action is the only thing that matters. Failing is worthwhile. Succeeding is worthwhile. Doubt is worthless.*

With that, he regained his determination and headed towards the direction he came. His gait felt lighter now, more purposeful. Nothing would, or could, stop him. He would make certain of that.

14

When Debra arrived back at the scene, little had changed aside from the number of vehicles and officers. Reporters circled the area like preying vultures, awaiting the kill. With more sun, she better grasped the area's vastness. A single path led into countless trees; the foreboding path accelerated her pulse. After parking, she spotted McCarthy in the distance and flagged him down. As he approached, she noticed disappointment etched in his face.

"Nothing?" she guessed.

"Less than," he replied, his voice a blend of frustration and exhaustion. "Every time we find something, it turns to shit."

"What do you mean?"

"Well, we haven't found any more clothes. Just the sweatshirt. We got the tracks, shoe size looks like it matches. But the prints are all over the place, not leading to anything, like he was running in circles."

"Nothing else?"

"Nada." He shrugged. "We're guessing he panicked and just started running, but I mean, that's a stretch, Deb. Big stretch I think. Any luck with the neighbors?"

"Nothing." This wasn't a complete lie. She had interviewed people in nearby homes, but the conversations were fruitless, and none had cameras pointed at the road.

"Well, at least we got sunlight for a while. We're going to catch this bastard, one way or another."

She reviewed the park and noted a few individuals in plain clothing. Pointing, she asked, "I'm guessing they are the start of the civilian cavalry?"

"Bingo. I'm bettin' many more are comin'. I'm actually okay with it in this situation, unless you tell me otherwise."

"Under one condition," she replied as she wheeled on McCarthy. "We can't get overwhelmed by volunteers. We have a lot of ground to cover and can't afford to get bogged down."

"You ain't kiddin'. There are about a billion and a half places to hide in that beautiful park. I've walked some of it myself."

"Bullshit," she said, surprised and bemused by her impulsive response.

"How dare you," McCarthy spat back with feigned indignity. "Not walked a bunch of it, mind you. But some. Pretty, but a lot of nooks and crannies as my momma used to say."

"Well, hopefully when we get close, maybe Jenna will find a way to break free, or yell, or something like that."

"Here's to hoping." McCarthy readjusted his cap and straightened his uniform. "I got to get back to it. You joining?"

"Not yet. I have a few more people I want to interview."

"Neighbors?"

"In a sense."

He studied her, his eyes squinted and face stern. "I don't like it when you talk that crap, Deb. Don't like it one bit."

She reviewed McCarthy's doubtful face and considered telling him the truth. The issue, however, was the possible consequences, especially given the fallout from the Johnston case. Though she did not expect McCarthy to tattle to the Chief, there was no reason to enlighten McCarthy and make him a fact witness in a later internal investigation, if it came to that. Better to keep him in the dark until illumination was necessary.

"Sorry," she said, deciding. "But I need you to trust me for now. I really can't help you much here, and I just have a couple more boxes I need to check."

"Fine, whatever." He tipped his cap. "Go play detective while we get dirty."

"Not too dirty," she scolded. "Dry cleaning bills have been out of control lately."

McCarthy sulked away while grinning and, within a few seconds, shouted orders at a young officer. She observed him as he dove back into the search, confident in her decision. Despite the rough edges, she had complete faith in McCarthy to smoothly handle "dirty work" such as directing search teams. His mind was more straightforward than hers, more direct. Her home was the weeds, for great treasure hides in tall brush.

Her watch read 10:50. Perfect timing. She would rejoin the search party soon, after interviewing a certain individual.

She hopped into her vehicle, shifted into drive, and navigated onto the roadway, careful not to strike officers on the scene. A few young officers stared as she drove off; the older officers knew better.

The sun shone above, revealing the surroundings' beauty. Tall green trees blurred past until she reached the vineyards, the stems bearing small fruit worth billions. It was her favorite time of year. A fresh hope bloomed with the fruit of the season, the possibilities for the area boundless. She hoped to harness that hope, drill it into her mind as she headed towards her destination, for she feared soon hope would be her pursuit's fuel.

She snapped out of her thoughts and saw the first glimmer of the vineyard. Even from a distance, the large blue and yellow "HOLLAND VINEYARD" sign stood clear against the green backdrop of rolling hills and sprawling vines. Cars littered its parking lot, an array of vehicles similar to any of those in a Hertz drop-off lot. Far more tourists visited Holland Vineyards than any other in Kenwood, and few Napa operations rivaled Holland, at least from a tourist-trap standpoint. From her previous investigation into Jacob Holland, she knew Holland Vineyards possessed a rare blend of history, quality wine, and amazing views.

She pulled into the turn lane behind two black SUVs. Even the entry gates were magnificent, a towering fusion of ornate wood and steel. The vehicles before her drove slowly as the passengers snapped pictures of the landscape. When she parked, she observed customers scurrying around the property and hanging out at each entry point, many posing for selfies. She envied their carefree ignorance.

The two-story main building shared more similarities with a mansion than a tasting room. The red clay roof accented the white stucco walls, giving the lofty structure a hint of hominess. Manicured gardens bordered the paved walkway to the main entrance: a large steeple with a circular balcony. The wooden tables flanking the front door were filled with happy people drinking wine, toasting the beautiful morn.

She headed to the front door as she heeded the buzz of the patrons, no sign of weariness or sadness in their voices, their upbeat tones in stark contrast to the nearby crime. An older man in wrinkled khakis opened the front door for her as she stepped into the main lobby area. The interior sprawled out like a maze, various paths leading to separate tasting areas. To her left was a small gift shop with assorted Holland Winery memorabilia. She considered approaching the young, bored clerk manning the gift shop, but instead focused on a redheaded girl behind the granite tabletop of the main tasting area who led a discussion with several customers.

Badge in hand, she approached the girl, who stopped and

looked at Debra. "Hi," Debra said as she flashed her ID. "Detective Foley. May I talk to you for a few minutes?"

The girl's eyes widened as the man to Debra's left scooted over a few inches. "Do I need to get my manager?" the girl asked.

"No, this shouldn't take long." She put away her badge and pulled out her notepad. "What is your name?"

"Jessica."

"Okay. Do you have a last name, Jessica?"

Her cheeks turned red, matching her hair. "Larson. Jessica Larson."

"Great. Now Ms. Larson, how long have you worked here?"

"Not sure," She appeared in frustrated thought, as if trying to solve an easy math equation. "Five years, almost six. Are you sure you don't need to call my manager?"

"That depends. Who is your manager?"

"Jacob Holland."

Perfect, Debra thought and asked, "So, Mr. Holland is working today?"

"Yeah, pretty sure. I spoke to him about some business this morning."

"Business?" Debra asked.

"Yeah, nothing big. Just logistics about an upcoming wine dinner we're hosting. He actually should be here by now, but I haven't seen him. Perks of the Holland name." As soon as she finished her sentence, she searched around the room, the redness rushing back to her face.

"That's okay," Debra said with a comforting smirk. "You can be honest with me. What time does Mr. Holland usually come in?"

"Around 10:40, 10:45." She twisted her body and looked up towards a clock on the wall behind the counter. "He should be here soon. Want me to call him?"

"Sure, that would be helpful."

"Okay, one sec." Jessica stepped away from the serving area, grabbed a nearby landline phone, pushed a few buttons, and pressed it against her face. As Debra waited, the man next to her looked her up and down, his eyes glistening in fear, interest, or both.

"Sorry," he muttered, his voice higher than she expected. He shifted his large body in the little barstool to better look at her. "Don't mean to interrupt. But are you, like, a real cop?"

She smiled and replied, "That's what they tell me."

"Huh. Kinda a weird place to be, no?"

"I end up working in a lot of weird places, let me tell you."

He nodded, his face scrunched in thought, probably trying to conjure another line. Before he could continue, Jessica arrived back. "He didn't pick up," she said, her tone a cocktail of worry and confusion. "He always picks up his phone." She turned her head at a tall coworker a few yards from her and yelled, "Hey, Brad."

Startled, Brad fumbled with a bottle before regaining composure. "What?"

"You seen Jacob today?"

"Yeah. Saw him driving to the butler's house a little bit ago."

Debra looked at Jessica, her curiosity piqued at this comment. Feigning ignorance, she asked, "Butler's house?"

"Yeah, one of Holland's relics. One sec." She called again as Debra tried to avoid making eye contact with her bar neighbor.

"Crap," Jessica intoned a few seconds later. "He's still not picking up. Tell you what. I usually start tours at 11:30. If we hurry, we can head up there and see if we can find him. It's a short drive."

"Yeah, that sounds good. I'd love to hear more about this butler's house and why Jacob might be there."

"Sure, I'll give you the quick tour." She grabbed a pair of keys from under the counter and yelled, "Brad, cover me."

He extended his arms, an exasperated look on his face. "Are you shitting me?"

"No, so suck it up or this lady will arrest you."

Brad stared at Debra and his body became rigid as she displayed her badge. "Ms. Larson isn't kidding," Debra joked, though the humor didn't appear to register with Brad.

She followed Jessica out a smaller door past the gift shop which led into a large private tasting room, an elegant mahogany table in the middle, brochures placed in front of each plush leather high-back chair. She led Debra outside and to a short walkway. A few feet ahead were several vehicles: a bus, a black Cadillac with "HOLLAND" in white on its sides, and a four-seater ATV.

"Is it all right if we take the ATV?" Jessica asked. "It's probably faster, and I need to get back soon."

"Sure, that's fine."

Debra climbed into the most comfortable ATV in which she had ever sat, its leather seat contouring to her body as if it had been designed especially for her. Jessica got into the driver's seat, turned the key, and they headed onto a paved road that crested the hill. The ride was smoother than Debra expected, the SUV purring effortlessly up the mild slope, the cool air gently tousling her hair. Sunrays beamed in from the side windows, warming her arm as they passed countless rows of beautiful grapes. Under different circumstances, she might have enjoyed herself.

"What's the butler's house?" Debra asked as they drove. She knew its background well but wanted to hear it described by someone other than Jacob Holland.

"So, that's a little hard to explain. Mind if I put on my tour guide hat for a second?"

"Not at all."

"Okay. So that building we just came from used to be the Holland family home. They didn't have public tastings for many years. They lived there until Mr. Holland Senior's accident." She paused for a moment and asked, "You know about Adam's accident, right?"

"Yes." She knew about it better than most, though everyone in Sonoma knew about the accident to some degree.

"Yeah, so after that, Mrs. Holland couldn't bear to live on the property anymore. Who could blame her? Too many memories. Anyway, so many of the buildings that used to cater to the Hollands' needs have been repurposed, the biggest being the main tasting room. But the only one that wasn't was the butler's house. Even though the Hollands' personal butler moved out with the family, they didn't touch the butler's house. No one knows why, but Jacob stays there a lot. He calls it his sanctuary."

"His sanctuary? What does he mean by that?"

"Not sure really," she said with a half shrug. "I think he writes a lot in there, tries different blends. I guess it's just his place to think."

"Any other buildings stay the same?"

Jessica considered the question for a moment. "Well, no buildings at least."

"What does that mean?"

"Well, the wine caves haven't changed much." She pointed to a smaller parking lot in the distance in front of an entrance that led seemingly into a hill, massive oak garage doors signifying the grandiose nature of the caves. "Also, you ever heard of the legendary Holland private reserve?"

Debra shook her head.

"Okay," Jessica continued, "the story goes that there's a massive private tasting room and cellar somewhere on the property. Only the family knows where it is. The story is the reserve contains one of the most expensive wine collections on Earth. Who knows? No one I've talked to has ever been in it. Could be just a fairytale."

"Sounds like a very specific thing to be made up."

"Yeah," Jessica replied, her face lighting up, "that's the thing. How could something like that be made up? It had to come from somewhere or something, right? Plus, what's weird is that I've been instructed not to talk about it with the patrons unless *they* bring it up first, and even then I'm supposed to be 'vague.'" She air-quoted with only one hand so the other stayed on the wheel, diminishing the gesture's effect. "Whatever the hell that means. Vague."

"Trust me, I know all about being vague in my line of business."

"Ha!" Jessica laughed. "It's a tough rule to follow. People that ask about the reserve tend to be very interested in it."

"I bet."

"Anyway, if there really is a reserve, it, the caves, and the butler's house are the only two things that haven't changed since the Hollands' moved out."

"You have any guesses on where it might be?"

"Oh yeah," she said, her excitement evident. "My money's on a secret passage in the wine caves. Makes sense. You can have a tunnel leading anywhere from there. But hey, what do I know?"

"A lot, from the sounds of it."

Jessica grinned. "It's easy to pick up gossip around here. Loose lips, especially after a couple of glasses. And here we are."

She parked next to a black extended cab truck. "Weird," Jessica said, "his truck's here. One sec." She shut off the ATV and walked to the door of the butler's house, a small white bungalow with a gray roof, flower-lined walkway, and inviting wooden front door. From its exterior, Debra doubted the bungalow was bigger than a thousand square feet, maybe no more than seven hundred, yet it emanated charm, and Debra bet there were few houses with better backyard views. She imagined it provided quite the sanctuary despite its diminutive size.

Debra watched Jessica for a bit and then focused on the

truck. She had seen the truck once before, and it baffled her then. In their few encounters, Jacob didn't appear to her as a "truck" kind of guy, and she doubted he needed to do much in the way of hauling and pulling cargo. Or maybe he did for his job? Either way, he couldn't have picked a more non-descript vehicle.

Lost in her thoughts, she jumped when Jessica hopped back into the ATV. "The door's locked and he's not answering," Jessica said. "I'm sorry. I'll keep an eye out and let you know the moment I spot him."

"Sounds good." Debra slipped Jessica a card. "I appreciate your help today."

"Anytime!"

"But please call me the moment you see him. I need to speak with him about something very important."

"Really? How important?"

"Can't get into that."

"Ah. There's the vagueness."

Debra grinned. "Exactly."

15

The minutes crawled. He cursed under this breath. Why did they visit the house, especially after he told Susan he would be in late?

He hoped his eyes betrayed him, but there was no avoiding it: Debra paid him a visit. The vineyard opened only thirty minutes prior and yet there she had been, riding high on his family's best ATV, already breathing down his neck, just after his first cup of coffee.

The damn AMBER Alert, he thought. That alarm hastened matters, like a sudden heartbeat spike during surgery, smudging an otherwise flawless blueprint. There was no downplaying matters now, no relying on best laid plans. His improvisational skills trumped strategy.

But first, a decision: Either avoid Debra's presence and blame the absence on his "illness," or kick off the party. Either way, he would face the bitch, likely sooner than later. The longer he delayed, the more suspicious he appeared. A missed knock is easily explainable; ignoring calls for hours would require a deeper level of creativity.

Screw it, he thought. *Let's pay the Piper.*

He glanced at his watch. They left four minutes ago, enough time to ensure they couldn't see him. Slowly, he cracked open the door and stepped outside. Scanning the surrounding, he saw he was alone on the hill. Relieved, he slipped out to his truck, grabbed his cell, and noticed several missed calls from the winery. Shortly after dialing back, Susan picked up with, "Holland Vineyards, how can I help you?"

"May, Susan," Jacob chastised. "May. We've been over this."

"Sorry, sorry Jacob," Susan replied, the embarrassment clear in her voice. "How may I help you, Jacob?"

"Better. I saw I missed some calls from you."

"Yeah, Jessica was looking for you. One sec."

There were a few seconds of fumbling, then the distant sound of a well-filled tasting room: casual conversations, laughter, and clinks. Music to Jacob's ear, music interrupted by Jessica's voice.

"Hey Jacob, you there?" she asked.

"Yup, I'm here," he replied with a cough. "I saw a couple missed calls from this number. I also heard knocks at my door, but I'm a little under the weather and could have been dreaming."

"No, no. You weren't dreaming. There's a cop here who was asking questions about you."

"What do you mean, a cop?" Jacob hoped his feigned surprise didn't sound fake. "What cop?"

"Her name's Debra Foley. She wanted to talk to you, wouldn't tell me about what."

"That's fine, Jess. I know her."

"Really? How?"

"I'll tell you later. Is she still around?"

"Yeah. Want me to grab her before she leaves?"

"Yeah, tell her to meet me in the big wigs room in five."

"Got it, boss."

"Thanks. See you soon." The line went silent, and he put his phone away. He considered whether the big wigs room was the proper place for the chat as opposed to one of the several smaller private offices. Too late to second guess, he decided. He had to follow his instincts.

As he pondered on his last contentious encounter with Debra, his mind drifted to Jodi. He wished she were there, comforting him as she used to before important meetings. Her existence put him at ease. Her voice, her eyes, her touch. Even her smell.

Her smell. An idea came to him. He hopped out of the car, rushed into the butler's house, and shut the door behind him. He walked into a small, sparse room with a queen-size bed, neatly made, surrounded by floral wallpaper. The light shone through a single dirty window, highlighting the room's scratches and dings. He kept it spotless, though, without a speck of dirt.

He fell on his knees by the bed. From underneath, he pulled out a small cardboard box. He opened it and riffled through cards, makeup, and jewelry until he found the item he sought: a small bottle of peppermint oil. Jodi used to refer to it as an "essential" oil; he never found it even desirable, much less essential. But it would serve a purpose that morning.

He readied his body, tensed his muscles, and steadied his breathing. Jodi was big into meditation, which he found more useful than her typical nonsense. He researched meditation and learned its benefits included suppressed heart rate and enhanced mood. She enjoyed hippie-dippy bullshit, but science supported meditation's benefits. And he needed it to work.

In the proverbial "zone," he pulled back his right eyelid and dripped peppermint oil onto his eyeball; the pain struck immediately, washing over the bottom half of his iris like a chemical bath. He focused on his breathing, fighting back the urge to blink. The pain in check, he repeated the process in his left eye. He stood upright before the mirror and concentrated on riding the anguish. Eyelids trembling, he did not submit.

Two minutes into the suffering, he let himself blink, bringing relief. Thin red lines crept along the whites of his eyes, slowly extending like rivers of blood. For good measure, he splashed hot water on his face, which helped stave off any lingering pain from the oils. He considered ruffling his hair but figured that may appear obvious and overboard.

He kissed the bottle and returned it to the box. He reviewed himself, searching for remnants of blood on his clothes or skin. Seeing none, he exited the butler's house and entered his truck, again reviewing the interior, lingering on every crevice. A trained dog like Debra would notice even a tiny drop undetectable by a normal person. He saw none, so he shifted the truck into gear and headed towards the main house, staying cognizant of his speed, not too slow and not too fast.

He parked on the side near a staff entrance to better avoid chit-chat with the regulars. Once in, he spotted Jessica and flagged her down.

"Hey Jacob," she said as she rushed towards him. "Damn, you look awful."

"Yeah, but I feel even worse. I doubt it is anything too serious, though. Is that police officer in the big wigs room?"

"Yup, in there waiting. Still want to take the meeting in that room?"

"Yeah, that's fine. Before I go in, did she say anything to you about why she's here?"

"Nope, just that it's important." She looked over his shoulder at the crowd gathering near the sign that read, "Tours Start Here." "Crap. I got to get the first tour started. Need anything else from me?"

"No, I'm fine. Great job."

"Thanks!" she replied with a warm smile before she stepped past him towards a ten-person group. He watched her approach the patrons with boundless energy, arms flailing as she went over the history of the vineyard. He liked Jessica, liked her very much. Several times he had considered asking her out, but he was not ready to move on from Jodi. Perhaps he would revisit the subject when matters quieted down.

He waved to a few regulars as he rounded the serving area and headed towards an "EMPLOYEES ONLY" sign. At the end of the hall, the big wigs room's door was ajar, so he let himself in.

The big wigs room never ceased to impress him. Two tall, spotless windows overlooked the prettiest part of the vineyard. Massive oak wine racks lined the walls, each holding rare and expensive vintages. Debra sat in one of the six expensive Italian leather chairs, two of which overlooked the vineyard. They didn't use this room to sell wine to average Joes; they used it to sell wine to companies, as well as the occasional celebrity and billionaire.

Debra watched him as he entered the room, her posture upright, her eyes fixed on him. He took a moment to admire how her graceful black locks fell around her neck and her skin shimmered in the sunlight. And her eyes, he remembered her eyes: dark green and stern, but with a hint of understanding. She was beautiful, but he couldn't let that fact disarm him.

She nodded at him and said, "Good morning, Mr. Holland." She gestured towards the chair nearest to her. "Please, have a seat." She looked him over and asked, "Are you feeling well?"

"Not really, but I'll live. Am I in trouble?"

"No, not at the moment. Like last time, I just have a few questions for you. You know the drill."

He did not like how she emphasized "last time," but complied with her request to sit. She sat upright and confident, her arms on the armrests, her stare professional and unwavering.

"So, what brings you in?" Jacob asked. "It's been a while since our little visits. I have missed them. Too bad Joe had to bring a stop to them." Joe Webster, his attorney, had slammed the door on her investigation into Jodi after three idiotic grilling sessions.

"I'm not at liberty to go into the details."

"You sure took the liberty of coming onto my property without an invitation."

"Please just answer my questions. Or do you need your bodyguard, Mr. Webster? He sure saved your ass last time."

He shrugged off her insult. "I've answered a lot of your questions. Over and over." Jacob twirled his index finger to signify the endless circle of her repetitive questions about Jodi. He then leaned back and eyed her. "Speaking of Mr. Webster, should I call him? I have him on retainer, you know."

"I bet you do. And you know the answer to that, Mr. Holland. You're not under arrest. I can't force you to talk to me. You can bring in your lawyer if you'd like. But this is a time-sensitive situation, so I hope you will be willing to help."

"Help what? You're not giving me much here." He scratched his head, his eyes on the floor. "At least with Jodi, I understood why you were talking to me. It got tiring after a while, but I got it." He returned his gaze to hers. "Is this about Jodi? Did you find out something? Figure out where she is?"

"No," she replied. He detected a hint of annoyance in her tone. "This is not about Ms. Johnston. But it's somewhat similar." She flinched as soon as she said "similar," as if she regretted using that word.

He jumped on that tell. "Similar?" He paused before saying, "Come on. You can't even give me a hint?"

She blinked twice and paused for a beat. "Again, I can't say, Mr. Holland." Though she did her best to maintain professionalism, her fatigue was clear. She spoke at a slower pace than normal, blinked faster and more often, and a few beads of sweat dotted her forehead. He wondered if her exhaustion could create an opportunity, an opportunity too risky to ever seize, but one that was so sweet he could taste it.

He leaned forward and tried to act casual to combat her severe demeanor. "First you believe I kidnapped my girlfriend, now you want me to answer questions without telling me why? And the questions aren't about Jodi?"

"I see you're back to being evasive with me."

Her accusation caught him off-guard, causing him to recoil. Any cracks in her persona intrigued him. But then again, did she purposefully throw in personality to appear less threatening and more welcoming? He couldn't get a bead on her.

"Detective," he began. "My family loves the police. How much have we donated over the years? But you can't fault me for being cautious. I'll definitely answer what I can, even if I don't know why you're asking. But if you're accusing me of something, I gotta get Joe on the horn. Especially after given our, what's the word? History?"

"Sure," she replied. "Let's call it history. What happened then is history." She waved dismissively, her face scrunched. "I won't hold it against you if you won't hold it against me. Deal?"

Jacob nodded. "Deal, with the right to rip up the deal whenever I want and call my lawyer. It's just the way it is. Everyone needs a bodyguard."

"That's your right," she said, unfazed, as she slid out a notepad and pen from the briefcase by the chair. "But, only the guilty need so much protection."

"Funny, I learned to always use protection."

She ignored his comment and leaned in to meet his gaze. "Ready?"

All business, he considered. *Some things never change.*

"Sure," he replied, putting his hands in his lap and leaning back an inch.

"Okay, first question. Are you familiar with Beverly Paxton?"

"Bev?" he replied. "Yeah. Recently divorced, one kid. A girl.

Jenna. Nice lady. We socialize from time to time. We share many interests. Books, wine."

"How did you first meet Ms. Paxton?"

"Hard to say." He shrugged. "I've known of her ex-husband, Ethan, for quite some time. Didn't know him directly, but my father, Adam, hired him often for various matters. Beverly was always nice to me, even as a kid."

"At any time did you enter into a romantic relationship with Ms. Paxton?"

"What?" he asked with sincere shock. How the hell had she learned so much so quickly? Her asking questions about Beverly made sense, but this line of questioning? Perhaps she was just grasping at straws, but that seemed out of character. In his experience, Debra was always prepared.

Debra repeated, "I asked were you ever in a romantic relationship with Ms. Paxton."

"No, I understood the question. I'm just stunned. Why would you think we ever hooked up?"

"You don't ask the questions here, Mr. Holland."

"Careful." Jacob patted his jeans pocket, which contained his cell phone. "Speed-dial, remember. And you know better than to call me Mr. Holland."

"Fine, Jacob. Please either answer my questions or end this interview so I can start the process of getting the answers in a more formal setting. That's probably what Mr. Webster would prefer, anyway, since you apparently listen to him like he's your daddy."

"Wow. Not into foreplay, are you?"

She blinked but otherwise didn't physically react to his comment. Her disregard for his banter annoyed him. "Jacob," she said. "This is not a game. I'm not interested in bullshitting with you. I'm interested in answers. Now, again, were you ever romantically involved with Ms. Paxton?"

"Of course not, what is wrong with you? First, who needs

the drama of a recent divorcee? Second, you may not have noticed, but she's a couple of decades older than me, and I'm not exactly the type who needs a sugar momma. But I get it."

"Get what?"

"You probably talked to someone who saw us together. Anyone would notice a guy in his 20s enjoying time with a woman in her 50s. Yeah, it's true, we've had wine together a few times."

Debra cocked her head. "You've had wine with her but weren't dating?"

"Right." He shot a finger-gun in her direction.

"I gotta say, the only people I have wine with are my girlfriends and husband."

"Good for you," Jacob replied. "Not all people are like you. See, a while back, I spotted her at the Grapes of Write and said 'hi.' We discussed literature and met every week or so for an informal book club." He half-shrugged. "Yeah, seems silly. Maybe even a little weird. But I could tell she was going through a tough time and wanted to help. I remember how she was nice to me as a kid. Kinda wanted to pay her back since she had it so tough, you know?"

"No, I don't know. That's why I'm asking."

He half-shrugged. "It helped that we were into different genres, if that makes sense. She liked romance. I was into the darker stuff." He smiled. "The three Ms."

"The three Ms?" she asked, a single eyebrow lifted. "What are those?"

"Murder, mystery, mayhem." He checked off each word with a different finger. "Those are all you need."

"So, you never met for any other reason other than to discuss books?"

He leaned in further, his hands on his knees, his eyes locked on hers. "I don't really get your question. There were a lot of reasons we met. I enjoyed talking to her. She seemed to like the distraction from the divorce. But none of those reasons involved sex."

"Would it surprise you that people I've talked to claim you're dating?"

"Not at all," he said with a dismissive huff. "This town's worse than a knitting circle. But is this all you want to ask me about, Debra?"

"Detective."

"Whatever. You're in my house, I'll call you what I want."

Debra flinched. Perhaps he was getting under her skin. Whether that was a good thing was debatable, but he had to stay "on brand" as he learned in one of his rubbish marketing classes.

"Well," Debra said after a few seconds, "If you want to act like a naïve child, then I'll spell it out for you. This town doesn't have too many kidnappings. Yet, bad things seem to keep happening to the women in your life. Tell me, what are the chances of that? The Chief may have bought your crap about Jodi, but I didn't and still don't."

His blood ran hot; red descended over his vision. She had barged into his territory with no proof, all bluster. Who did she think she was? A nobody, that's who. She brought up Jodi's name but wasn't even skilled enough to figure out the truth. And yet she had the gall to call him a child?

His fists balled. "How dare you…" Then he caught himself. It was an obvious trap. She subtly implied that something "bad" happened to Beverly. He composed himself and continued, "Wait a minute. You used the word 'kidnappings.' Plural. Did something happen to Bev? Is she hurt?"

Disappointment flickered in her eyes. "I can't get into that."

"Bullshit," he shot back. "You brought it up. What the hell happened? I'm calling her right after this to find out."

"All I'm going to tell you is that something bad happened. And unless you have good answers to my questions, I'm digging deeper into your relationship with her. I'll find out if this friendship was one of literature or something more. I'll go even deeper than I did with Jodi, I can promise you that."

"You wouldn't dare," Jacob replied with a grin. "Not after the spanking the Chief gave you. I'm sure your ass had to hurt for a while after that one."

She combated his grin with a haunting, knowing smile. "That was because he was convinced Jodi ran away. This is different. I have much more discretion."

"You have the advantage here, Deb. I don't know why this, as you say, is different. But you're not going to scare me. I've done nothing wrong."

"I'm not trying to scare you, Jacob, but you're obviously trying to intimidate me. You like to pretend that you don't care about what people think of you, but that's crap. This room," she pointed towards the windows and traced her fingers to the wine racks, "is proof of that. You put me in here to intimidate me. You use this room to impress people. But how many customers will be left to impress when people believe you hurt women?"

"So, someone hurt Bev?" He expected this second trap.

"Yes, someone hurt her. And I'm trying to figure out who. Maybe it was you. Maybe she's sitting somewhere next to Jodi." Her tone darkened as she asked, "So, tell me, Jacob, where were you last night?"

He didn't hesitate. "I was with my girlfriend, Sherri. Sherri Sloan. The girl I am actually dating. I left her house near Sonoma early this morning to visit my mother. She's in a nursing home."

"Your mother?" Debra scribbled some notes. "You visited her this morning?"

"Yes. I've been up for a while." He smiled. "I actually visited our wine caves before visiting her to check on stock. Have to prepare for a big rehearsal dinner we're hosting in there in like a week. That's why I feel so bad. Don't think I got enough sleep." He wondered whether telling her about the wine caves was the right call, but he figured he should cover all his bases. They'd only find his office with a warrant, and if she were ever in a position to obtain one, he'd be long gone.

For the first time in the conversation, Debra appeared surprised. She sat in silence for a few beats before asking, "You are dating someone named Sherri Sloan? How long?"

"A while now, like a year, but we've tried to keep it under wraps. Like I said, knitting circle."

"And you were with her last night?"

"Yup. We watched some terrible movie she liked. *The Notebook*, perhaps? Isn't that based on a novel?"

"Yeah," Debra replied, frustration growing.

"Well, you know how they say the book is always better than the movie? That wouldn't be hard here. Anyway, I was with her last night. Call and ask if you'd like." He grabbed a nearby pad and pen that lay on the desk between them. He scribbled down the number and handed it to Debra, who took it with a tentative grasp. "I'm supposed to see her again tonight. Now, let's get back to my question. What bad thing happened to Bev?"

Debra's eyes stared deeply into his, unwavering, unyielding. She may not accept his story, but it bought him time. "I'm not going to tell you, Jacob. But I'm sure you'll learn soon enough. And I'll learn soon enough also. I'll figure out if you're telling the truth, or, as you said, just knitting a circle for me. Until then," she stood and extended her hand, "please call if you remember anything else. You still have my number, I'm sure. If you don't, Mr. Webster does."

He took her soft hand and said, "I do, and I will. No need to involve Joe yet. Let me know if there is any way else I can help. We are always willing to share our family's good fortune with the police."

"I'm sure." She nodded and turned to leave.

With her back to him, Jacob called out, "Hey Debra."

She stopped but did not turn to meet his gaze.

"Say hello to your Chief for me," he said through a grin.

She did not respond, instead scurrying away without a second glance, leaving him in silence, the sun warming his back, the racks of wine encircling him like a blanket. He sat back down and sunk into the leather, contemplating every sentence of their conversation. Overall, it went well, aside from one component: Sherri. He wondered if he played that card too quickly. Her involvement complicated matters. So much relied on her and it concerned him.

Sherri wouldn't crack, and this wasn't an official police investigation. He didn't swear to tell the truth. If shit hit the fan, he'd claim he panicked because Debra targeted him in the Jodi investigation. Alone, that lie wouldn't be enough to arrest him. Perhaps on some bogus obstruction of justice charge, but that wouldn't stick, and he'd get out on a small bail. Debra would need much more evidence to lock him up for anything serious, and if that happened, he would disappear. And, if needed, he would make Sherri disappear.

First things first. He pulled out the cell phone, dialed the number, and waited three rings before Sherri picked up with a cheery, "Hey, baby!"

"Hey, hot stuff. How's it going?"

"Oh, can't complain. Not sure you'd wanna hear it, anyway! How you doin', handsome?"

"Not great, actually. Do you remember that detective I told you about? Detective Debra Foley?"

"Oh, Heavens yes! The bitch that tried to frame you when your old squeeze ran away."

"That's the one. She just interviewed me again, this time implying that I may have kidnapped a little girl. I don't have all the details, but that's the gist I got from the conversation."

"My God! Are you all right?"

"I'm fine. Look, it's obvious now that someone has a vendetta against me and is paying this Detective a bunch of money to stop me from inheriting Holland Winery. Why else would all this be happening?"

"No clue, baby doll. I just can't imagine what you're going through, you poor, poor thing."

"I'm fine, but listen. Remember how I asked you to cover for me earlier?"

"Yeah."

"If she calls, I need you to tell her that I was with you last night. If not, I could be in a lot of trouble for terrible things I didn't do. She grilled me a lot about last night. Not sure what happened, but it sounded bad."

She paused, then quietly asked, "How bad?"

"Real bad. I mean, they'll never be able to pin anything on me, but they could ruin me. Getting to trial would take a long time, years even, and all the while my reputation is ruined. Our future is ruined."

"Baby," her voice cracked. "I'm so, so sorry. I won't let that happen, swear on everything. That bitch will have to take me down, too."

"That's why I love you so much. But this is why I wanted to keep things between us quiet for a little bit. Once we get past all this nonsense, we'll be able to do whatever we want. I'll take you wherever you want."

"Even New York City?"

"Yes," he said, hoping he could hide his disdain. "Even New York."

"Alrighty, sweet thing. I got it."

"Try not to stress. If things get too hot, I'd get you the best lawyer in town."

In fact, I know one who is about to have a lot of time on his hands.

"Okay sweetie," she replied. "I trust you."

"Thanks, babe. I trust you, too. Also, with all this crap, I'm probably going to have to bail on tonight. Let's lie low for a few days."

"Boo!" she replied, the "oo" lasting nearly three seconds.

"I don't like it either. But it won't be long."

"Yeah, yeah. We'll see. Don't you go forgetting about me."

"Never!"

"Hey, one last thing. What if she calls today? Do I tell her we talked?"

"Good question." He considered, surprised by her awareness. "Yeah, tell her I called. They'll probably get our phone records, anyway. Tell her the truth: That I was freaked out by the interview."

"Okay, love you!"

"Love you, too." He broke the line, sat deep into the chair, and stared out into the endless rows of vines ascending towards the heavens like angels awaiting wings. Before contemplating further, he took a few deep breaths and allowed his heart and mind to slow. The entire morning, he ran on emotion and instinct. Now, he needed forethought and clarity.

First question: How to remove Ethan? Jacob's hope was to keep Ethan disposed until the police presence dissipated. But, with Debra hot on his trail, the plan required modification.

Second question: How to handle Debra? He knew how she operated. Once she set her sights on something or someone, she was like a dog with a bone. If he had more time, he'd love to break her down and take her, like Frank Chambers in *The Postman Always Rings Twice.* Time, however, was of the essence. He needed a distraction, a reason to get people off of the vineyard and out of his business.

An idea struck him. He pulled out his cell phone and dialed Jessica, who picked up after one ring.

"Hey Jacob, what's up?" she asked through background clamor of conversation and engine. He deduced she led a tour.

"Nothing much," he replied. "Sorry to bug you, but can you do me a quick favor when you get back to the tasting room?"

"Sure, anything."

"Great. That cop was asking me a bunch of questions about something that happened last night but wouldn't tell me what. I'm worried a friend of mine may be hurt."

"Oh no, that's awful!"

"It is. Could you just call around the various vineyards to see if anyone has heard anything? It would put my mind at ease."

"I'll get started right after this tour. I'll also find someone to cover the rest of today's tours."

"Thanks so much. I'll be out in a bit."

"Sounds good."

He ended the call and smiled. Circumstances had dealt him a bad hand, so now it was time to bluff or bust.

16

Before departing the vineyard grounds, Debra sat in her car for several minutes, analyzing the entire conversation. Jacob's alibi, his callous demeanor, his odd reaction to her mentioning Beverly. On a surface level, it all sort of made sense, but something below the current troubled her, like a piece of glass buried in a sandy surf. She had to keep going, following Ethan, the most obvious trail, especially if Jacob had an alibi. Still, there was another lead she needed to explore.

She glanced at her notes of the conversation and dialed the number Jacob gave her. A spunky voice picked up after the second ring.

"Sherri here!" a twangy voice answered.

"Hello, is this Sherri Sloan?" Debra asked.

"Yes, you got the right Sherri. How can I help ya?"

"Good morning, Ms. Sloan. My name is Detective Debra Paxton with the Sonoma police department. Do you have a few minutes to answer some questions?"

"Why, yes. Yes, sure."

"Thank you. Do you know a Mr. Jacob Holland?"

"Very much so."

"How do you know Mr. Holland?"

"Well, I guess intimately as they say!" She laughed hardily with a hint of reservation.

"Does that mean you are dating Mr. Holland?"

"That's right. Been datin' for a while."

"All right. I'll be honest with you, Ms. Sloan. I've talked to several people today about Jacob and none have mentioned you."

"Can't blame people for what they don't know. We've kept it on the, what do they call it, down-low? Jacob's a private person, and you know this town. It's like a knitting circle."

Debra processed the comment before asking, "Sorry, did you say knitting circle?"

"Yeah, honey. Isn't that the right expression?"

"Sure. I just don't hear it often. How long have you been dating Mr. Holland?"

"Oh, a while now. Maybe a year? It's serious. We're so in love." She sounded like she was trying to convince herself.

"I understand. And where were you last night?"

"With Jacob. He came over and we drank wine and watched a show."

"A show?"

"Yeah. I think." Silence. "A show."

"What show?"

"I mean, I'm not sure." Her voice stuttered. "An old one. Maybe *Friends*?"

"You don't remember exactly what you watched last night?"

"Well, to tell you the truth, I wasn't too interested in the show, if you know what I mean."

"I don't, but that's fine. So, you had wine and watched *Friends*. Is that all?"

"Yup, that about sums it up as they say."

"All right. When was the last time you spoke to Mr. Holland?"

"Oh, a few minutes ago."

"Really?" she replied, her surprise genuine.

"Yup. He called right after you talked to him. He was freaked out, if I'm being honest. Who wouldn't be? A cop asking him a bunch of questions."

"Okay, what exactly did he say I asked him about?"

"He didn't know. He sounded scared that you were talking to him. I know ya thought he had something to do with Jodi skipping town. I promise, he didn't. He wouldn't pull the wings off a fly."

Who would? Debra wondered.

"I understand," Debra said. "But this isn't about Ms. Johnston. Did he say anything else about our conversation?"

"Nope. It just freaked him out so much he canceled our date tonight. He said a little girl was kidnapped. It's just awful."

Debra noted the inconsistency: She had never told Jacob about Jenna's kidnapping. In their conversation, Jacob had only guessed that Beverly was hurt. Of course, it was not inconceivable that Jacob recalled the AMBER Alert from that morning and either reviewed it or put two-and-two together. Yet, Sherri mentioned Jacob called her right after speaking with Debra, leaving him little time for deduction. Either way, while not damning, she certainly would remember Jacob's revelation.

"Okay. It is awful. Is there anything else you'd like to tell me, Ms. Sloan?"

Sherri hesitated before responding, "What do you mean?"

"Listen," Debra instinctively leaned into the phone. "I get you care about Jacob and you want to protect him. And if he's innocent, I want to protect him, too. But this isn't just about a kidnapping. The little girl Jacob mentioned? Last night, someone killed that girl's mother before taking her. Now we're worried whoever took her is going to hurt her, or worse. I'm sorry to be so blunt, but I have to be direct. So please tell me anything else you recall."

Several seconds passed before Sherri replied, "Um, no. No. That's it."

"Okay," Debra sighed. "You have this number if you remember anything else. Call no matter the time."

"Sure thing."

"Goodbye, Ms. Sloan." Debra hung up and considered the call. Once again, very little made sense. Why did Jacob tell her they watched *The Notebook*, yet Sherri said they watched *Friends*? Minor details like that could mean nothing or everything. Either way, something didn't add up, but the disparity didn't amount to probable cause. She needed more.

She remembered Sherri said they had wine. Wine seemed to be Jacob's constant. Everything he did involved wine. Everything.

She killed the car's engine, stepped out, and returned to the tasting room. Inside, she quickly spotted and flagged down Jessica, who stood behind the bar, deep in conversation on the phone. Jessica muttered a few seemingly apologetic words before hanging up and jogging towards Debra.

"Hi, Detective," Jessica said. "I thought you left."

"I did, but I figured I ask one last thing. Can you tell me about your wine?"

"My wine? You mean Holland wine?"

"Yes, that's exactly what I mean."

"Okay." She focused on Debra with squinted eyes. "That's a broad question. Is there a specific varietal you had in mind?"

"No. Let me ask this. Is there a difference in the manner that Holland Vineyard bottles its wine?"

"Manner? Like, the bottle itself?"

"Yes. And the cork."

"No, actually. That's a good question, in fact." She nodded, seemingly impressed. "From the top-end to the bottom, Holland uses the same high quality bottling materials. Here, I'll show you."

The women walked to the bar, Jessica passing behind it. She pulled out a bottle of wine and said, "This is our base Pinot. Not crazy expensive. But Jacob insists we use the highest quality glass and cork. Especially the cork."

"Really? Why the cork?"

Jessica shrugged, her expression bemused annoyance. "I don't get it, but Jacob is obsessed with corks. He says they make a major difference with oxidation and insists on Grade A, Portuguese wine corks no matter the wine, which can be expensive. He'll even inspect the corks for color and lenticels."

"Lenticels?"

"Like, horizontal cracks. Too many and he'll reject an entire shipment. Suppliers hate him, but we do so much business that they really can't complain."

"Makes sense. This may sound strange, but may I have one?"

"A cork?" She looked baffled and her voice shook. "Sure, sure I guess." She reached behind the bar, pulled out a bottle opener, and uncorked the Pinot.

"Here," Jessica said, presenting the cork. "This is the same cork we use for all our wines."

Debra took the cork. "Thanks."

"Would you like a glass now that it's open?"

Debra chuckled. "No, I'm fine."

"Hell, we'll take it if she won't," a customer near Debra said.

"Be my guest," Debra replied as she waved to Jessica. "Thank you again for your help. I'll let you know if I have any other questions."

"Sounds good. Happy to help." Jessica stared at her for a long while before turning to the customers pleading for a glass of the newly popped pinot. She handed them the bottle and hurried to a nearby corner where she pulled out her phone and placed a call. Debra tried to eavesdrop, but the merriment drowned out the conversation.

Debra reviewed the cork as she exited the tasting room. The corks' top was stained crimson, but the color, texture, and lack of "lenticels" appeared nearly identical to the cork she retrieved earlier from the scene. The sole distinction was the cork she held displayed a large "HOLLAND VINEYARD" logo, whereas the earlier cork was blank. Yet, she still lacked any semblance of probable cause. She could envision the empty stares from the grand jury even as the most prominent wine expert compared and contrasted the two corks.

But probable cause was not her guideline to continue an investigation. She had learned enough to keep trusting her suspicions, but for now, she had no further avenue to explore. There was only one place that contained direct evidence of Jenna's disappearance: Sugarloaf. And, perhaps fresh air would float her towards more roads to follow, for she sat at a dead end.

17

The phone's vibration interrupted Jacob's thoughts. He picked up and said, "Hey, babe."

"Hey is for horses, silly!" Sherri had told that joke at least a million times. Jacob now shuddered whenever someone said "hey."

"Everything okay?" he asked.

"Yeah, I guess so. Kinda." She paused. "That cop called me like you said she would."

"Yeah, what did she say?" Jacob asked, unsurprised.

"Asked questions about us. It's weird though. She talked about the little girl, but also said the mom was murdered. So, like, now they're worried the person who took the girl is going to hurt her. Maybe even kill her."

"That's awful," he replied, trying his best to sound stunned.

"Yeah. Yeah, it is. But I'm not gettin' it, Jacob. I mean, it don't make sense."

He gripped the phone so hard the case indented his fingers. "What doesn't make sense?"

"Some of what you said. Like, the mom's dead? I mean, I

trust you, babe. No matter what. But I don't get how all that has to do with you gettin' the vineyard."

"It's complicated, honey."

"Yeah, that's what you said. And it kinda made sense when it was about your ex running away. But this? I mean, a little girl and a dead mom. How could they fake that?"

He clenched his fists to keep his anger at bay. "I'm not saying they faked it, babe. I don't know all the details. My guess is someone paid that detective to investigate me and make it look like I did something, which could make things complicated when my mom passes."

"No, no. I get it, sugar. It's just that she said this all happened last night. And I read the AMBER Alert this morning. So, like, they paid her when? This morning? And who? I just got this weird feeling in my stomach."

Jacob couldn't hold back any longer. "Yeah, what's that feeling? The feeling that you're dating a murderer? A kidnapper? That's what you think I am? Some monster?"

"No, no," she replied, her voice quivering. "It's just—"

"Just what. Just you believe I'm capable of killing. Are you crazy? That's shit my mom would say." He now screamed. "You're no different than her."

"Baby, please, I didn't say you did nothing."

"But you're doubting me." His voice became that of a sulking child. "After everything I've done for you. The car, the house. Get your crap out today. Right now."

"What? Get out of what? The house?"

"That's right. I want everything out by this afternoon or I'm calling the cops on you."

"Jacob," she said after a long hesitation, her voice quiet and calm. "Let's not lose our head. I'm with you and I'll keep on being with you. Please, don't act crazy. I'm just trying to tell you what I'm thinkin', because it may be what others will think, you know? Only you think like you. The rest of us aren't so, what's that word you used? Complicated."

"Actually," he sighed. "That makes sense. You're right, this will look bad if I don't figure it out quickly. Tell you what, do me a favor and lie low. Don't talk to anyone for a day or so. Okay? I'll see what all I can find out and we'll discuss. Does that work?"

"Sure baby, it does. I'm here no matter what."

"That's good to hear. I'm sorry."

"Me too, hot stuff. Please do what you have to do to clear your head. And call if I can help with that."

"I will. Love you."

"Love you too, baby." She broke the connection, and he chastised himself for acting so irrationally. Especially because she was right. The flaws in his plan revealed themselves like a teacher's marks on an incorrect formula that reached the right answer. No matter the destination, the path he took made a difference. Cooler heads needed to prevail.

He noticed a silhouette of a woman in his periphery. "How much did you hear?" he asked.

"Nothing," Jessica replied with a stutter. "I heard some shouting, and I ran down to see if you were okay. Everything fine?"

"Yes, just a fight with the girl I'm dating. Anyway, what's up?"

"So, two things. First, that cop, Debra, came back in after she left."

"Really?" He turned to face her, his interest piqued. "Why?"

"She asked to see a bottle of wine and took a cork. It was a strange conversation."

"A cork? Did she say anything else?"

"Nope."

"Weird, but okay. What's the second thing?"

"I made some calls like you asked. Richard over at Landmark

told me there was police activity a little past them off Adobe Road."

"Interesting. I told you that cop asked me some questions about a missing kid, right?"

She nodded. "Yup."

"And you got that AMBER Alert this morning?"

"I did."

"They got to be connected, right?"

"They are. Richard asked a few cops what was going on and one of them said they were looking for a missing child."

"Get Richard back on the phone. I have an idea." Jacob stood and stepped past her, confusion plastered on her face. When he reached the tasting room, he grabbed a glass and cheese knife while yelling, "Excuse me, may I have your attention."

He dinged the glass and waited for the murmuring to cease. When it was sufficiently quiet, he yelled, "As many of you know, I'm Jacob Holland. If I haven't had the pleasure of meeting you, thank you so much for enjoying our wine and our vineyards. But for now, I must ask you to leave." He reviewed the befuddled looks of the crowd with pleasure. "How many of you got today's AMBER Alert?" Several hands raised. "Well, I looked into the situation. Our friends at Landmark tell me the police are looking for a missing girl near their fine vineyard, off Adobe Road. I am organizing a search party to help in the efforts to find her. So, we are closing early, but I encourage all in this room to join in the search. This is a small community and we stick together. Cheers!"

The crowd responded with, "Cheers!" and slowly began finishing their drinks. He flagged Jessica, who jogged up to him.

"You never cease to surprise me, Jacob," she said.

"Good. I can't speak for you, but I like surprises."

She smiled coyly, which Jacob appreciated. It was becoming clearer that Sherri was a mess that needed to be cleaned, and he would soon need her replacement.

"So, what next, boss?" she asked.

"Start calling the nearby wineries. Kenwood, Ledson, all of them. Get as many as you can to join. Time is of the essence."

"Will do. Anything else?"

"Not for now. But great job. Thank you for everything you do."

"Anything." She grinned and stepped away, pulling her phone out as she departed. He surveyed the room and decided which hands he needed to shake before leaving. Business first, always.

Less than thirty minutes later, the tasting room was empty aside from two employees, including Jessica. He spotted her in the distance, on the phone. When she placed it down, he approached her.

"Hey," he said. "Were you able to get ahold of anyone?"

"Yup, all the wineries we talked about and a few farther away. Everyone sounds on board to help. Landmark was already shutting down because of the police presence, so we gave them a good excuse to get rid of customers without pissing them off."

"Good, I like the guys over there."

"Me too."

"Anything else we need to do around here?"

"No, I think we're all set. I dismissed all the employees. Many of them are going to help with the search. Really cool thing you did here, Jacob." She grazed his forearm with her hand before pulling away. "I mean it."

"Thank you. I appreciate it."

"I'm going to join the search party, if that's okay."

"Sure. Need a lift?"

She considered and said, "No, that's fine. I'll take my car in case I need it."

"Sounds good. See you there."

She smiled, waved awkwardly, and left. The tasting room was now barren, aside from stray bottles of wine. He noticed one of his favorites—a young but still flavorful pinot—and figured a glass would calm his nerves. He poured, the liquid flowing like a cerise waterfall. When the wine hit his palette, his body unwound in unison. His muscles loosened and his breathing slowed. The wine was not exactly what he wanted at that moment, but it made for an acceptable substitute.

As he indulged, he enjoyed the silence of his family's tasting room. Normally, it was filled to the brim with customers and employees. The quiet shepherded memories. Long repressed memories. Memories from before his father's accident and the subsequent renovations. Memories of his childhood home's layout and how much fun he had running through the halls, a play gun in one hand, a shield in the other, emancipation of youth guiding his steps. He took his first steps in these halls, said his first words, thought his first thoughts. His next home was bigger but less impressive, and the landscaping could not rival rolling hills and vines. Those days were the last he remembered of peace, before his mind went askew and the world shifted a shade. When they left, they left a piece of him behind, perhaps the only good piece within him.

Not that it mattered. His father's death just sped up things. Eventually, this property was too valuable to remain a home. Yet, he couldn't help but reconstruct it in his mind, overlaying where rooms used to be as he scanned the cavernous interior. So much of his family legacy had transformed, sacrificed at the altar of business. Every day, strangers trampled the footprints he left as a child.

He sipped and realized he was not pondering *his* legacy. The structure was his mother and father's legacy. They would pass it to him, but he didn't build it. No, he would build his legacy elsewhere, starting with his work in the private reserve.

He downed the rest of the wine, appreciated the silence one last time, and headed towards his car.

***

He parked outside the yellow lines blocking the entrance into Sugarloaf and surveyed the chaos with glee, the flames from the fire he lit. A large cop waved his hands at a group of non-uniformed people obviously there to render aid. Jacob noticed a couple who were in his tasting room earlier when he delivered his speech. Near the large cop stood Debra, her arms crossed, her face pensive.

He opened the door to his car and got out, waving a single hand in Debra's direction. Her expression morphed from confusion to conclusion to anger as she stepped towards him.

"Hello, Jacob," she said, her tone steady if a little surprised. "What exactly are you doing here? Come to tell me something you forgot?"

"No, ma'am." He waved at the patrons he recognized, who returned the gesture. He pointed to several cars pulling up to the scene and said, "I told you earlier. My family is always willing to help."

"This isn't helpful and you know it."

"I disagree, Deb. So does the Chief. Called him on my way over here. We golf a couple times a year. I told him about our little conversation and he didn't seem too happy about you wasting that little girl's time by interviewing someone who obviously had nothing to do with her kidnapping. Especially given our, what was the word I used earlier? History?"

"Is that supposed to scare me, Jacob?" She inched closer and stared him in the eye. "You feel like a big man because you called my boss to tattletale?"

He met her gaze. "You've already falsely accused me of a crime once. Pounded me hard over and over even when it was clear I had nothing to do with Jodi skipping town. I'm not going to let it happen again."

"Funny, I don't remember an accusation. Just questions. Guilty conscience eating at you?" She stepped back and grinned. "Speaking of golf, rumor around town is that you suck."

He balled his fists and dug nails into his palms to stave off the rage. "That may be. One can't be good at everything."

"Apparently."

"Enough of this. None of that matters. I'm here to assist, and I've made several calls to recruit others. Insult me all you want, but Bev's daughter's out there." A tear fell down his cheek. Sometimes he surprised even himself. "I met that girl once. Jenna. Beautiful, smart baby girl. I'm not going to let her deadbeat dad hurt her more than he already has."

Debra was silent for a few seconds and then said, "Touching, Jacob. It almost looked like you believed it." She shoved past him and pulled out her phone. He guessed her plan was to call the Chief and see if she could change his mind. He doubted it, though. Too many factors working against her.

The tides shifted in his favor. The news would spread like wildfire among the Sonoma populace, and everyone, save Debra, would pin the kidnapping on Ethan. Soon, the public would descend upon the area, everyone wanting to help. If he made any mistakes, the stampede would cover them, and if he left any DNA or fingerprints, now he had a plausible excuse for being there. There was only one wildcard: The Queen, and she glared at him as she spoke into her cell phone, her eyes surveying his every move. Like Sherri, he may have to take care of her. But one step at a time. Taking the trash out too soon invited stink.

18

A terrible headache blasted Ethan. He squeezed his eyes hard to fight it, but his efforts did little to combat the ache. The pain went deep, deeper than he had ever experienced. Nauseousness soon followed the headache, but he kept any vomit at bay.

For a while, he sat there, praying. He prayed that he slowly awoke from a terrible dream. Prayed that his daughter was safe in her bed and that he was safe in his, next to Sarah. But his hope was fleeting. Even with his eyes tightly shut, he knew his arms and shoulders ached, and he knew why they ached, for the rough texture of the barrel rubbed against his inner forearms.

With his reality plain, he took a few moments to think of Jenna in the darkness of his shut eyes. In the still and quiet, he pondered questions he had not before. Did Jenna know about her mom? Had she seen Beverly's dead body? Worst of all, was it possible that Jenna witnessed the knife plunge into Beverly's heart? The possibility of Jenna seeing her mother's murder through her innocent eyes brought back the nausea.

If Ethan somehow broke free and found Jenna, she would have only him. Both his parents were dead. Bev's mom was dead and Alzheimer's robbed her father's mind. He was it. He would be her entire world. The prospect both excited and terrified him. For all his complaints about Beverly, she was a terrific mom. One of the best, in fact. Whether he could fill her shoes alone, he wasn't sure.

You're putting the cart before the horse, he reminded himself. He worried about things that would be a blessing if they came to be. To become her entire world, he had to first take her away from this hell and shield her the best he could.

Don't give up hope, he decided. He was awake, which meant he was not dead, which meant he still could rescue Jenna. And to do that, he needed to remain calm and thoughtful. Jacob would slip up eventually, and Ethan needed all his strength to pounce when that moment arrived.

Gradually, the headache lessened as the effects of Jacob's drugs subsided. He opened his eyes a slit, and the room's florescent light invaded, forcing him to close them. After a beat, he opened them again, blinking rapidly to counter the blinding light. Jacob, apparently, had removed Ethan's blindfold.

The massive wine barrel obstructed most of his vision. At most, he could look left, right, and heavenward. Above was nothing of note. Just florescent light fixtures. A television hung above the corner of the opposite wall.

To his sides, Ethan noticed pictures that hung on the wall against which he sat. Initially, Ethan could not make out the images. The first obvious oddity was the number of pictures. From top to bottom, 4x6 pictures covered the wall. That his periphery vision blurred much of the images did not help matters.

Ethan blinked hard, squinted his eyes, and focused on the one closest to him that was within the boundaries of his vision. He saw the picture displaying three people: a man, woman, and child. The man stood with his arms crossed. The woman angrily pointed at the man, her mouth open, tears in her eyes. The little girl sat with her back turned to both adults, playing in the small vineyard outside Ethan's pinot palace.

Reality struck Ethan like a hammer. The picture displayed the moment he picked up Jenna the weekend prior and the fight he had with Beverly over the fact that Ethan hoped to keep Jenna a day longer than his court-sanctioned weekend. Worst, it was a different picture than the one he noticed earlier in the day, before Jacob knocked him out.

Ethan's heart pounded as he reviewed the other images. One was of him and Jenna at Landmark, playing bocce ball. She had just landed right next to the jack and was jumping in celebration, Ethan's arms extended towards her. Another was of Beverly and Jenna eating dinner at a restaurant the family used to frequent, Jenna taking a bite of her favorite grilled cheese sandwich, Beverly sitting quietly and watching her like a hawk. The next picture displayed Jenna sitting alone in the front of their Sonoma house, playing with her Barbies. Even though she held her favorite toys, her face appeared distraught and longing, as if her play-things were not distracting her as well as she hoped.

Ethan could not see all the pictures, but the pattern was clear: a collage of stalking images. Ethan's life surrounded him, documented in detail by Jacob, the man who murdered his ex-wife and kidnapped him and his daughter.

Ethan tried to scream, but the duct tape prevented it.

Ethan ground his teeth as he noticed something else unusual in his periphery. He refocused on the barrel and saw a large, yellow sticky note stuck about halfway up its frame. After blinking twice and leaning in to help his tired eyes, Ethan read the note.

Hello Ethan,

I like to underestimate the dosage initially to avoid an accidental overdose. So, if you wake up, know this: I'm watching you, and I'm watching Jenna.

The note did not contain a signature. Ethan read it several more times, and with each successive read, his fists balled tighter.

After the fourth read, he could not take any more. He slammed his head into the barrel, making sure the note landed in the middle of his sweaty forehead. He waited a moment for moisture from his head to seep onto the note, then he ripped his head sideways, flinging the note from the barrel. The act tore the skin from his brow, and beads of blood and sweat tickled him.

With the note out of his sight, he tensed his shoulders and arms before ramming them backwards, his elbows striking the walls. The tight handcuffs tore the skin from his wrists, and pain rushed throughout his arms. This only fueled his rage more. Over and over, he pulled, tearing more and more flesh, causing more and more pain.

The agony soon unbearable, he relented and rested his head on the barrel.

So much for calmness, he thought, before pulling again.

19

SIX MONTHS PRIOR

He considered all the effort, all the planning that led to this one moment. His heart slammed against his ribs as he tried in vain to keep his breathing steady. The hand holding the wine glass sweat, leaving streaks.

To calm his nerves, he took a swig of his Pinot Gris, but flinched when the liquid grazed his tongue. He wasn't a fan of white wine, never had been. White wine lacked the complexity and nuance of red. A white wine with the prettiest golden hue could not rival the beautiful crimson of even a mediocre pinot noir. He loved how red wine danced in his glass as he swirled, the streaky legs memorializing the ritual. Wine was his lifeblood, and it made sense to him that his preferred varietals should so match.

"You okay there, babe?" she asked.

"Huh?" He looked over at Jodi, whose gaze fixated on him. "Sorry, I was lost in my thoughts." He admired her: a tall, blonde bombshell with the right amount of curves and a brain to boot. A perfect subject.

"What were you thinkin' about?"

He smiled at her and replied, "You. Us. How's the fish?"

"It's fantastic. Best you've ever cooked." Jodi's favorite food was seafood. He was more of a meat, potatoes, and red wine guy. But he agreed that the meal turned out well: Chilean sea bass on a bed of lettuce with avocadoes, asparagus, and a beautiful Oregon Pinot Gris. Now, it was time for dessert.

"So," he said, "aren't you going to ask?"

"Ask what?" she replied with a coy smile.

"Ask why we are eating in the butler's house instead of the main dining area, or a restaurant, or anywhere else."

"Well," she cleaned her mouth with a napkin, "I was curious. I've never seen this retreat of yours. Always wanted to see it, but it's your special place and I didn't want to push it." She shrugged. "I was kinda more excited when you told me than curious. Figured you wanted to let me in on this little secret of yours."

"Secret," he intoned while leaning back. "That's an interesting way to put it. Yes, I'm here to reveal a secret, but it's bigger than this little house."

"Bigger?"

"Yes. Much bigger." He set his napkin on the table, stood, and took her left hand into his right. The new diamond on her ring finger created a little light show even in the dimmed room. "This ring," he held her hand up and pinched the diamond, "means you will be a Holland. For better, for worse. You will not only get to know me, but the entire family and our secrets. That includes our biggest one."

He released her hand and enjoyed her crinkled forehead and raised eyebrows, her go-to expression of confusion. He appreciated her overwhelming beauty. Sapphire eyes with flakes of jade. Tanned, soft skin. Everything about her was nuanced and perfect. For a moment, he questioned his path, for after the culmination of his intentions, she would never be beautiful again.

Though that may not be the case. Beauty was in the eye of

the beholder. Perhaps her sacrifice would enhance her beauty in a deeper way, a level past physical.

Regardless, there was no going back. The plan was already in place. No use trying to slow a freight train. It was better to enjoy the ride.

Besides, she was too perfect a specimen.

"Your biggest secret?" she said, interrupting his thoughts. "What does that mean?"

He smiled. "Some things are better seen than heard. Follow me real quick." He moved towards the bedroom slowly, listening for her steps behind him. Soon, she was next to him, her heat tickling his arm.

"See that." He nodded towards a large chest across from the bed.

"That? That's your biggest secret? I mean, I don't really see how that's much of a secret. It's just a chest."

"Sometimes the biggest secrets are the most obvious. Watch." He grabbed a handle on the chest's side and dragged it away from the wall; four wheels guided it. Under the chest rested a small door, an iron handle in the middle.

"Wow," she gasped. "You're full of surprises."

"Better than being full of shit."

Her laughter cut the nervousness. She looked so beautiful when she laughed. Many girls he dated before tried to repress laughter, holding back out of fear of tarnishing their looks. Not Jodi. With Jodi, every laugh was an event, a blast of lightning to his soul. She hunched over, her right hand on her stomach, her left on her chest, her smile large with white teeth outlined by ruby lips.

She had to be the first. He could no longer avoid the reality. He loved her unconditionally, and that love was a liability. She was like a mild earthquake, unbalancing his equilibrium, and he needed every bit of stability for what lay ahead.

"I said you're full of surprises," she replied. "You could be full of other things as well, including shit."

"Eh, agree to disagree. Listen." He took her hand. "What I'm about to show you is important. It means a great deal to me and my family. I've never shown anyone else this, never even considered it. But you're not anyone. You're the one. My only one."

His speech caught her off-guard. A gentle, content smile replaced her giddy one. "I love you, babe," she finally replied.

"I love you, too. Now, be careful going down." He bent over and, with force, pulled up on the handle, opening the door. "It is dark, and the way is dangerous."

Before them extended a steep staircase leading into pitch blackness, bottles of wine lining the path, the dim light darkening their maroon liquid. He had gone down to his private reserve countless times, but this time seemed different, as if all other descents were but appetizers to this main course. Jodi's obvious uncertainty added to the excitement. He felt like a kid about to ride the roller coaster he previously only admired from pictures.

"What's down there?" she asked, her voice shaky but curious.

"That's for me to know and you to find out." He extended his hand, and she took it.

He stepped gingerly. The creaky wood trembled more than usual, likely due to the weight of two people, yet he did not feel unsafe. His father commissioned the staircase to specs that would outlast Jacob's lifespan. But Jodi's hand continued to quiver, so he kept stepping, his grip rotating between a firm grasp and a gentle massage of her palm with his thumb.

"You okay?" he asked.

"Yeah," she replied. "Not great at seeing in the dark. Don't really like it, either. My brother used to turn off all the lights, then jump out and scare the crap outta me."

"Don't worry, we'll be near light soon."

As if on cue, a speck of light appeared before them, brightening the path. A few steps later and their feet struck ground. A candle in the distance illuminated a sparse table with two port glasses and a single wine bottle in the middle, unlabeled. In the penumbras of the lights glimmered a myriad of other bottles that encircled them, resting in large oak racks. The chill caused him to shiver no matter how many times he experienced it. A deep, soul-shaking shiver that clothes did little to halt.

"You too cold?" he asked. The entire room was temperature controlled to remain at 55 degrees Fahrenheit.

"A little," she admitted with a shudder.

"Here, take this." He took off his coat and placed it over her bony shoulders. "That should help."

"It does. So, this might sound dumb, but is this what I think it is?"

"Yup."

"Wow." She gazed around the room. "Not sure what to say." She turned to him and asked, "Who else has seen this?"

"Aside from you, no one not named Holland. Well, and the guys who built it, but I'm guessing they signed NDAs. I also keep strong tabs on the stock down here, which I don't need to tell you is invaluable. Once every two weeks, I check every bottle against a list. To date, the only wine missing is what we drink."

"How far down does it go?" She pointed to the darkened area untouched by the candle's shine.

"Not too far. Just a few more feet."

"You know, I pictured something bigger. I like this much better."

"Me too. Quality over quantity. The wine in here is worth many, many millions. But we won't be drinking any of these, sorry to say."

"Oh?" The candlelight accentuated her sharp features, including her raised eyebrow. "What are we drinking?"

"Sit and I'll explain."

She nodded and sat. He followed, and once sitting, he lifted and reviewed the unmarked bottle on the table. He first studied it, ensuring it was the bottle that contained his secret "ingredient." He also sniffed it to ensure the ingredient remained odorless, not that he was concerned about Jodi distrusting him.

Satisfied, he poured Jodi a large glass. "So," he began, "remember how I've talked to you a few times about my dream of becoming a winemaker?"

"A few times?" She laughed.

"Fine, you win. Remember how I've talked to you a million times about my dream of becoming a wine maker?"

"I think you've said something about that, yeah."

"Well, my dear, this is my first attempt."

"Oh yeah?" She grinned playfully, her eyes twinkling in the flame's ballet. "So I guess I'm the guinea pig?"

"Now, now. I would never call you a pig. But my test subject, sure. You're the first. Probably the only for a while. You have a great palette and don't pull punches, exactly what I need."

"Thank you for the compliment." She raised the glass for a toast, but his glass remained on the table. "You're not drinking?" she asked.

"Not yet. I guess I'm nervous. Kinda like a writer reading a first draft for an audience. I'd rather see how you react."

"Suit yourself." She lifted the glass a second time and drank in one long pull. At first, she maintained a composed smile. Slowly, it morphed into an expression of reserved disgust, her cheeks tightening, her mouth a slit. She could only maintain her restraint for a few seconds before bending over and dry heaving.

"What?" he asked with feigned concern. "What happened? Are you okay?"

"I'm sorry, Jacob," she replied in stilted syllables. "I think something's wrong with the wine."

He grabbed the wine and brought it to his nose, pretending to sniff. "God, I think you're right. I'm so sorry, babe, I'm so sorry."

"It's okay," she replied, her voice more collected. "I'm fine. It was just weird, you know? Never tasted anything like that."

"Yeah, definitely not what I was going for. I think maybe it became sour somehow. I'll tell you what, let's wash that down with something else." He stood, walked to the racks, and took a few moments to survey. He decided on a bottle and brought it to the table, displaying its label like a sommelier in a fine restaurant. "How about this? A '95 Richebourg?"

"Jacob," she replied with a gasp. "What's that wine worth? Several thousand dollars, right?"

"Something along those lines."

"I can't drink that, Jacob. It's too expensive."

"Don't stress. It's actually one of our lesser bottles here." He pulled a bottle opener from his pocket and twirled it into the cork.

"Is that a bottle opener in the pocket or are you just happy to see me?"

He laughed in response, but her observation unnerved him. He didn't consider how strange it might look to be casually carrying a corkscrew in his pocket. Would less trusting individuals question such irregularities? He had to focus more on the minutiae and pay better attention. Every detail from this point forward mattered.

"Yeah," he finally replied as he removed the cork with a *pop* that sounded louder than normal in the tight cellar. "I figured we might indulge in more than one bottle down here. You know me, Mr. Boy Scout."

"That probably sounded better in your head."

He poured a large glass and slid it over to her; she snatched it and pulled the glass towards her face to better study it. "Ah yes," she said, sarcastically feigning pretentiousness. "Great legs on this one."

"It's not the only one."

She kicked him under the table.

"My point exactly." He filled the glass and lifted it in her direction.

"So, what are we toasting?" she asked.

"The future."

"Good. I like that."

They clinked glasses and drank, each taking a moment to savor the incredible liquid. Bursts of pepper, dashes of dark cherry, hints of tobacco, undertones of wet earth. There was nothing he disliked about this burgundy. Everything about it was incredible.

"Wow," she finally intoned after several moments of silence.

"Not bad, huh?" he asked.

"Not bad? This might be the best wine I've ever tasted."

"It's definitely up there."

The comfortable silence lingered for a while longer as they both enjoyed the wine's ride. Whenever drinking an amazing wine, Jacob liked to picture the vintage year. 1995, a good year. Oklahoma City bombing. O.J. acquitted. Large, world-changing events that resonated in the wine.

He watched her with glee. At first, she tried to fight it. He could tell in the subtle changes to her demeanor. Her hand flicked her hair but rested on her temple for an extended moment. Her eyes drooped and her blinks slowed, each successive blink taking longer and longer. She swayed gently, almost indecipherably, in her chair, while trying to steady herself on the table.

Jodi finally broke the quiet. "Hey Jacob, can you do me a favor?"

"Anything, babe. What's up?"

"I really hate to ask this, everything is so romantic. It's just, can we go upstairs?"

"Why?"

"I'm not feeling good."

"What do you mean?"

"I'm not sure," she replied, her voice woozy and soft. "You know, just not good."

"No," Jacob replied as he leaned over the table. "I need you to tell me exactly what's wrong. Every symptom in detail."

She glared at him, her expression a mix of confusion and concern. "What do you mean? Symptom?"

"In the clinical sense. I need to understand what's off. Dizziness, pain, everything. It'll help me in the future." He sat back and raised his glass. "The information will aid you too, actually. The more you know, as they say."

Her eyes flickered, filled first with confusion and then panic. "What's gotten into you?"

"You." He slammed the bottle opener into the table, the bang echoing throughout the hollow room. The pointed end remained stuck in the table, the instrument sticking upright. The noise startled her, causing her to jump in an odd, unsteady sort of way. When her stability returned, she rested her arms on the table.

"Jacob," she said, her voice shaky.

"Answer me. Do you feel light-headed?"

She nodded, the muscles in her face tightening as the rest of her body relaxed.

"How about tired?" he asked.

She nodded again.

"Dizzy?"

"Yes," she replied.

"Good." He smirked, closed his eyes, and sipped his wine. He heard her stand and try to scream, but her voice came out muted and ineffectual. The next sound was her body hitting the floor.

Then, beautiful silence. He enjoyed the rest of his wine to the soft melody of Jodi's breathing and occasional groan. Passed out, she looked even more beautiful, angelic even. He didn't lie: He would enjoy spending every day with her.

Jacob set down the empty glass and lorded over Jodi. Carefully, he removed the jacket from her body. He grabbed gloves from a nearby cabinet before flipping Jodi onto her back and removing keys from the Tori Burch purse that lay at her side. To ensure she slept, he shook her and, aside from a light moan, she remained motionless, her chest lifting with soft, stilted breaths.

He ascended the stairs and, from within the wooden chest, snatched handcuffs and rope. As he bound her, he considered injecting more medicine, but erred on the side of caution. The bindings would prevent motion and screaming, and he read damning reports about the medicine's side effects. He could not risk renal failure, the worst possible outcome.

When finished, Jacob kissed her on the forehead and whispered, "Sweet dreams, my Princess. I love you." He then stood and headed up to the kitchen, closing the trapdoor behind him and sliding the chest back to its spot, ensuring little appeared array.

The kitchen needed cleaning. The fish would stink if left out. In retrospect, fish was a poor choice for Jodi's final meal. No matter. A thorough cleanse would both hide his tracks and ease his mind.

As he cleaned, he analyzed the next steps. Every step required precision. He could not deviate unless forced. Any variation could throw off the plan's delicate symmetry.

After he scrubbed to a spotless shine and replaced the dishes, he reviewed the room and searched for any major signs of Jodi. He found none. With Jodi disposed of, it was time to take the next step towards eventual perfection. He strolled outside and slid into her car. Before starting the engine, he studied the interior, scanning for signs of his presence. One can't be too careful when driving the car of his poisoned fiancé, especially given the Sonoma and Healdsburg cops could be snoopy, and he already had too much blood on his hands for one night.

The night was quiet and cold, so he drove with the windshield down and allowed the sweet Sonoma breeze to cool his anticipation. He had to remain calm. Eagerness could lead to calamity. All it would take is a cop spotting him driving a few miles over the speed limit for the plan to unravel. And while he was an excellent liar, he much preferred the luxury of keeping his mouth shut. A closed mouth told no lies.

About ten minutes north of Santa Rosa, his first destination came into focus. Shiloh Ranch National Park was one of Jodi's favorite hiking areas—with few tourists and stunning views at the top, Jodi spent countless hours biking its trails. He parked about one hundred meters past the entry; the park was closed, but he could hop over the low gate.

Despite the lack of cameras in the vicinity, he slid the hoodie over his head as a shield. He jumped the gate and trekked until he found a high, memorable tree with sprawling branches and a nearby bench. His head on a swivel to guarantee his safety, he sat Jodi's phone next to the tree and placed a rock on it, careful to avoid crushing the delicate machinery. He stepped back to review his work: In the dark, the phone was practically invisible unless one searched specially for it.

He returned to the car and drove away. Accelerating with confidence, he kept a watchful eye on the odometer and the clock. The minutes were now precious, and he had to finish the job quickly.

He took back roads for the next fifteen minutes until he

spotted his destination. The junkyard had been in his family for years, primarily run by his Uncle. Jacob recalled several sweaty summers laboring in the yard for extra dough. He enjoyed the work, for he relished using his hands and lacked any aversion to getting them dirty. That night, his youthful employment would be invaluable.

He pulled into the junkyard and parked near a smattering of broken-down pieces of crap. He stepped out and searched for his target: a teal minivan, a navy truck, a dusty SUV. None of which were useful. Finally, he saw the green Mini Cooper he had scoped out a few days prior. He had waited patiently for such a car to arrive. Eventually, he would have proceeded even without a substitute vehicle, but once he saw this car, he knew it was time. The car was an omen of impending rain as well as his umbrella. Its color was wrong, but the year, make, and model were more important.

He ran over to a nearby workshop, grabbed an adjustable screwdriver, and used it to take the plates off the yellow Honda, which would replace Jodi's plates. That would work as a temporary Band-Aid—while his uncle could sell underwear to a nudist, he did not track inventory well. A couple of days later, with more time to spare, Jacob would return and crush Jodi's car. But for now, he had to hurry.

A drawer in the workshop had keys to the tow truck; Jacob took the keys and hopped in the wrecker. Before pulling out of the junkyard, he made sure he had Jodi's plates; then, he drove away.

He wanted to hit the accelerator, but he knew the wrecker wouldn't comply. He also didn't want to risk a breakdown, for that would create an escapeless obstacle.

A maddening twenty minutes later, he saw the park. He parked about a mile away from the tree this time and removed his hooded jacket. Underneath, he donned a jogging suit, which matched his gloves.

The crisp night made for a pleasant jog, and the thumping of his steps calmed his nerves a bit. An avid runner, he found that the best way to slow his mind was to move his legs. Often, running was his only escape from the madness. But he didn't want to escape it that night, for his madness was to become his glory.

Soon, he was near the tree. Though he worried a little the whole run that the cell phone would disappear, it remained where he left it.

It's all going according to plan, he thought.

He picked up the phone, dusted it off, and placed it in his pocket before jogging to the wrecker.

He left the wrecker in the parking lot of the Healdsburg Walmart after discarding Jodi's plates in the largest lake in Foothill Regional Park. If the cops later found the plates, well, that may just add to the story. But that was a concern for another day. He was almost done. And God, did it feel good.

He walked about half a mile until he was in front of one of Jodi's favorite coffee shops, which wasn't open. Nothing was open, actually: Healdsburg was a sleepy town, perfect for his purposes.

He found a dark area with no obvious cameras. He pulled out Jodi's phone from his pocket, swiped it to unlock, and typed in her passcode, which was just her birthday. Poor Jodi. She was always too trusting.

He set up a text message for Jodi's parents, typing in, "Gonna take a long vacation. You won't hear from me for a while. I love you." After hitting SEND, he placed the cell phone on the ground and crushed it with a few stomps of his feet. The cracking sound of crunched machinery was beautiful, an abrupt coda to a masterful symphony.

He picked up the cell phone remnants and put them in a nearby trashcan. As he headed back to the wrecker, he allowed himself to enjoy the moment. He guessed the night's temperature was in the low 40s, and the chill air filled his lungs and ignited his passion. A long night awaited: He had to drop off the wrecker at the junkyard, jog back to the butler's house, and start cleaning any signs of Jodi other than what remained in the private reserve. But as his final chapter faded away in the trucker's rearview mirror, he anticipated his planned sequels.

20

LAST NIGHT

Jacob sat near but was careful not to touch Beverly. Subconsciously, he recognized he was growing fond of Bev, but could not let those fleeting feelings distract him. He had a friend, George, in high school who transferred from Texas and spoke of his days in Future Farmers of America and how he grew attached to the cattle he showed. Jacob determined that he, like George, must learn to distance himself from his prey, for the show trumped his feelings.

"You sure we won't be interrupted," he asked, placing a short stutter after "sure" as a sign of sincerity.

"I am," she replied. "Ethan's coming down this weekend, but other than that, no one is coming by."

"You didn't tell anyone about us, right?"

"No, Jacob. Look, I've also got a lot to lose here. Ethan is an incredible attorney. I can't give him any ammo he could use to change our divorce agreement, not that he would try." She shook her head and said, "I'm just being paranoid. I doubt he would do that just because I'm dating someone else. I just need to be mindful."

"No," he said, his voice flat. "I get it."

"Good." She sighed. "I'm glad you understand. All of this is odd, I get it. That's why I asked you to be patient with me. And slow. We'll get there."

"I have no doubt."

She squeezed his arm, and he fought the urge to pull away. "I haven't told you this, but I really appreciate that you haven't complained about how slow we've taken it."

"I care about you. And, as weird as it sounds, I care about Jenna, too. As long as I'm with you, no matter the circumstances, I'm happy." He repressed a smirk.

She let go of his arm, giving it a light rub before doing so, and asked, "So what now?"

"Well, first things first. You want to see my surprise?"

"Sure."

"Great. Don't move." He stood and strolled towards the kitchen, cognizant to maintain a strut of eagerness. He grabbed the bottle he brought as a "gift," retrieved a wine opener from the cabinet, and pulled out the cork. In his periphery, Jacob noticed a familiar sight: A bottle of Holland Vineyard's recent pinot release.

"Hey," he called out. "You already open a bottle of wine?"

"I did," she replied. "Thought it would be a bit of a surprise. Hope you like what I got!" Her playful tone annoyed him, and he knew he would have to dispose of the Holland bottle before leaving that evening.

Repressing his frustration, he returned to the living room with his surprise and handed it to Beverly. "I don't get it," she said after reviewing the bottle. "What is this? It doesn't have a label or anything."

"This, my dear, is my own personal, I don't know, experiment I guess. Experiment's not the right word. Like, recipe maybe? Sad to say, but my mom is passing soon, so I've been thinking a lot about how I can put my mark on the Holland legacy. This is my first step."

"So wait," she replied as she leaned in close to him. "This is a vintage you put together?"

"Yup."

"Well, what is it? What varietal?"

"Let's call it a blend for now. I don't want to give away specifics unless I have the formula down pat. But try it and tell me what you think." He carefully placed the wine opener's screw into the cork, circled, and yanked it out.

As he poured her a glass, she asked, "So, no name for it yet?"

"Good question," he replied with genuine surprise. "Not yet. How about the Bev?"

"Oh stop." She waved the glass in his direction. "Bottles up." She took a swig, and her expression, like Jodi's, slipped from pleasure to pain, though not as suddenly. Beverly's shift was gradual, like a ferry operator slowly realizing a cruise ship wasn't going to stop.

"You okay?" he asked.

"Yeah," she replied. "It's just, I don't know. I guess I've never really tasted wine like this. I can't describe it."

As with Jodi, he grabbed the bottle, gave it a deep, feigned, sniff, and said, "Dammit, this bottle isn't good. I can tell. Something's wrong. I'm so sorry."

"No, no, it's fine," she said, her hand outstretched towards him. "I'm glad it's not me. I figured I was missing something there."

"No, no, you're not. I'm just embarrassed." Though he wasn't. Her reaction as compared to Jodi's illustrated how far he had come in such a short period.

"Hey babe, sorry to change the subject, but do you have your phone?"

"My phone?" She asked, her tone curious. "Yeah, in my

pocket." She pulled it out and displayed it for him. She paused, eyes unfocused, and asked, "Hey Jacob, what was in that wine?"

"I told you, it's a secret for now. I can't tell you the blend."

"But, only grapes? Nothing else?"

"Of course. I'm not some weirdo here."

"It's just, I'm not feeling that well."

"Oh yeah? What's wrong?"

"Not sure. I'm dizzy. I'm tired."

"Here, lie down for a bit." He took the glass from her hand and placed it on the table, careful not to spill any. She lay and looked up at him as haze oozed over her eyes.

"You know," he started, "I've enjoyed getting close to you. Thank you."

"Thank me?" she asked, her voice fading. "What does that mean?"

"None of this would have been possible without you."

"Jacob," she replied, the word elongated and soft. "I don't, I don't understand."

"And you never will. But for now, just rest, my dear."

She didn't protest. Her eyes closed and she lay limp. Before putting things into motion, however, he had to connect the first piece of the puzzle. With his hands still in gloves, he grabbed her thumb and placed it against the cell phone's home screen, which sprang to life.

Step one, done.

In his pants pocket rested step two. He stood and walked towards Bev's purse. When he arrived, he placed in it a bottle containing several small pills, the prescription made out to a fake person. He hoped this would be enough to convince any nosy forensic pathologist.

Step two, done.

The most challenging step remained. He headed up the stairs and to Jenna's bedroom door, conscious of making too much noise. Outside her room, he composed himself, attempting to balance concern and maturity. Ready, he knocked several times and said, "Jenna. Jenna, are you there?"

A meek voice responded with, "Hello?"

"Jenna, this is Jacob. I need to talk to you."

A few seconds later, Jenna cracked open the door and stared up through blonde curls with big hazel eyes. Her dolphin pajamas clung to her tiny frame, meaning she likely sprouted up and was between sizes. She looked older every time he saw her.

"What's wrong?" she asked, her voice worried.

"It's your mom. She passed out."

"What?" She flung open the door and stared at him. With the light from the hallway, he could see portions of her bedroom, which looked typical: pink bedsheets, purple stuffed animals, and Frozen posters.

"Yeah, not sure what happened. She just fell over. Was she sick today?"

"No." She stepped out and gazed upwards, worry lines over her smooth features. "She went running this morning. Looked okay."

"Here, come downstairs." He motioned to her to follow and, hesitantly, she complied. As they descended the stairs, she saw and ran to her mother, shaking her limp body.

"Momma!" she screamed, shaking more forcefully. "Momma, wake up!"

"I tried," he said with a contrived comforting voice. "She's breathing, so that's a good sign. I need to call the hospital. Can I borrow your phone? I forgot mine."

"Yeah," she said and ran upstairs. He loved her innocence. At no point did she question anything about the situation. Her only thoughts were of protecting her mother. A beautiful sentiment, if meaningless.

When she arrived, he handed him the cell phone unlocked. As he grabbed it, he purposefully pressed the side bar, locking it.

"Dammit," he said. "What's your code?"

"2-2-3-5." Focused on her mother, she didn't even hesitate. He didn't expect it to be that easy. He tried the code, and it worked.

"Got it," he said. He was glad that she willingly gave him her code. That made things easier. Wouldn't have mattered either way, though. He could have used her face.

Everything in place, he slipped her phone into his pocket, pulled out a rag from his back pocket. As he walked behind her, she didn't break sight of her mother, her meek muscles straining as she tried to wake Beverly. She didn't even notice when he stood right behind her.

Step three, done.

***

Jenna moaned as Jacob slipped on the final handcuff. Interested, he watched her awakening, faster than he expected. His concerns about overdosing caused an underdose. No matter as they were in the private reserve, and he had plenty of medicine left.

In fact, he thought, *perhaps I can work this to my advantage.*

He recalled the voice memo feature on his phone which he used to record tasting notes. After pulling out his phone, he navigated to this app and placed his finger on the record button.

Gradually, her eyes opened, her expression first of confusion then curiosity, and, finally, fear. "Jacob?" she asked with a trembling voice. "Where's mom?"

"She's gone," he replied.

"What do you mean? I don't—"

"She's gone. Gone for good. But your Daddy's on the phone. Wanna talk to him?" He hit the record button and placed the speaker near her mouth.

"Help me!" she screamed. "Help me, Daddy! Please, Daddy, help!"

He pressed the pause button, said, "He can't hear you, Jenna," and restarted the recording.

"Daddy please, help! Get me out!"

He clicked off the recording. "That's better. Now it's time to go back to sleep for a while. Don't worry. I'll be right here when you wake back up." He tousled her hair, leaned in, and whispered, "But I doubt you ever will."

She started screaming, but the rag muffled the sound.

Jacob stood over Bev's sprawled-out body and considered whether it needed any additional fine tuning.

No, he decided. *She's perfect.*

He glanced at the living room that he had worked so hard to destroy, a nice balance between scuffle and all-out brawl. He didn't want to go too overboard on the ancillary chaos. The focus should remain on what lay before him.

His pulse quickened and sweat beads formed in his palms like little pools of tension. It had only been a couple of minutes since he sent the text to Ethan, though it felt like much longer. Whether he responded changed things a great deal. He had to be sure Ethan would drive this way before he put the finishing touches on Plan A. Plan B, regardless, was available, but he far preferred Plan A.

Bev's phone lit up and displayed the name "Ethan." A good sign, but not enough. For the next several minutes, Jacob ignored call after call, each building the excitement like ads before a movie. He knew the main event would start soon.

And as that thought crossed his mind, the text he had been waiting for arrived: "Why the hell aren't you picking up? I'm coming over."

Jacob placed the cell phone next to Bev's hand, lifted the blade, and grinned. As he did so, she fidgeted and moaned, her head rolling back and forth. He studied her, noting the symptoms. She opened her eyes, which stared blankly at first. As she focused, she noticed him.

"Jacob?" she asked, unsteady.

A feeling surged through him, unfamiliar and disconcerting. It possessed all the hallmarks of fear: increased heart rate, heavy breathing, and trembling hands. But no, it was not fear. It was excitement, which swelled as he plunged the knife into Bev's heart.

Ethan read the text again: "I need you to come over. It's about Jenna."

Light blinded him; swerving hard right, he veered back into his lane and dodged the incoming car. He refocused on the road through the sound of a blaring horn, not that Ethan could fault the other driver. The early hour did not excuse reckless driving.

To combat the desire to look at the text, he instead dialed his ex-wife's number. After five rings, her joyful voice said, "Hi, you've reached Beverly's voicemail! I'm not here—"

He broke the connection and redialed; again, he got her message with the same feigned exuberance. He tried four more times, but she did not answer.

Dammit to hell, he thought. *Why isn't she picking up?*

He dialed a different number. Two rings later, a groggy voice said, "Hey baby."

The muscles in his back uncoiled. "Hey sweetheart. Thanks for picking up."

With a giggle, Sarah said, "You don't have to thank your girlfriend for answering the phone."

"Sorry," he replied and cursed under his breath. "Been a while since I did this dating thing." He hoped that sentence didn't come off as pathetic as it sounded to him.

"Silly," she replied, unfazed. "You reach Bev?"

"No. I keep calling, but she's still not picking up."

"Ugh. I'm sure she sent you that text just to be dramatic."

"You're probably right," Ethan reluctantly concurred, "but I have to make sure everything's okay. I'm really sorry."

"Don't apologize. I mean, it's your daughter. Who wouldn't freak out about a text like that? Just call me when you get there, okay?"

"Promise."

"Figure out what's going on and then get your butt back to bed with me. Love ya."

"Same." After ending the call, he placed the iPhone in the cup holder and concentrated on keeping his breathing steady, using the flashing road dashes to time his breaths. Five dashes in, five dashes out. Panic did nothing but muddle the mind, and he needed to stay clear.

Jenna's okay, he thought. *She's okay. God, please let her be fine.*

Images of Jenna blasted his mind as he navigated the wine country roads, fog distorting the signs and lampposts, making them appear ethereal. Through hazy and temporary surroundings, he witnessed flashes of Jenna's birth, first steps, garbled words, and laughter, all convalescing in a blur of memories.

Over the engine's roar, a tiny voice dominated. The voice fluttered in his ear, tickling his neck. The voice repeated the same thing, over and over: "Hero," Jenna's nickname for him.

Normally, the trip to Ethan's old Sonoma home could take up to two hours through the often-gridlocked California highways, especially at that time of year with the out-of-towners making their yearly pilgrimages. Ethan's drive took less than forty-five minutes. For the first time since purchasing it three years prior, he tested the acceleration and handling of his Mercedes coupe, and the car responded as if she had awaited the moment.

He pulled into the driveway and parked in front of the house he once referred to as his "pinot palace." Two-story, all white with tall windows throughout, he recalled how he once loved to stare out at the surroundings and get lost among the endless green and distant mountains.

He jogged up the stone stairs to the oversized wood front door and rang the doorbell, which chimed with a deep *dong-ding-dong*. After a few seconds, he rang twice. Ten seconds later, he banged on the door in a fit of frustration, knuckles throbbing after hitting harder than he intended.

"Bev!" he screamed. "Open the door, dammit!" No response. He cupped his hands and peered through the door's frosted windows but noticed no movement through the distortion.

Quickly, he pulled out a jangling set of keys from his pocket and located the one with a maroon base. Bev gave him explicit instructions to only use the spare key "in a big emergency." He figured a mysterious text about his daughter qualified, and if it didn't, to hell with her arbitrary definitions.

He inserted the key, turned, and realized the door was already unlocked. He stepped inside and shuddered; his once immaculate home was a disaster. Overturned chairs littered the room. Dirty plates rested on every table. Food, booze, and grit caked the floor. The maid service he paid for obviously had not visited that day. The entire scene reminded him of his last year of marriage.

This is no place for a child, he concluded. *Once this is all over, I'm filing a motion to modify custody.*

In the corner of his eye, he spotted something unusual near the living room sofa: the color red. Liquid oozed, its borders creeping outward like a new moon. At first, he thought the liquid was spilled wine, but the consistency was too thick, the redness too bright.

"Bev?" he whispered as he stepped towards the sofa. He looked behind it and found Beverly sprawled on the floor. Tousled brunette hair covered her face and blood stained her white top with crimson streaks that ran down her jeans. His eyes fixated on the handle of a large kitchen knife sticking out of her chest.

Air escaped his lungs as if he were slugged. He stepped back. His vision twisted. Pressure built against his chest. His composure lost, he fell to his knees and covered his eyes, unable to face the blank expression of his daughter's mother. He wept into the back of his hands. His palms stifling his pleas. He wished to drown in the sea of his salty tears to escape the sight of Beverly's vacant eyes.

After the initial rush of grief, he inhaled deeper breaths between briefer cries, slowing his pulse. The tears continued to flow, but clarity slipped between them.

Stand, he chastised himself. *Stand, now.*

He stood, knees wobbling, and braced himself against the couch. Once stable, he screamed, "Jenna! Jenna! Where are you?" He frantically reviewed the room but found his dead ex-wife was his only companion.

A noise startled him; it was brief, so he didn't register the sound at first. It happened again, and he realized two cell phones lay near Beverly. One, an iPhone with a pink case, he recognized as hers, but it remained silent. The second—an old school flip model—rang, and its caller ID displayed an incoming call from "Jenna." While gritting his teeth, he grabbed the bulky phone and answered.

"Jenna, where are you?" he asked.

A pleasant male voice replied, "Hello, Ethan."

"What? Who the hell is this?"

The man said, "My name is Jacob," and chuckled. "If you ever want to see Jenna again, you'll do exactly as I say."

"Screw you," Ethan shot back, his calmness suffocated by the weight of his ex-wife's body and daughter's apparent disappearance. "Tell me where Jenna is or I will hunt you down and cut your damn head off."

Laughter met his threat. "Now, now, Ethan. No need for dramatics. Yelling at me isn't going to get you any closer to Jenna."

"Tell me where she is!" His whole body shook as if he stood over the epicenter of an earthquake and struggled to keep from falling into the slithering crack.

"I will, I will. You have my word. But first, I need you to do a few things for me. Then, you can have Jenna back."

"I'm not doing shit for you."

"I understand your hesitation." The caller's smile was clear in his voice as he spoke, further infuriating Ethan. "But you must understand," Jacob continued. "If you refuse me, I will have no more need for little Jenna here. For now, she's useful. You wouldn't want her to become a liability, would you? Just look at what I did to Beverly."

"Go to hell, psycho. I'm done—"

Before Ethan could finish, a young female voice screamed, "Help me! Help me, Daddy! Please, Daddy, help!" The voice sounded muffled and strange, but Ethan recognized it immediately.

"Jenna!" Ethan yelled. "Jenna! Talk to me. Has he hurt you?"

"Daddy, please, help! Get me out!"

"Jenna!"

Silence.

"Jenna, are you there?" Ethan screamed. "Jenna!"

A man's voice instead answered, "Now, are you ready to cooperate?"

Ethan bent over and braced his hands on his knees, the dizziness returning. Vomit rose in his throat, and with a swallow he forced it back.

"Fine, fine," Ethan said. "First, please, just tell me where she is," Ethan pleaded, his voice cracking every other word. "Where are you keeping her?"

"I'm not going to let you depose me, Ethan."

Depose me? Ethan thought. *How did he know...*

"She's in the bed of my truck," Jacob replied flatly. "Now, listen closely. You won't have to do much, but you can't mess up anything. I'm not kidding, Ethan, anything. One screw up and Jenna's a goner. Got it?"

"Yes," Ethan said. "Yes. I'll do anything. I swear."

"Good stuff!" Jacob exclaimed cheerfully, like one guy talking to another about a big play in the big game. "Glad to have you onboard. Relax a little and you might even have some fun with what's going to happen next. Just give me a sec..." The line went silent. "Can you hear me?" Jacob asked, his voice distant.

"Yeah."

"Great. Sometimes this Bluetooth crap acts up. Technology's a weird thing, man. Endless pain in the backside, but occasionally, it can really do some amazing stuff. Like, for example, I can see you right now. You still wear a sweatshirt from law school? Impressive that it still fits so well."

Ethan instinctively looked down at the navy-blue sweatshirt emblazoned with "BERKELEY LAW" in large, gold font.

"I hope you're not attached to it," Jacob said. "Because it's about to be ruined."

"How can you see me?"

"The security app on Jenna's phone. Enough chit-chat. Ready?"

Ethan closed his eyes and guided his breaths. In-and-out, in-and-out. "Ready."

"Okay, first thing. See the knife in your ex-wife?"

Ethan fought the urge to curse. "Yes."

"Pull it out."

"Why?"

"No more questions," Jacob replied flatly. "Just do it."

"Okay."

"And don't try anything silly, like covering your hand with that sweater. Grab the knife with your bare hand."

"All right." Ethan placed the cell phone on the sofa's side table and walked towards Beverly's body, which was sprawled out in a pool of blood that soaked into her brunette curls. Her eyes remained open. Panicked, lifeless hazel irises stared up at him as if begging for his intervention. He repressed an impulse to close her eyes and stayed on task. He grabbed the knife's thick wood handle, imagined Jenna's face, and pulled.

The knife slid out easier than he expected. He stumbled backwards, his eyes burning; he rubbed them, and when he pulled his hands back, blood dotted his fingers.

"Good job!" Jacob yelled, his voice coming from the side table. "Pick the phone back up."

Ethan complied. "Now what?"

"The next step is easy. Just smear the blood from the knife onto your sweatshirt."

Ethan exhaled a sigh of relief at this command. He pressed the knife against his chest and ran it up and down his sweatshirt as he dismissed a desire to ram the blade into his heart. He rotated the blade after a few strokes and repeated the process. When finished, he tossed the knife, knowing his fingerprints littered the handle. He reviewed his sweatshirt and noticed the blood streaks morphed two of the Es into backwards Bs.

"Atta boy," Jacob said. "You're almost there. Just two more things. After I hang up, drop Beverly's phone and your own in the pitcher of water on the table near the sofa. See it?"

Ethan assessed the ornate Waterford pitcher, a wedding present they had rarely used. "Yeah, I see it."

"Good. Drop both in there the moment you hear the click. Keep this phone on you as I may need to call you again. Then you'll have exactly ten minutes to meet me at the first entrance to Sugarloaf Park. The one just past Landmark. You know where that one is, right?"

"Yes." Ethan knew it well.

"Splendid. You have ten minutes starting now. One minute longer, and I'm leaving with Jenna."

"Okay. I understand."

"Cool. Great talking to you, Ethan! I look forward to seeing you in person."

The line broke, leaving Ethan little time to act. He knew anyone using the security system's app could only see, not hear, a feature he selected to protect privileged conversations. After dropping Beverly's phone into the pitcher, he reached into his pocket and held the HOME button on his cell phone; Siri dinged as he pulled out his phone. Trying not to move his lips, he said, "Text Sarah, 'call the police.'"

Siri's mechanical voice replied, "Ready to send it."

"Send," Ethan said as he lifted his phone over the pitcher and dropped it in. He glanced once more at Beverly's lifeless body, slid the flip phone into his pocket, and ran out the door.

After jogging to his car, he hit the accelerator and peeled out of the driveway, his tires kicking up dust; in the rear-view mirror, he watched the silhouette of his pinot palace fade away as he sped down the neighborhood street.

He veered onto Arnold Drive, causing the Mercedes' wheels to leave the ground for a moment before the vehicle stabilized. Once his safety was certain, he hit the gas.

His mind raced with questions. Who possessed a motive to take Jenna? Could the kidnapper be a convict Ethan put away during his years as an assistant district attorney? He doubted this. The obvious setup was too complex for the pond-sucking scum he prosecuted. Maybe a spurned businessman distraught because Ethan got their case thrown out on a motion for summary judgment? Possible, but not likely: He would have remembered an opposing party crazed by such animus.

You're thinking too much, Ethan reminded himself. It was pointless to search for logic within the illogical. Logic did not drive a person capable of kidnapping an innocent child.

The car's dash clock read "3:45." The sun wouldn't rise for almost three hours.

Why don't you have a flashlight? he lamented. For the first time in his life, he wished he owned a gun.

Lost in his thoughts, he almost missed his turn. He swerved right and the vehicle's wheels again lifted as he turned onto Adobe Canyon Road; to his left, he passed one of his favorite wineries, Landmark, and repressed memories of "Daddy-daughter dates," though he swore he heard Jenna's sweet laughter as he sped past the beautiful grounds.

Pay attention, he thought. *There will be time for reminiscing later.*

He spotted the first entry to Sugarloaf Park and pulled into the concave parking area. Next to him idled a black Chevy extended cab truck. He was not alone.

Before getting out, he scanned the car's interior for anything that may be of use. It was spotless, free of distractions and anything helpful. He balled the fingers of his only available weapon.

He stepped out of the car, steadied his breathing, and studied the pitch-black surroundings, the interior light of the truck providing slight illumination. He listened for any noise, especially a girl's moan. Against his wishes, the night remained silent and still.

He crept towards the truck, searching all around for any sign of an attack. He suppressed a wish to scream, to cry out for his daughter, though the notion of making the kidnapper scream guided his steps.

When he reached the truck, he peered into its empty and clean cab. No sign of Jenna. He circled to the back of the truck and gazed into the bed; a dingy blanket covered something bumpy.

He reached in and pulled back the sheet; underneath lay piles of empty wine bottles.

Sharp pain invaded the crook of Ethan's neck. Then, darkness overtook.

21

NOW

Exhausted, Debra sat on the stone near the wooden bridge and contemplated the day before and night ahead. She rested her face upon her hands and fought the urge to fall asleep on the bridge. The fatigue was now so extreme it had morphed into a palpable thing, a sludge that impeded her thinking and slowed her movements. She considered her decisions that day and wondered if her exhaustion had caused her to act too impulsively.

They had collected no more evidence. No one in the search party had identified any suspects, and no one spotted Jenna or Ethan. As she sat, the mental countdown clicked away in her head. Fifteen hours gone, thirty-three left. Well, that's only if one listened to statistics. But Debra refused to view Jenna as a statistic. Jenna was a beautiful young girl who needed Debra's help, and Debra would not let off the gas regardless of how close they came to a statistical barrier.

The commotion swelled around her. Cops yelled at each other. Civilians shuffled about, likely destroying evidence. Normally, this would be a concern, but here, everyone proceeded with the same conclusion: *What more do we need?*

Ethan did it, and if they destroyed footprints as they searched, what difference would it make? Finding Jenna was far more important than collecting a few more bits of evidence to support an open and shut case.

Debra had no reason to question this logic. Her conversations with Jacob and Sherri, while strange and off-putting, didn't provide anywhere near probable cause. No judge in his or her right mind would issue a subpoena to search someone's property because that person read books with a murder victim. The contradictions in Jacob and Sherri's stories about the night before wouldn't get Debra much further.

If another cop approached her with similar suspicions, she would have dismissed them. She focused on Jacob because of her gut, not logic. He set off her radar, always had.

Yet, even the most likely scenario missed pieces. They collected Ethan's clothes and shoe prints near the entry to Sugarloaf. After those discoveries, it was as if Ethan and Jenna disappeared into the ether.

She considered three possibilities. First, Ethan discovered a way to elude detection and cover his tracks. This conclusion seemed implausible as nothing in Ethan's file showed he possessed such skills at his disposal. The counterpoints were Ethan's intelligence and awareness of the law. Perhaps he better understood police procedure than she gave him credit.

The second possibility: Jenna and Ethan hid near the entry, but no one had found them. The entrance into Sugarloaf was narrow, but there were plenty of spots to hide. Though encouraging, this possibility was unlikely. Even assuming Ethan could find a suitable hiding place, she doubted he could keep such a young girl under control and quiet for an extended period. Unless he found another way to maintain her silence.

The third, and most improbable, scenario was that the "evidence" amounted to mere distractions, that someone planted evidence to distract them away from the truth.

Typically, she would dismiss any such notion as rarely, if ever, are violent crimes pre-planned. Most of time, violence is borne from impulse, fear, and anger. But at this point, she had to entertain all possibilities. She typically laughed at conspiracy theories and enjoyed the simplicity of Occam's razor, but, in her job, sometimes she needed to forego logic and dive into the murky currents of chaos, for that's where her subjects swam.

But she was wading in treacherous waters. As much as she tried to understand the mind of sociopaths, killers, and rapists, she was not one and could never fully comprehend. If she dove too deep, she could drown.

Sociopaths on her mind, in the distance, she spotted Jacob, his face tired and concerned. She bought the fatigue. Concerned, that was a different subject altogether. Even discounting their off-putting interactions that day, she disliked the way he walked onto her crime scene and the confidence he carried as he instructed his dapper group of tipsy patrons and well-to-do wine professionals. She did not want to judge a person's best intentions, but when driving through Hell, one had to keep their eyes on the road. Besides, nothing she knew of Jacob led her to believe there was a selfless bone in his body. Everything he did was first and foremost for Jacob and Jacob alone. The trick was discovering the method behind the madness, for Jacob, she had to admit, was very good at hiding his true intentions.

Jacob noticed her studying him, waved first quickly and then he slowed as if catching himself, and walked over.

"No luck," he said, his voice flat and, to her ear, unsurprised. "Sorry. I really thought we could help. I'll be out here again first thing tomorrow morning unless something comes up at work."

"That's fine, Mr. Holland."

"Again with the Mr. Holland. My Dad's dead, Deb."

She stood and glared at him directly in the eyes, watching their every movement. "Fine. Are you leaving, Jacob?"

"Yes, I really have to go." He looked at his gold watch. "It's getting late, and I have a date tonight," he said. "A hot date, actually, and I need to get cleaned up beforehand. I'm sure Sherri will be proud of the work I put in today, but I've never met a girl who liked a smelly man."

She considered his comment. In his world, decency was the threshold for pride. "No, that's fine. There's not much you can do once it's dark. You have my cell number if you can think of anything."

"I do. Good luck, Detective. We got off on the wrong foot, but I really admire you and I care about Jenna. I hope you find her, and soon."

His words caught her off guard as they sounded genuine, though his lie tempered the earnestness. He extended his hand, and she reluctantly took it. As they shook, he met her gaze and glared even deeper, like a lion before taking the first bite. And perhaps she imagined things, but she thought she caught a hint of a smile.

He strolled away, his gait light. "Hey Jacob," she called after him, causing him to stop on a dime and turn, his eyebrows raised in interest.

"Yes, Detective?"

"Where are you taking Ms. Sloan?"

His eyes flickered as he hesitated, as if he hadn't expected the question. "Not sure to be honest. We didn't have set plans, exactly, and it's been a long day. I was going to suggest staying in."

"Don't you millennials call that, 'Netflix and chill?'" He blinked as he beheld her, his look one of surprise. She appreciated that her joke frazzled him further.

"Wouldn't know," he finally said after an extended pause during which her question floated like a piñata. "I guess I am technically a millennial, but I've never related well to them."

"Not surprising," she replied with a smile.

"What does that mean?" He appeared confused about whether to take offense.

"Nothing, nothing at all. I just agree with you. You don't strike me as a millennial type."

His large smile returned, but with a chilling edge. "May I ask you a question, Detective?"

His question caught her off-guard, and she replied with a meek, "Sure."

"Why are you giving me so much shit? I mean, there's no way you could think I'm involved in this crap. I mean, look." He pointed towards his posse of winos. "I rallied all those volunteers. Why would I have done that if I had something to do with this?"

Jacob's inquiries no longer surprised her. She expected these questions. The whole spiel reeked of calculation. Nothing he said sounded genuine.

Debra shot back, "You did it so you could ask that question."

Jacob blinked and replied, "What question?"

"The question, 'Why would I?'"

Jacob's haunting grin returned as he asked, "You ever heard of confirmation bias, Debra?"

Debra silently nodded.

"That's what's happening here," Jacob continued. "You thought I had something to do with Jodi skipping town, so everything you looked at pointed in that direction. And because you think I did something with Jodi, you think I'm guilty here." Jacob stepped close, deep into Debra's personal space. His hot breath warmed her forehead. "Is this really a road you want to go down? Remember what happened the last time you fucked with me."

Debra inhaled, balled her fists, and replied, "I remember. I remember you screwing with my investigation. I remember you dodging all my questions. I don't forget crap like that."

"Your investigation, huh?" Jacob cocked his head and eyed

her with an inquisitive look as a schoolboy might. "And what about Peter's investigation?"

"What?" Debra stuttered. Her fists unclenched. "Peter?" Her attempt at surprised ignorance came out flat and hollow.

"Don't play dumb with me, Detective. I know you hired Peter Sullivan to follow me. Thankfully, I have the means to pay him way more than you." Jacob stepped back and grinned. "He's been invaluable. Quite capable, he is."

"I know Peter," Debra replied. "But I don't know what the hell you're talking about."

Jacob shrugged. "Have it your way. But just think about what will happen if the Chief finds out you hired a private detective against his orders. I'm guessing that conversation wouldn't go well for you."

Debra mirrored Jacob's shrug in mocking fashion. "I've made it this far."

"That you have. Goodnight, Debra."

"Yes. Goodnight, Jacob. Tell Ms. Sloan I said 'hi.'"

"I'll be sure to do that." He stood motionless for a bit, his eyes studying her with an odd blend of anger and admiration. After this assessment, he turned and walked to his car, his stride less confident than it had been when he approached her.

She mulled the conversation over in her mind. The son-of-a-bitch found out about Sullivan and not only stopped him, but basically stole him from her. Now, Jacob possessed the ultimate trump card. If she got too close and spooked Jacob, he could effectively end her career in one fell swoop.

But, the truth was unavoidable: He had lied to her. Sherri told Debra that Jacob canceled their date, and yet he left the search party to attend this canceled rendezvous. Perhaps they un-canceled, though his reaction to her question about their plans diminished that possibility. In describing his plans for the evening, he appeared a man searching for an answer among many possibilities.

She recalled *Indiana Jones and the Last Crusade's* climax. In it, Indy, searching for the Holy Grail, chose the least adorned cup out of a wide selection. Jacob, in picking his answer, seemed to employ similar logic, hoping the dullest response would elicit the least attention. Unlike Indy, Jacob chose poorly.

Even with Jacob's bombshell, she was comfortable with her decision. She clicked into her cell phone and launched the tracking app. She had placed the tracker in the bed of his truck when he was deep into the search and far from his vehicle. She doubted he would notice it as it was the size of a small cell phone.

Onscreen, a map of Kenwood and the surrounding area appeared, with Jacob's car right in the middle, heading North, likely towards Santa Rosa. She recalled Jacob saying Sherri lived near Sonoma. They could be meeting up in Santa Rosa, but his file did not show that he owned property there, which meant Santa Rosa was an unlikely destination for a "Netflix and Chill" session.

No, she did not know his destination. But it wasn't to meet Sherri.

She made her decision. In the corner of her eye, she spotted McCarthy and flagged him down. At first, he gave her a "What the hell" look, but then hustled over when he realized she was serious.

"What's up, doc?" he asked. She hated this greeting.

"Any updates?"

"Nope. I woulda told you. Same shit, different hour."

"Yeah, I know what you mean. With that, can you cover for me?" she replied.

McCarthy stepped back. "The hell you mean, cover?"

"Look, just say there's an emergency with my kid if anyone asks. I'm not doing any good here, anyway."

"Yeah. This emergency. Wanna give me some more details?"

"I do not." She still did not feel comfortable explaining the situation to McCarthy. He was unpredictable when exhausted.

"You know," McCarthy responded, frustration building in his voice. "You've been pulling this shit all day. Disappearing when we need you. Then we get you for a few hours and you take off again. You gotta do you, but this is getting tiring, Deb."

"I get it," she smiled and patted him on the arm, in response to which his massive shoulders relaxed and dropped. "I'm sorry. It won't take long. I just really need to check something out or I'll be distracted and no help. We'll blink and be at the forty-eight-hour mark, and I'm doubling up work here, work being performed by people far more capable than me. Like you."

His hard features softened a little and, after a few moments, said, "Fine, fine. I'll cover for your ass again. But you owe me."

"Next time we're out, drinks are on me."

"Be careful what you promise, Deb. I'll drink away your next paycheck with the shit you've put me through today."

"And I'll be right there with you."

"Yeah, yeah," he said with a dismissive gesture as he walked back to the scene. She headed towards her car and double checked her tracking app. Jacob continued to head towards Santa Rosa with no signs of slowing down.

She navigated out of the app and into her contacts, clicking on "Hubby." Three rings later, her husband's voice answered: "Well hey there, stranger."

"Hey back. You follow the news at all today?"

"I have and figured it was better to just let you do your thing. I picked up Charlotte. She's doing good, working on some homework."

"Mind if I talk to her?"

"Sure. Once sec." She heard him call out to Charlotte, and soon her little voice answered the phone.

"Hey, Mommy!" she said.

"Hey, baby," she replied, her muscles relaxing at the sound of Charlotte's voice. "How's it going?"

"Great. Daddy let me eat a big bowl of ice cream."

"Did he?" She heard Bill scream "hey!" in the background.

"Yup, chocolate."

"Awesome, baby. That's great. Go finish your homework."

"Okay. Love you!"

"Love you too. Put your Dad back on."

The line fumbled before Bill said, "I'm guessing you'll be home late."

"Yup. Late as in I have no idea how late, so don't wait up. I'm really sorry."

"It's okay, baby. You do whatever you need to do to find that girl, okay?" The line went silent for a few seconds before he continued, "Every time I see that little girl, I think about Charlotte."

"I know, baby," she replied, tears building in her eyes. "Me too."

"At least she's got the best looking for her. So, get off the phone and go do what you do. I can't distract you."

She had never loved him more. "Give Charlotte a big kiss for me, okay?"

"I will. See you later, hot stuff."

"Can't wait." She cut the connection and stared at the phone for a few minutes, Charlotte on her mind. Debra hoped Charlotte understood why Debra had to work so many late nights, why the job trumped everything so often. Charlotte was an introspective girl, giving Debra hope for understanding. Charlotte was also only seven-years-old, so it would be impossible for Debra to comprehend the depths of such a young girl's mind. After this case, Debra would dedicate more time to motherhood. Charlotte deserved it.

Debra shook herself out of thought and put the car into drive. As she drove, she allowed her mind to wander and ponder things unrelated to the investigation. Charlotte's first words, first day in preschool, first picture she drew of Debra. In that crude image, her smile dominated the scene, a fact she found funny since random dudes often told her to "smile more." That her smile was the first thing Charlotte thought of brought an actual smile to Debra's face.

She realized that she drove without concentrating on the road. The clock indicated that, somehow, almost fifteen minutes had passed. She clicked into the tracking app, which displayed Jacob's car. She did a double take when she saw the direction he drove.

22

"Hello, Mother." Jacob stepped into the same room he visited earlier that day. He closed the door gently behind him, turned towards his mother, and smiled. "Happy to see me again? Twice in twenty-four hours. That's got to be a record."

He stepped towards and took a seat next to his mother in the same chair he sat in that morning. He leaned close to her ear and whispered, "You know, I was thinking. I can't bear seeing you like this anymore. I know you. You wouldn't want to live like this." Jacob pulled back and said, "Plus, let's say you passed away in the next day or so. I'd be so, so devastated." He clasped his heart for dramatic effect. "My heart just wouldn't be able to handle that."

He dropped his hand from his heart to his lap, a smile crossing his face. "What was that phrase you always said? 'There's always a silver lining?'" Jacob considered and nodded. "Yeah, that's the one. Anyways, you think anyone is going to investigate a guy mourning the loss of his mom?" Jacob shrugged. "Well, maybe that bitch Debra. But I'm guessing the

Chief will come down on her even harder this time. Hell, maybe he'd even fire her." Jacob chuckled. "Hey, a man can dream."

Jacob pulled out a few pills from his pocket, grabbed a bottle of water that rested near his mother, and forced her to swallow the pills, which were a far higher dosage than what he gave her earlier. He'd be surprised if she lasted a day. Then, he'd be off scot-free, with a built-in excuse to avoid questions or interviews. Technically, they could run a toxicology report, but why would they? He would decline any request for an autopsy, and why would they even want one? An old lady died in a nursing home. Not exactly newsworthy.

He sat for a while in silence, thinking about the last words he planned to say to his mother. A couple minutes later, he said, "You know, you called me a demon earlier. I'm guessing you were trying to hurt me with that. Since Dad died…" He paused and grinned. "Since he died, you always tried to hurt me. But you can't hurt me with words. Shit, what you said wasn't even an insult. What's more powerful than a demon?"

On that note, Jacob stood, bent down, and kissed his mother on the forehead. He whispered into her ear, "I'll miss you, I really will." He then turned and left, realizing with glee that he would never have to visit this godforsaken room again.

Before he left, he stopped by the front desk, now manned by an older gentleman.

"Excuse me," Jacob mumbled.

The old man focused hard on Jacob's face and said, "Yes?"

Jacob replied, "My mother is Gretchen Holland. Do you know her?"

The man nodded. "Quite well, yes."

"Would you mind checking on her when you have a sec?"

Without hesitation, the man said, "We always do. We check on all our patients."

"I know y'all do, I know y'all do. It's just, I don't know."

The man lifted a single bushy eyebrow. "What don't you know?" he asked, his curiosity seemingly genuine.

"There's just something about the way she was breathing," Jacob whispered, hoping he sounded embarrassed. "It just sounded different, but I'm not a doctor."

The man nodded, and a smile cracked the corner of his lips. "You don't need to be a doctor to get that kinda feeling."

"Okay, good." Jacob sighed. "So, I don't sound silly."

"Not at all. We'll give her some extra attention, promise."

Jacob smiled widely and said, "Thanks. I really appreciate it. And call me if anything changes."

The man nodded and said, "Will do."

Jacob waved, turned, and left the nursing home, he prayed for the last time. With each step, his thirst swelled. He had searched those godforsaken woods for hours without a single drop of wine, cognizant of how imbibing would look to the fellow searchers. The consequence of that decision now hit him, and his desire for his creation weighed him down. When thirsty, he acted far more on impulse than logic. He could not permit himself to give into this primal desire. He was far too close to his forever release.

23

Debra waited in the well-lit parking lot near a four-way stop. She had no idea if Jacob would travel in this direction. It may not even matter. Even if he stopped in front of her, the short glimpse she would get into the car might not reveal much.

In thought, she almost missed the blip on her app that represented Jacob creeping in her direction

Her heart raced as his vehicle approached. He beelined to her. In anticipation, she shut down her car and clicked off every light, including her cell phone, reducing any chance he would spot her.

Based on her calculations, he would arrive in her area in three minutes. The seconds dragged as she ticked them off in her head, the "Mississippi" she placed between each tick seeming much longer than the already burdensome word.

Then, she spotted light approaching, headlights from Jacob's black pickup truck, approaching in the lane closest to her. She focused her sights on the exact spot where he would stop.

Soon, he idled before her. His windows were tinted dark, but in the illumination, she saw he was the only one in his vehicle. Within seconds, Jacob turned, heading towards the freeway.

She considered the options. He could have dropped Sherri off somewhere, or he was on his way to pick her up. There was one way to confirm or eliminate these possibilities. She grabbed her phone and dialed the number. After a few rings, a groggy voice answered, "Hello?"

"Ms. Sloan, this is Detective Foley. Sorry to call you at this hour."

"I would hope so, golly." She shuffled and Debra heard an item smack against the floor, likely a phone or clock. When Sherri's voice returned, she sounded flustered. "I was dead to the world."

"Dead to the world? You mean you were asleep?"

"Yes. What is it, like, one in the morning?"

That answered Debra's question, meaning she did not have to push any further. But now she needed a reason for the call.

"Yes," Debra replied. "Something like that. I am just checking with all my interviewees to see if they recalled any additional information. Normally, I would wait until the morning. But this is a case where every second counts.

"Yes, yes," she replied, her voice now strong and tone near apologetic. "I saw what happened on the news. Like I told ya earlier, I want to help. I do. But I got nothin'. Jacob don't, either."

"That's fine, I just wanted to verify. Thank you again, Ms. Sloan."

"Okay. Good luck."

"Thanks." Debra broke the connection and sat in contemplation. While she made progress in her investigation, much of it was a Pyrrhic victory. Her moves placed her in a position with no available aid.

First, there was the issue of Peter Sullivan. If Jacob suspected that she tracked him, a single call to the Chief and her career was likely over. She could not remember an instance of a detective going rogue and hiring a private detective, but she figured the department would not view such an extreme move in a favorable light.

The tracking device also created a major issue. She couldn't obtain a subpoena without additional authorization, and she couldn't obtain authorization without revealing why she needed it. She couldn't play another card without confessing to the tracking device. And once she admitted she tracked Jacob without a warrant, not only would her investigation end, but her job would be in jeopardy, too.

Jeopardy, she considered with a chuckle. If the Chief found out she planted a secret tracking device on Jacob Holland's car after she circumvented his orders by hiring a private detective, he'd fire her twice just to be certain.

Two options remained. First, abandon Jacob and join the search party, preserving the possibility of re-opening the investigation if she discovered probable cause. Though appealing, this possibility was not workable. If she had more time, perhaps. She appreciated the slow-burn approach. Here, though, she faced a deadline, and it rapidly approached.

The other alternative was to keep following Jacob and hope she'd find an excuse that would support her investigation without revealing the tracking device. There were many exceptions to the general warrant rules, and she knew them by heart. The case against Jacob wasn't her primary concern. If she rescued Jenna, the prosecution would make something stick. She may be reprimanded, probably even fired, but that mattered little. Part of her grew tired of the grind. If finding a child resulted in having to leave the force, she could imagine worse outcomes.

Before deciding, she had a text to place. She lifted her phone and navigated to her contacts, searching for "Peter Sullivan." Pulling up the contact information, she composed a text with two words: "Fuck you." She paused for a moment before sending, wondering if doing so was a mistake.

Nah, she thought. *Fuck him.*

She hit SEND, and sat back, breathing deeply, composing her thoughts in anticipation for what may arise over the next several hours. If Jacob hoped telling her about Peter would act as some sort of deterrent, he was badly mistaken. If anything, Jacob hiring Peter to curtail her own investigation solidified in her mind that he had something to hide. Whatever he hid, Debra decided her goal was to find it.

She decided. She would go it and go it alone. There was no turning back, no playing by the books. She planned to follow Jacob wherever he went until she found Jenna or was satisfied that he did not take her. Along the way, she might also find out where Ethan is and how he's involved.

Looking at her phone, she saw that Jacob traveled the highway now, heading towards Kenwood. She drove after him, keeping a watchful eye on the tracking app, careful not to get too close, especially since he had seen her in her civilian car.

An alert interrupted her navigation app. She had a new text from Peter Sullivan which read: "I'm sorry." She waited to see if he would send another text elaborating, but none came. With a smile, she placed the phone back into the cup holder in a position where she could glance at the updating navigation map and concentrated on the road.

As she drove, her thoughts drifted again to Charlotte as she stifled a chuckle at the notion of being anything other than a cop. She bled blue. But she needed self-reflection and time away. She had not taken a "true" vacation in nearly three years, a fact that her husband and Human Resources rarely let her forget. She wanted to fly far away, her family by her side. Maybe Florida? Disney World sounded good.

Yes. One way or another, she was heading to Disney World,

her daughter's hand in one hand, a drink in another, the memories of Jacob left two thousand miles away.

24

Before heading into his office, Jacob used his phone to search for stories about Jenna's kidnapping. Once he entered the tunnel, he would lose reception.

It did not take long for him to strike internet gold. Jenna's story was now national intrigue. Her face was plastered throughout the web, on news outlets both small and large. Many popular online forums also dissected her disappearance, on which couch detectives reviewed the details of the case and debated various scenarios. Most stories and posts, however, related to Ethan. The discussions focused on the how and why rather than the who. To his relief, not one story or forum post even contained his name or referenced the Holland Vineyard. He was an invisible puppet master entertaining the ignorant masses, exactly as he planned.

Jacob slipped his phone back into his pocket, made his way through the tunnel, and stepped into his office. He saw that Ethan continued to struggle, which Jacob admired. Ethan's fatigue was also clear as his efforts came in short bursts after long rests, and Jacob noticed blood trickling down from the rope to the floor, staining Ethan's jeans. That would require cleanup. Another complication.

"Relax," Jacob warned Ethan as he displayed the gun from earlier in the day. "I told you there was no escaping. Or did I? I apologize, it's been a long day and my head's a little fried." Jacob pointed the gun at Ethan's skull and continued, "I'm guessing you can relate. The hangover from that crap can be a bitch."

Jacob rubbed against Ethan's left wrist and analyzed the blood that now spotted Jacob's fingers. "My, my," he said. "You've been a busy boy. I saw your feeble efforts to break free from your chains. Would have visited earlier, but I've been busy."

Ethan stopped struggling and glared at Jacob. Ethan's eyes did not flicker or stray. They remained fixed on Jacob, beaming with hatred and rage. A caged animal would do anything in its pursuit of freedom.

"Easy there, tiger," Jacob said, the idea of Ethan as a beast still stuck in his head. He raised the gun, his palms exposed, and said, "I come in peace." The stare remained, unnerving Jacob.

"Are you not interested in seeing your daughter again?" He pointed to the television screen and said, "See, she's alive and well. I mean, I guess depending on how you define 'well.'"

Ethan grunted, surprising Jacob. At first, the sound was incomprehensible, like a child trying to say its first complicated word. Then, Ethan grunted louder, and Jacob understood. Ethan asked Jacob to "fuck off."

Perhaps a different approach would be necessary. He placed the gun on the table, moved to Ethan, and crouched to look at him eye-level.

"Listen, I'll be frank with you. No more bullshit. I'm doing this because I can tell you are a guy who doesn't like BS-ers, which means you don't care for me much. That's fine, I'm not here to be your friend. But we both have goals for this evening, and they align. You want to see Jenna. I want to take you to see her. Get the alignment? So, here's my proposal. A settlement offer in your parlance." He walked to and picked up the gun, massaging its barrel. "The only way I'm going to be able to take you to Jenna is if you follow my every direction. See, she is in a remote location. I can't haul you, so I need you to comply. Because here's the rub." Jacob lifted the gun and studied it. "I don't need you, Ethan. My better judgment says to cut you loose. You'd be far less of an issue dead, and it wouldn't be hard to dispose of you. I'm sure you're aware I have resources." Jacob knelt before Ethan and caressed his biceps with the gun barrel. "But here's the thing, while I don't need you, I want you." He bowed his head and whispered, "Really want you. So, I'm willing to take some risks if you'll play ball. Besides, what's your alternative? I'm not entertaining counteroffers."

Ethan's eyes fell back and forth between the gun and Jacob's face. Swimming in varying emotions, every second a different one coming up for air. Eventually though, Ethan nodded in resignation. As he did so, his entire body relaxed, giving in to giving up.

Jacob smiled. "Good boy. Now, let's get you out of these bindings." Jacob rounded the wine barrel, unlocked the handcuffs, then undid the ropes, which took longer than he expected as holding the gun unbalanced his grip. Once free, Ethan stood and stared at Jacob, those rage-filled eyes returning and burning hotter than hell. Thankfully, Jacob was ready, the pistol raised towards Ethan's head.

"Are we really going to go down that road, Ethan?" Jacob asked. "Because it's long and winding and you won't like the destination." Ethan's fists balled and then released, his muscles stiffening. Ethan raised his hands to the duct tape over his face and started clawing at it.

"Stop that," Jacob demanded, and Ethan listened. It was hard to argue with your mouth bound and a gun pointed at you. "I didn't tell you to do that. This will only work out if you follow every instruction without question. First command. Take off those jeans." Ethan complied, but slowly, his eyes unwavering and locked onto Jacob.

Once Ethan's pants were off, Jacob said, "Good. It's time to go for a ride."

Before starting the car, Jacob reviewed Ethan sitting in the passenger seat, his shackled arms behind him. Jacob almost felt sorry for him. His broad shoulders slumped and his gaze toward the floor. He was a defeated man who was putting himself in a situation that likely would result in his death, and he did so for the small chance of seeing his daughter one last time. Jacob respected that. Admired it, even. Even though he loved Jodi, he would have never put her needs before his. That would be counterproductive. And yet there Ethan sat, willing to do whatever it took, at any cost, for one more moment with his daughter.

"Hey," Jacob said to Ethan, who did not move in response. "You there, big boy? You're being awfully quiet. My mom used to say that the quiet boys were the ones you needed to keep an eye on."

The silence continued for a while until Jacob said, "May I ask you a question?"

No response.

"We're going on a short trip," Jacob continued. "After we arrive, we probably won't talk for a while. Might as well chit-chat now. We have time."

Ethan's muscles tensed a bit, but he did not turn toward Jacob.

"Here, let me help you." Jacob pulled a pocketknife from the center console and cut away the duct tape, also nicking Ethan's lip. The blood swelled and dripped. Jacob dabbed at the cut with a tissue also from the center console. Ethan remained stoic, his eyes locked on the road.

"Sorry about that," Jacob said. "Butterfingers. Anyhoo, my question stands. Because I don't get it. I knew Beverly. Don't stress, nothing physical or anything, all for the purposes of this." Jacob rotated the knife back and forth between the two of them. "But I liked her. She was sweet and intelligent. Pretty hot too, for her age as they say."

Ethan replied with a flat, "What's your point?"

"My point," he brushed the tip of the knife against Ethan's right biceps, "is you love your daughter, in a way I can't grasp. You bolt out in the middle of the night because of a text. You put your ass on the line for any chance to see her. It seems you're willing to do anything for her, except love her mother."

"I'm not telling you shit."

"Now, now. There's no use fighting it. I'm bored." He pulled the taser from his pocket and placed it near Ethan. "Remember this bad boy? How about you stimulate me so I don't have to stimulate you. That work?"

Ethan gritted his teeth before replying, "Fine."

"Great! So, tell me. What happened with Bev, man? I want all the juicy details."

Ethan replied, "Nothing happened. There wasn't one thing to point to."

"You regret anything?"

"Yeah. I made mistakes. People make them."

Jacob considered this. It was true that Ethan was a helluva attorney who had bailed Jacob's father out on multiple occasions, both personal and business-wise. Was there something to that? His dad was an emotional guy too. Jacob always wondered what he was missing because of his lack of certain emotions. Maybe it went the other way. Perhaps those bound to emotion were missing the tools to do what was necessary.

"Just tell me," Ethan said unexpectedly, startling Jacob. "Is Jenna really alive? Don't bullshit me. There's no point to it anymore."

"Yes," Jacob said, his voice steady. "I know I talk a lot, and you really don't have a reason to trust anything I say. But I swear to you, Jenna is alive. She will also remain that way as long as everything goes to plan. And it will go to plan as long as you keep doing what I ask."

Ethan listened to this but did not turn his head. That's when Jacob realized the real reason Ethan was not resisting. Though Jacob held a gun, he wouldn't be surprised if Ethan could overpower him. Even with his hands handcuffed behind his back, Ethan might have stood a chance: Though similar heights, Ethan outweighed Jacob by forty or fifty pounds, and none of those pounds were fat. Jacob would understand that move, because either way Ethan thought he was dying tonight, so why not go down with a fight? Ethan, without a doubt, was a fighter. But even if he could escape, he had no idea where Jenna was. Therein lay Ethan's dilemma: If he attacked Jacob, he would be attacking the only person with knowledge of Jenna's location, meaning she may end up safe from Jacob but later succumb to thirst or hunger. Jacob was safe at the moment but would need to remain on guard as they approached the private reserve.

"Hey," Ethan said, again startling Jacob.

"Yes?" Jacob replied.

"Who are you?"

Jacob shrugged. "Guess there's no reason not to let the cat out of the bag. Jacob Holland, at your service. You did some work for my dad back in the day, remember?"

Ethan nodded. "Adam Holland. You look like him. Did litigation and IP work for him."

"IP?"

"Intellectual property."

"Aw, yeah," Jacob replied with a sarcastic wave. "Dad was

always convinced that someone was out to steal his stuff. Recipes, logo. Everyone wanted a piece of his 'art,' as he called it. Kinda arrogant, really. You'd have to think your shit doesn't stink to believe others would want a sniff. Didn't matter. He had no vision."

"And you?" Ethan asked, his sarcasm overriding his weariness. "You have vision?"

"Better believe it," Jacob said, his smile wide. "I've got better vision than Superman. I'll show you soon enough, trust me."

"Why are you doing this?" Ethan stuttered as he asked this, obviously afraid of the answer.

"You will have to elaborate a bit. That's a broad question."

"Why did you kidnap Jenna? Why are you kidnapping me? What does all this get you?"

"Oh, it gets me plenty," Jacob insisted with a grin as he hit the ignition. "Exactly what, you'll find out soon. As to your first two questions, well, it's nothing personal. Jenna and you just fit a particular profile I needed. Also, I was pretty familiar with you, and Beverly was an easy target. It all came together well. I am sorry, sometimes people are in the wrong place at the wrong time."

"I mean," Jacob said before hesitating. "I guess there's a little more."

Ethan asked, "Yeah, what's that?"

Jacob shrugged and said, "Don't know how to say this. You just kind of remind me of my father. Shit, you even look like him a little." He gripped the steering wheel as he said, "And I fucking hated my father."

Ethan looked at him for the first time since they got into the truck, his eyes narrow and face stern. "You're a psycho, you know that?"

Jacob shrugged. "Just cause I know what I want doesn't make me a psycho. Look at all the shit you've gone through today for someone else. And I'm the crazy one?" Ethan did not reply.

Throughout the short and bumpy ride to the butler's house, Jacob kept one eye on Ethan. Out of precaution, Jacob steadied the gun with a bead on Ethan's head, making sure there was enough distance so that Ethan couldn't easily swipe it away.

They arrived and Jacob parked. Before exiting, he sat there for a few minutes and looked at Ethan, who returned the glance. "You're at the home stretch. You're very close to Jenna. Follow my instructions for the next few minutes, and you'll have her in your arms again."

Ethan's eyes widened. "In my arms?" The man in his 50s suddenly looked like a child. Jacob felt bad. He didn't mean for Ethan to accept the cliché at face value. But why not let him dream a little longer?

"Yes. Now," Jacob pointed at the door, "after you."

Ethan glared at him.

Jacob laughed. "Would be kind of difficult to open in your predicament." Jacob stepped out of the truck, rounded it, and opened Ethan's door, the gun extended and at the ready. "First thing's first," Jacob said as he grabbed the roll of duct tape at Ethan's feet and wrapped a fresh roll around his mouth, ensuring he couldn't scream once he exited the vehicle.

"Get out," Jacob commanded, beckoning Ethan with the gun.

Ethan instead sat, glaring at Jacob. In response, Jacob placed the gun right on Ethan's forehead, pressing the metal against his flesh so hard it indented inward. This did not faze Ethan. He did not lean back or move sideways. He sat with that same hate-filled glower.

For a moment, Jacob considered killing Ethan, but that act would create a nearly insurmountable obstacle. First, if Ethan forced Jacob to shoot in front of the butler's house, the shot would resonate for miles around. People two vineyards over would hear it. He would have to dispose of the body before cleaning any of the blood and brain. That path was unacceptable. He would have to convince Ethan to follow.

With the gun still in his hand, Jacob reached into his pocket and pulled out his phone. With the phone's screen in his periphery, he navigated to the cam fixed on Jenna's face. He showed it to Ethan, whose shoulders slumped in response.

"You obviously aren't grasping the gravity of the situation," Jacob said. "Let me clue you in." He placed his phone on the dashboard so the video faced Ethan. Jacob slammed the door and locked it, ensuring Ethan couldn't escape.

Quickly, Jacob made his way through the house and down to the private reserve. There, he looked into the camera that rested on the arm of the chair on which Jenna sat. He waved at the camera with the gun in his hand, a smile plastered on this face. For emphasis, he kissed Jenna on the head and whispered, "It's going to be all right." Whether or not Ethan could hear, Jacob did not know, but the words were far less important than the act itself.

He returned to the car. In it, Ethan sat limp, as if the sight robbed any remaining strength.

"Now," Jacob said. "You've seen that she's okay, and I'm in a position to change that fact. Are you ready to listen?"

Ethan nodded.

"Great! Now," Jacob gestured towards the butler's house. "After you."

Without further acknowledgment, Ethan stood and straightened, his expression defeated, his eyes watery.

"Atta boy," Jacob said as he closed the door. "I'm glad you came around. Now," Jacob shoved Ethan towards the butler's house, "march."

The men proceeded in silence, Jacob following with the gun's barrel pressing against Ethan's spine. Ethan could do little more than shuffle, lengthening the journey. As they walked, Jacob realized that, for the first time in a while, he didn't have to plan anything. His date with Sherri was set for the evening, so he had hours to kill. Rest would be wise, but he figured it would evade him. Excitement rushed through his body, causing his neck hair to raise and hands to tremble. The end was close, so close. Soon, he would enjoy the fruits of his labor without interruption.

They arrived at the entrance to the private reserve. With the gun aimed at Ethan, Jacob lifted the door. Once open, he rushed behind Ethan and pressed the gun against his back and grabbed his collar.

"Jenna is down there," Jacob said. "Let's go see her."

Ethan did not resist. Step by step, they descended into the private reserve, Jacob's grip tightening with each step. When they arrived at the bottom, He screamed and rushed forward, taking Jacob with him. Before Ethan reached Jenna, Jacob slammed the butt of the gun onto Ethan's neck. He lumbered sideways and hit the ground with a loud *thump*.

"Listen to me," Jacob said. "Any more antics and I'm done with both of you. Now, in that chair, or else Jenna gets a bullet to the brain. Got it?"

Ethan stood and the men stared at each other for a moment before Ethan's body went limp and he fell into the chair. He looked defeated, the fire in his eyes seemingly extinguished.

"That's good," Jacob said, his tone comforting. "I'm a man of my word. You're with Jenna."

Ethan barely moved as Jacob placed the rag against his face. Once Jacob ensured Ethan was out, he performed the same process he did with Jenna, using the same chains and rope. He had perfected the method to the point it was second nature.

With Ethan detained, Jacob relaxed. Despite the hour, he needed a reward.

He picked out a nice burgundy, poured a tall glass, and drank, allowing the wine to take him on its journey.

25

When Debra arrived at the Holland Vineyards, she saw no sign of any employee or customer.

She sat and weighed her options. She had no warrant, and no real basis to get one. Therefore, entering the property would jeopardize the admissibility of any evidence she recovered.

It all came down to reason. Would a judge consider it reasonable for her to hop a gate to knock on a door to conduct a follow-up interview with a witness she already interviewed? That would concern even the most pro-cop robe.

A distant light interrupted her internal analysis. She squinted, focusing closely on it. It appeared to emanate from in or near the wine caves Jessica flagged earlier, though the darkness made it impossible to be certain.

The light pulled out slowly, cautiously, and drove for a bit, seemingly down, then right, then up again. The trek was short, and the headlights remained within the Holland Vineyard property the entire time. When the headlights finally came to a rest, Debra knew their exact location: the butler's house.

Debra refused to permit legal logistics to stop her from doing her job.

Either Jacob was innocent, so there would be no evidence to gather, or he held Jenna, which meant Debra had no time to waste. And so, she decided.

She grabbed a flashlight and proceeded to pat her sidearm, ensuring it sat in its holster, easily accessible. Ready, she approached the large gate which appeared even more glorious in the flashlight's glow that accentuated its opulent finishing, including the Holland family icon: The initials of each of the three family members joined to form a letter H. The initials for Jacob's father were black, whereas the initials for Jacob and his mother were white. Soon, Jacob's mother's initials would also be painted black, leaving Jacob as the sole heir to a massive fortune. Rumors persisted that Jacob would sell once his mother passed, but those who knew him dismissed this chatter as baseless: Jacob loved his family's work, and, according to gossip, had many plans for expansion.

Despite the massive size of the main gate, the side gates were eye-level. She jumped the one to the right of the main gate, collected herself, and dimmed her flashlight. She found the road that led to the butler's cabin and started her journey.

The night was still. A cool breeze swept by Debra's ears. An occasional vine scratched her skin as she passed, one drawing blood. With each step, she shined the flashlight to the left and right to help avoid any obstacles, though the vines were impossible to completely avoid.

The house looked even smaller than she remembered, darkness concealing much of its structure. She figured it only had three or four rooms, no more than one bedroom.

The interior was dark. A large, waist-high generator ran next to the house. Its soft whine shattering the night's tranquility. She wondered why such a small house needed such a large generator.

She stepped away and headed towards Jacob's truck parked

near the house and removed the tracking device she placed in the truck bed. It was small enough to slide into her pocket.

She flashed the light around the vehicle's base but found no helpful evidence. There were a few footprints, but they didn't tell her much. She then shined her light into the car from the driver's side and noticed a speck on the passenger's seat.

She rounded the car to get a closer look. The tint of the windows made it difficult to see, but the color of the stain appeared deep red.

Blood in his car, she thought. Fresh blood, too. She considered if that was enough to establish probable cause.

No, she thought. *I need more.*

She reviewed the backseat and the trunk but found nothing of note. The backseat held the cover for the bed.

Frustrated, she stepped away from the car and focused again on the house. Shut blinds covered the windows, yet as she approached, she realized that the blinds did a poor job of shielding the interior. She peered first through the window next to the front door. Inside, she discerned through the slits certain objects that, when she cobbled together the visible portions of the room, she peered into a living room with a television and couch.

She passed the generator and approached the rear of the house. There was a larger window there, but the blinds were tightly pressed. Two things caught her attention. First, she detected the outline of a bed, which appeared made and empty. Also, she spotted a ring of light towards the back of the room. The light, alone, was not unusual, but its positioning and the rectangular shape of its glow piqued her interest. It shone too low to the ground and too weak to be from a lamp.

She circled the house and gazed through a window on the other side. These blinds revealed the most of the three. The kitchen appeared standard fare and utilitarian, with no fancy appliances or dishware. In the corner, though, Debra spotted something unusual: an empty trash bag. The bag just lay on the floor, no trashcan in sight. Something else caught her attention. Squinting, Debra realized something at the top of the bag glimmered.

Debra got as close as possible, pressing her face against the cold glass, as she studied the contours of the small item by the bag. After over a minute of analyzing, she almost gave up, and then it hit her. A small bracelet with green stones lay on the floor. She remembered from Jenna's file that her birthday was in May, just like Debra's. Emerald was May's birthday stone. Debra pictured a parent gifting such a bracelet to a child. Perhaps after a bad divorce as a keepsake.

The scenario played out in her mind. Jacob kidnapped Jenna, put her in a trash bag, and carried her into this house like garbage. Then, while unloading her, the bracelet slipped off and Jacob didn't notice. Perhaps he would have had the day gone differently, but because of her investigation, he didn't have enough time to clear all his tracks.

It wasn't a lot. Probably not enough for a judge. But it was enough for her.

She headed to the front of the house and tried the door. Locked. The lock appeared small, meaning it would be easy to kick down the door, though she hoped to find a quieter entrance. The front and back windows were also locked, but the kitchen window was unlocked.

She lifted it and noticed the opening provided barely enough space for her to squeeze through. She poked her head in, grabbed the countertop, and jumped; her shoulders scraped against the windowpanes as she negotiated her body into the house, leaving blood smears against the white paint.

She stood motionless, her hand on her gun, ready to pull it once Jacob jumped out of hiding. She locked onto every shadow and every sound. Convinced she was alone in the kitchen, she relaxed a little.

Where the hell is Jacob? she wondered.

She used Lysol wipes that sat next to the sink to clean away the blood before it stained the paint. There was no point in leaving behind evidence of her little visit. She placed the wipes in her pocket and bent down to review the bracelet. She did not touch it to preserve fingerprints. A silver trinket dangled from the middle of the bracelet, engraved with "JP."

That should be enough for any judge, she thought, but also doubted that conclusion the next moment. If there's one thing she's learned, it's that judges are far less predictable than juries. Either way, she had done her job. A judge might throw some evidence out, but if she caught him red-handed, she figured any judge would allow enough in to ensure a verdict.

She had no alternative. Even with pictures, she would have to convince her boss she stumbled upon this evidence without breaching any protocols. And obtaining a warrant would create a massive delay. At best, a warrant would take several hours, and that was assuming a judge accepted her story without question. Jenna did not have that time.

No, Debra needed to press on. Like she learned while raising Charlotte, a parent should stop a fit before picking up the mess, for decluttering in front of an upset child was a recipe for endless cleaning.

She walked through the kitchen into Jacob's neat and sparse bedroom and discovered the source of the light she witnessed outside: the outline of a trapdoor. She studied it with the flashlight and noticed an iron handle, as well as a nearby chest. She placed her ear against the door but heard nothing.

Her next steps were critical. She could approach aggressively, yelling out her title and ordering anyone to raise their hands and drop any weapons. The problem with this plan was the possible confusion and chaos. Jacob was already an unpredictable person; who knows what he would do in an unpredictable situation.

No, she preferred to maintain an element of surprise. Jacob was unaware of her presence, and she planned to keep it that way.

She clicked off her flashlight, unholstered her gun, and used the free hand to lift the door, which moved quietly. No alarms sounded. She rested the door at its maximum open position, maneuvered her way onto the steps, and descended as she closed the door behind her. There was a slight clunk as she shut it, causing her to jerk her head back towards the door, but she did not see anyone.

Down the stairs and, despite her efforts, each step resulted in a creak that seemed to echo throughout the whole room. Her gun remained in front of her as she scanned the area from right to left.

The walls, including those near the steps, were lined floor to ceiling with wine. But the wine didn't interest her. As she descended into the reserve, she got a better look at the table near the steps, which held many pieces of medical equipment such as bags with tubes and needles at the end. IV drip machines surrounded the table.

As she approached the last step, two bodies came into view. Jenna and Ethan sat in orange padded chairs with armrests that extended in front of their chests. Debra had seen these types of chairs before but could not place them. Their arms were chained behind them, an IV pump attached to each.

The lights went out.

She reached for the flashlight when she sensed a prick against her arm; then, her entire body tensed up and tossed, throwing her to the floor. Her gun slid away as another current raced through her, again contracting her muscles, curling her into a ball. Her face smooshed and she let out a stuttered scream.

Before she recovered from the shock, something smashed against her head, slamming her face to the floor. The wood crashed against her forehead with such force that she almost passed out. She lay there, unable to move, blood pooling and seeping into her hair.

As she lay defenseless, cold metal pressed against her wrists and shins. Before she could move again, it was too late. Jacob chained her, just like Jenna and Ethan.

The lights flickered back on, and Jacob stood before her, a shit-eating grin on his face.

"Well hello, Detective," he said, his tone dripping with condescension. "I always appreciate visitors, but I do ask that you call next time."

She flailed on the floor and scooted towards him. To what end, she did not know. He had won.

"Fuck you," she screamed.

"My, my," he replied. "Such rudeness. Maybe I won't extend an invitation. I'm impressed, though. I have no idea how you found this place, and I admire your efforts to be sneaky. Even a decade ago, you might have succeeded. But nowadays, there's an app for that; including one that notifies me whenever someone approaches the house or opens the door to my private reserve." He shrugged.

Her muscles were fried, her vision distorted. She rested her head on the floor and allowed visions of Charlotte to fill her mind.

Instead of going to Disney Land, her little girl may have to grow up without a mother. How would Bill explain it? Especially if her colleagues can't figure out what happened to her. Will Charlotte grow up thinking her mother abandoned her, ran out without saying goodbye? That reality was far worse than being killed on duty.

Lost in her thoughts, she barely noticed Jacob's face near hers. "Whatcha thinking about?" he asked. In response, she spit at him, catching him off guard. He stumbled away while wiping his face.

"Well," he said and wiped the spit on her forehead. "I guess we'll have to do it the hard way."

For the few moments she had left, she recalled happy times. Charlotte's first steps. Her first report card, filled with As. Her joy in learning about animals and colors and Mommy's job.

Greatness awaited her. Debra prayed her failings wouldn't screw that greatness up too badly.

Jacob's fist connected with her head, throwing her backwards. Through the haze of her daze, she saw the blurry image of Jacob head to the other side of the private reserve, search for something, then approach her, duct tape in one hand, a blindfold in the other.

"Now, now," Jacob whispered as he unrolled the duct tape, his voice playful. "Time to have some fun."

2 6

With Debra bound and gagged, Jacob headed out of the private reserve and to the bedroom. There, he dropped the façade and allowed the panic to wash over him.

"Bitch!" he screamed as he smashed his fists against the table.

How had he screwed up so badly? Were there any other officers in tow? Jacob had to find out what Debra knew and why she invaded his reserve. But one thing was certain: He refused to go to jail. Not tonight, not any night. He stroked the pistol in his hand and affirmed that promise.

The cold steel calmed his heart, as did his conclusion. If tonight went south, at least, more than it already had, Jacob would exit the light and step into the quiet of the dark. He'd rather face nothingness than a prison cell.

But that was absolute worst-case scenario. He needed additional information before deciding anything. Similar to Ethan and Jenna, he chained her and placed duct tape across her face. The difference was she was not yet sedated, and he did not want to waste medicine until he finalized his plan.

Before continuing, he needed to put himself in her shoes, learn what she might have learned. First, he reviewed the bedroom. Nothing was out of place. His bed appeared untouched. His laptop remained closed. The chest rested in the same spot. He saw nothing that would clue her into his intentions. He closed the door behind him as he stepped out of the private reserve.

When he walked into the kitchen, he immediately recognized his mistake. How did he miss that stupid bracelet? He chastised himself for leaving the bag out in plain sight. The day had been a blur, but that did not excuse such a big screw-up, tantamount to leaving a smoking gun on the dining table. Not only that, but the blinds peering into the kitchen were cracked, the window itself open. The maid always opened a window whenever she cleaned and often forgot to lock it before she left. Jacob should have fired her years ago, but like the bracelet, he had gotten sloppy. Too sloppy, in fact, and that would change immediately.

So, she spotted the bracelet from outside and crawled inside, Jacob deduced. This conclusion brought him a semblance of relief. If she possessed a warrant or alerted other officers, he doubted she would crawl through windows and sneak down stairwells. She would have come in guns blazing, her pig friends following. And it all made sense, too: She had nothing on him, forcing her to go alone. Both his respect and hatred for her grew and grew.

Still, he wanted to make sure she didn't bring backup. He exited the cottage and scanned the area, paying close attention to his truck. He noticed a few tracks she left behind but saw no evidence of any other police presence. Her vehicle was also missing. He guessed she left it near the entrance and jumped the fence, which he would have done, too. This excited him, as she left no indication she ever stepped onto Holland Vineyard since this afternoon.

To verify his conclusion, he opened his truck and grabbed a flashlight from the dash. When he turned it on, he noticed the small bloodstain on the seat. This confused him at first, but then the conclusion hit him like a brick.

Dammit, he thought. *Why did I have to cut off Ethan's duct tape?* He also should have bandaged Ethan's wrists. The waves of excitement so swept him that he did not notice the waiting shark. These small messes piled up and weighed him down.

Flashlight in hand, he jogged down the small hill and towards the front gate. He didn't need to turn on the flashlight for the jog as he knew the route by heart. Once at the gate, he flicked on the flashlight and caught Debra's car. She parked it off but near the road, close enough to be spotted by rubberneckers. Thankfully, it was dark, and Debra drove a nondescript vehicle, much like his truck.

While jogging back to the house, he considered another item he needed to check. He headed to the private reserve and descended the staircase. There, Debra struggled without regard to her circumstances. He admired her for a while, unable to repress his respect. She may not be aware, but the fact that she lay in his private reserve was a huge accomplishment, for she was the reserve's first uninvited guest. He considered mentioning this to her but decided against it.

To slow her floundering, he flipped her onto her side, grabbed her hair, and slammed her head against the floor. Her skull ricocheted, and she lay there stunned for a moment. Once she regained her composure, though, she started resisting again as if he had never touched her. He needed a different tactic, a more direct one.

He flipped her back onto her stomach and mounted her, pressing his knees against the back of her shoulders for balance. Even with the duct tape, he heard her muffled scream, but there was little she could do to resist. He pet her head softly, causing her to violently shake in an attempt to remove his hands. The whole scene was absurd, and he couldn't help but smile.

Searching her person as he squirmed, he pulled out a small

device, keys, and two blood-stained Lysol wipes. It took him a few seconds of reviewing the device before he understood.

"Clever girl," he whispered into her ear.

From the other pocket, he pulled out the item he feared. Her cell phone lit up to an unlock screen filled with text message notifications and he refused to touch it any further to avoid locking himself out. A workaround was required, and the best tool to do so lay at his feet.

He stood, releasing her, allowing her to thrash about again. Watching her conviction, he considered another option. Unlike Ethan, Debra looked light enough to carry up the steps, and he still had plenty of time before sunup. He could place her in the car and drive far, far away, and then arrange for her death to look like a suicide. Certain unsavory folks could handle that for the right price, and Jacob knew a few of them. He appreciated the simplicity of this approach, even though it involved third parties.

But, there was one big drawback to this plan. He tasered, struck, and drugged her. It would be a miracle if a forensic pathologist missed each of these three calling cards.

Besides, he wanted her. Her physique impressed him as he sat and scanned her helpless body, tight from working out and a physical job.

He grabbed the bottle of burgundy he opened before, poured himself a fresh glass, and headed back up to the bedroom. There, he took a moment to enjoy.

27

Debra understood it was pointless but kept thrashing. The pointlessness was part of why she would not submit. The moment she gave into the reality of her circumstance, the moment she accepted her plight, was the moment Jacob won. And so she flailed. Her shoulders stung from where Jacob pressed. The duct tape tickled against her lips as she screamed. Her head throbbed from the blow to the ground. But none of this phased her. She flapped in place, well aware that she likely soon would suffocate.

Right before she ran out of energy, she heard a distant noise. It was clear enough for her to decipher: someone raised the trapdoor leading to the stairs. Then, heavy steps plodded downward, closing in on her. A blindfold covered her eyes, but she instinctively cocked her head in the direction of the visitor. This gave her a second rush of energy, and she yelled, "Help!" knowing that the person descending the stairs likely was not there to help her.

Then there was stillness. She ceased her resistance, desperately focusing on her hearing, hoping to detect any faint noise that may clue her in on who approached. They ripped the blindfold from her eyes, and she was momentarily blinded, even in the dull light of the reserve. She blinked hard to compensate, focused on who pulled off the blindfold, and her heart sank when she saw Jacob's shit-eating grin above her wrecked body.

"Hey there, Debra," Jacob said as he sat next to her. "You free? I was hoping we could chat for a bit."

Debra tried to spit, forgetting duct tape covered her mouth. She then screamed, "Fuck you!" as loud as possible, though the distortion caused the words to coalesce into a prolonged, "Mmmmm."

"Now, now," Jacob whispered with a pat against her sore shoulders. "Where are your manners? You're a guest here. Try to maintain some semblance of decorum."

She shifted her shoulder aggressively to toss off his hand, causing a fireball of pain.

Jacob turned away from her and stared off into the distance. Softly, he said, "I can't lie to you, Deb. I'm tired. It's been a long day. You know?" He turned back to her, the grin returning, and continued, "Yeah, you know. So how about we do this the easy way. Because the hard way is going to take a lot out of me, and even more out of you."

Jacob lifted and extended his hands, revealing their contents. In one hand, he held a small box-cutter knife. In the other, a gun.

"So, here's the rub. I'm going to cut the tape off of your mouth now, and I'm hoping we can have a pleasant conversation. But if you act up, you may leave me with no choice then to use the backup plan." Jacob shook the gun as he said this. "So, what'll be?"

Debra considered her options. The last thing she wanted to do was "chat" with this lunatic, but she may need to in order to get answers. Slowly, she nodded towards the knife.

"Works for me." Jacob leaned in and cut off the tape, gently slipping it off her face, careful not to pull too hard. With the tape removed, he said, "Now, if you scream, the best case is I'm going to put the tape back on. Worst case…" he tapped the gun against her forehead. "Got it?"

Debra nodded, wordlessly. She did not want to engage until necessary.

Jacob said, "Now, I really only have one question." He placed the gun on the ground before slipping his hand into his pocket and pulling out a cell phone. Debra immediately recognized it as hers. "What is the passcode to this?"

Debra inhaled, pushed down the pain, and said, "Why would I tell you that?"

She prepared for the strikes, but they did not come. Instead, Jacob just sat silently, beholding her. Almost whispering, he said, "That's enough, Deb. I know you wanna fight, and I get it. I really do. But all that's behind you. You're mine now. What happens next to you is completely up to me. I can make things really, really hard on you in here. But that's not the road I wanna go down. Does that make sense?"

Debra sighed, then nodded, her eyes on the ground.

"So, what's it gonna be?" Jacob asked.

With a slight shrug, Debra said, "0652."

Thanks, Deb. I know you're hurting. I'll make sure you get a little rest in a bit." He turned his attention from her and to the phone. Within a few seconds, she saw his muscles tighten, his brow furrow. She couldn't help but smile.

"Think that's funny, huh?" he said, his tone dark. The next moment, Jacob's hand was on the back of her head, and she barely had time to process before her head slammed against the ground.

She swam in a sea of blurred shapes and bright dots. Then, the pain rushed in, and she opened her mouth to scream, but Jacob's firm hand against her mouth prevented it. He grasped her face so hard that his fingernails dug into her cheeks.

"Hush now," he said. "Enough with the games. I want you to

know that. I don't care to hurt you, and I don't care to not hurt you. You're like a bug under my shoe. I'm not looking to smash you, but I will." He dug his fingernails in deeper as he said, "Believe me, I will."

He released her head, and it fell against the ground, exacerbating her disorientation. She scrunched her face to stave off the pain, but it did not help.

"So, are you finished with your bullshit?" Jacob asked. "Or do you want to continue this dance? Because I can go all night, baby. Don't fret about that."

Debra spit blood and said, "I think I'm done."

"Good, then. What's the passcode?"

"0306."

"Say that again."

"0306," Debra repeated. "March 6th. The month and day I joined the force."

Jacob nodded, seemingly pleased. "Got it. Makes sense." He then leaned back, and again it did not take long for his muscles to clench. He whispered, "You know, Debra. I'm not a patient man."

"You're not a man, period," she shot back. She barely had time to finish the sentence before he was on her, his hand around her throat. He pressed hard, so hard her trachea shifted out of position. She gasped as hard as she could, but no air came into her throat. She tried to scream, but found that cost her precious air. Every moment, she expected Jacob to relent, but he did not. He choked harder and harder, his eyes wide, his breathing deep. Blackness bled into the periphery of Debra's vision, enveloping her like a dark hug. She decided to not fight it and instead recede. After closing her eyes, she slowed her breathing, and thought of Charlotte's most recent soccer game. She had scored two goals, and they had celebrated by going to her favorite restaurant, a burger place Debra hated. Although Debra suffocated, she sensed the hint of a smile on her lips.

The memory faded as she fell from Jacob's grip. She inhaled, the air rushing into her lungs, filling them like deflated balloons. She sounded like someone who had just crossed the finish line of a marathon, her rasp no different from that of a longtime smoker.

She looked up at Jacob's face, and he gasped as hard as her, the frustration clear in the lines of his forehead. "Why do you make me do that?" he asked, sounding like a spoiled child.

Once her breath returned, she balled her fists and said, "I might be a bug to you, but you're less than that to me, Jacob. Do what you want to me. I'm not telling you shit." She glared at him and said, "By the way, that phone is police issued. Get the passcode wrong a third time and it wipes. So good luck figuring it out. Better hope you don't fuck up."

She saw the anger build within him. His hands balled, his vision narrowed. She braced for the attack, hopeful he would kill her quickly. But his rage passed. His shoulders lowered, hands released. Then, the smile returned, which unnerved Debra more than his desire to kill her.

"I should have known," Jacob said in a flat tone. "Threatening you was silly. You're not going to give up the ghost just because I hurt you. You're a mother." Jacob focused on her with haunting eyes, eyes of a man untethered to her concepts of mortality and goodness. "Mothers, they got too much on their minds to care about themselves."

For several seconds, Jacob sat, his eyes again distant. Then he stood and walked to the other side of the room. Debra tried to cock her neck to see what he was doing, but he was beyond her sight. So, she instead listened. She heard scratching and clicking and a faint moan. Several seconds later, a face appeared before her, a face she assumed was Jacob's. Upon closer inspection, though, she realized it was not Jacob's face. It was too soft, too young, too pretty. Blonde hair covered the little girl's eyes, but Debra knew from the picture that beautiful blue irises lay beyond her closed eyelids.

Jacob pressed a gun against Jenna's temple, and Debra screamed as loudly as possible.

"Settle down," Jacob coaxed. "Keep that shit up and I'll blow her brains out right in front of you." He pushed Jenna's face closer to hers, and Debra instinctively and shamefully turned away.

"Now," Jacob continued. "Here's what's gonna happen. You're going to tell me the passcode to your phone, or I'm going to blow her head off. Then, guess what? I'm going to find pretty little Charlotte and do the same to her."

At the sound of her daughter's name, Debra collapsed onto the ground, fully giving in and giving up.

"So," Jacob whispered in her ear. "What's the passcode, pretty please."

Without a second thought, Debra said, "0812."

"Aw," Jacob replied. "Charlotte's birthday. I probably could have put that together if you gave me enough chances."

Jacob's knowledge of Charlotte's birthday only emphasized the stark reality Debra now faced. This wasn't a situation in which only her existence was on the line. She had sworn to uphold the law, even if it meant sacrificing her life when she accepted the badge. Jacob knew about her family, knew about her daughter. He likely knew where they lived and where Charlotte attended school. Knowing that, resistance was no longer an option. Fighting back was no longer an option. Debra would do whatever Jacob asked until he mercifully killed her, and she prayed that would happen without pain and without the involvement of her daughter.

"Thank you," Jacob whispered in her ear, obviously satisfied that he was able to unlock her phone. "I promise you this. As long as you cooperate, I will not hurt Jenna, and I will not hurt

Charlotte. Believe me, doing so would just add needless complications. But if you misbehave, all bets are off."

Debra nodded, completely defeated. She felt the adhesiveness of the tape press against her face, and she did not resist. She sensed Jacob step back and stand up above her, obviously staring down at the feral dog he successfully domesticated.

"Atta girl," he said with a chuckle. "Don't stress. I'm not interested in bringing in Charlotte. You and I are gonna have enough fun for three people."

28

Jacob couldn't believe his luck. As he drove, he reconsidered his previous dismissal of religious beliefs. Perhaps divine intervention was real?

No, he decided. *Only divine anticipation.* Perhaps an unworldly force did not bestow his unnatural ability to recover. Perhaps he was the unworldly force. It made sense. His ability to turn problems into opportunities was unparalleled, this most recent example perhaps being the best. A cop ambushed him in his basement, the one cop who suspected him, and he not only turned the tables but will now create another distraction miles away from his beloved reserve.

Though, again his mind returned to Sherri. What should he do with Sherri? He had decided to keep her, but that was before the nosy bitch detective crashed his party uninvited. Debra replaced Sherri. He had no qualms about that. Debra may even prove to be the better subject. Sherri was younger, though, and fit.

The issue was trying to accomplish too much too quickly. He had some knowledge of bankruptcy law and understood the number one killer of successful businesses was growing too fast, believing profits would never end. Yet, all it takes is one bad investment to bring the whole enterprise down. Many paper millionaires disappeared overnight just because they picked the wrong New York broker.

In his private reserve lay three excellent specimens, the best he's had since Jodi. Going for a fourth too soon would create liabilities, especially if others knew that Debra suspected him. Plus, he told only Debra about his fake alibi, so he had closed that loop. Well, he assumed Debra didn't tell anyone. He'd find out in a future discussion.

Either way, Jacob was not a suspect to anyone but Debra, so now, status quo was his friend. He was also no longer in a rush now that he had his beautiful threesome to play with.

He pulled off of Sonoma Highway and parked across from the sign that read SONOMA VALLEY REGIONAL PARK. Before exiting, he pulled the rag from his coat and wiped down every surface, searching for any hairs. Clothes covered his every inch, including his gloved hands, but tonight taught him that one cannot be too careful.

Once the car was wiped clean, he pulled out Debra's phone and a Ziplock bag from his pocket. He opened the bag, slipped out Debra's phone, and unlocked it with her passcode. She had over a dozen missed messages, most from an Officer McCarthy. He read them, and they were thankfully uninteresting; none had anything to do with him. He read several chains of messages and none mentioned his name. This was encouraging as Debra likely was going rogue in pursuing him. He expected nothing less from her. Like him, she eschewed authority in favor of blazing her own trail. He respected that about her, respected many parts about her if he was being honest. Challenging prey is a hunter's joy.

Once satisfied that he understood her recent

communications, he clicked into the message string with Officer McCarthy and wrote: "Thanks for the updates. I'm following up on a lead in Glen Ellen. Ethan may be in Sonoma Valley Park." He hit SEND, wiped down the phone, and placed it in the cup holder.

He considered whether there was anything else for him to do. This park was far smaller than Sugarloaf, though its location was beneficial, miles away from Holland Vineyards but still within jogging distance. He also figured planting evidence would be a waste of time. And he had little time to waste.

He stepped out of Debra's car, zipped up his jogging gear, and headed towards his reserve. By his calculations, he should arrive well before any employee.

Jacob had another loose end to tie up. He dialed her number, making sure she was there so he didn't waste any time. She picked up on the fourth ring.

"Hey babe," she answered, her voice groggy. "How's it goin'?"

"Not well, not well at all," he replied. "You home?"

"Yeah. What's goin' on?"

"I can't talk about it on the phone. I'm like three minutes away from your place. Are you there?"

"Yeah, yeah. But what do you need, hunny?"

"I need you to be there when I get there in three minutes, okay?" He broke the connection and, a few minutes later, he pulled into the driveway of the cottage which, he had to admit, Sherri had done a nice job decorating. He jogged past the rocking chair and banged on the front door, which creaked under his force.

"Sherri!" Jacob screamed as he pounded his fist against the wood. "It's me, Jacob! Open up, please!"

He heard scurrying inside as someone frantically attempted to click the lock. Sherri flung the door open and asked, "Now, what is all this commotion?"

"It's been a long day," he replied with a sigh. "Can I come in?"

"Of course. Get your butt in here now, mister." She pulled him inside by the collar of his shirt and slammed the door behind him.

"Jacob," she murmured. "I've never seen you like this. What's going on?"

"There's no 'they,'" he replied. "There's only a 'she.'"

"That detective?"

"Yeah, that detective," he buried his head into her shoulder and pretended to sob. "She's making crap up about me now. I'm not sure even lawyering up will slow her down this time. She won't stop until she finds a way to nail me for something I didn't do."

She patted his back and whispered, "That's awful, baby. That bitch is why I'm so darned tired. She woke me up."

"What do you mean, she woke you up? How?"

"Oh, she called at, like, one in the morning."

"What did she say? Anything about me?"

"No, sweetie. Apologized for waking me up and asked if I remembered anything new. I told her no, and she hung up. That's it."

Jacob considered this and wondered what it meant. Probably nothing, but the conversation was one to remember. "When things calm down," he said, "we're going to sue her and the damned police department to hell and back. I'll be able to pay off all the family debts and some. We'll make this right, I promise. But I have to get out of here and lay low for a bit. Wanna come with me?"

"Of course!" she exclaimed. "I'll go anywhere with you. I love you."

"And I love you. I love you so much that I want to show you a secret. A family secret."

"Oh? A secret?"

"Yeah, follow me." He led her down the hallway. There, he pulled down a cord that hung from the ceiling, revealing a stairway up to the attic. "Ever been up there?"

"No," she said. "I don't really go places I'm not supposed to."

"Yeah, that's one thing I like most about you. Here," he guided the staircase down and stabilized it on the floor. "Follow me."

She did, and they both ascended the stairs into the warm attic. Though generally barren, in the corner rested a small safe.

"See that?" he asked.

"Yeah," she replied.

"Let's go see it."

They walked to the safe and Jacob pushed in the code. He opened the door, and large clumps of cash fell out. The bills were only twenties and hundreds, no small denominations. He withdrew thousands and thousands of dollars over the course of months to fill up that safe as a backup if the shit hit the fan. He could not remember how much he stashed in there, but it was in the six-figure range, more than enough for his purposes.

"Oh my gosh," Sherri whispered. "Oh my gosh. How much is that, Jacob? I've never seen so much dough."

"Yup," Jacob replied. "Not sure exactly how much is in here, but there's a lot. Quite a lot, in fact. Enough to get out of this hell hole and start up somewhere new until things cool. Somewhere fresh. I won't be worth what I am, but we'll have each other. Is that okay?"

"Baby," she squeezed him, and he grasped her hands to make sure they did not reach anywhere near the gun in his back waistband. "You're all I need. Just you. Money don't mean anything."

He pulled away, studied her eyes, and said, "I'm glad to hear that, babe, but let's get some while we can. Can you grab me some trash bags?"

Sherri nodded, stared at the money once more, and scurried down the steps. Jacob waited patiently. As he considered what he told Sherri, part of him wished he was running away with her. They could sneak into a foreign country and live out the rest of their days on a sunny, remote island, with locals catering to their every need. He knew enough people who could easily acquire fake passports. Well, almost every need, for while the dream sounded good in concept, Jacob had more work to do, and he could not abandon his well-earned trophies.

A minute or so later, Sherri reappeared carrying a package of Glad trash bags. She stumbled on the last step, regained her composure, and extended the bag towards Jacob.

"Here," she presented it to Jacob, "Is this what you need?"

"Yes," he replied. "It's perfect. Help me put money in, and then I'll tell you my plans. Our plans, really."

The two worked for the next few minutes to shovel the money into the garbage bag, which filled quickly. Sherri pulled out a second bag, and they started on that one. The second bag filled pretty well, but not all the way.

"Perfect," Jacob said.

"Yay!" Sherri replied, clapping her hands. "Is there any more left? Anything else you need to tell me about?"

"Nope, that's it."

"Good Lord," she placed her hand on her chest. "All that money." She stared at the bags, dumbfounded. "I just can't believe it, can't believe it."

"Yup." He shook the bags with a grin. "And it's all ours."

"So what's next? What's the plan? You said you had some plan."

"This," Jacob dropped one bag and used his free hand to aim

the gun at her. She examined it with a look of panic, her eyes wide and trembling.

"Jacob, what are you doing?"

"I'm sorry, Sherri, I really am. I didn't want to do this, but that bitch detective left me no choice. Please forgive me."

"The detective?" Her voice quivered and her eyes drifted from his face to the gun. "I don't understand, Jacob." Her eyes flicked towards the money. "We're getting away from her."

"She's not going to stop."

"But, you just said—"

"She's not going to stop until she figures out what I did."

She sat there with a blank expression for several seconds, obviously processing Jacob's statement. "So," she said, her eyes locked on the gun. "You killed Beverly? And took Jenna?"

"Yup," Jacob admitted, deciding a confessional was in order. "I intended for you to join Jenna, but things just didn't go as planned, and now you'll have to go. I hope you understand."

Unexpectedly, her panicked expression morphed into resignation, causing her to look much older. "You know," she said, her tone oddly calm, her demeanor defeated, "did I ever tell ya about my stepdad?"

"No," Jacob replied, his interest piqued.

"Never met my real pops. My stepdad started off real nice, gettin' me to think we'd be best of friends. Seemed to treat my Momma good, too. But then, once they got hitched, something changed. He turned mean. The beatings started. Momma and I kept waiting for the man he was to come back, but he never did. He was just bad to the core, and we missed it." She stared up and him, her eyes filled with tears. "There was a feeling in the pit of my stomach about you, Jacob. That you were bad news, like my stepdad. But I pushed it away, thinking not every man could be evil."

"You're right," Jacob replied. "Not every man is evil. Just us lucky few."

With a content grin, he pulled the trigger.

Once he got back to the butler's house, he hopped in his truck, drove it down to the main building, and parked in the spot closest to it. He got out and checked the doors to the tasting room. Locked. As he rounded the building's exterior, he searched for any sign of life. He was alone, so he headed back to the truck.

He pulled out his cell phone and hit the number for Jessica. It was early, but she was an early riser. After five rings, she answered with a breathless, "Hello?"

"Hey Jessica, on your morning run?"

"You know me too well. What's up?"

"Hey, so, I'm sorry for calling this early, but that little girl has been on my mind."

"Yeah," she replied. "Me too. Poor thing. I spent all day yesterday at the search party. Didn't find anything."

"When did you leave?"

"Like seven? You were still there when I left. When did you head out?"

"Not too long after you. I may join them again. I got a good night's sleep and feel rested. How about you?"

"It's up to you. I'll work if you want me to. I get it's a busy time of year, and I want to do whatever's best for the company."

He liked the sound of that. "I was thinking about closing down again. From what I've heard, they haven't found anything yet and may expand the search."

"Oh yeah?"

"Yeah. It's just such a horrible situation. We helped out yesterday and I think we should again. Does that work for you?"

"Definitely. That's the right move."

"Great. Will you do me a favor first?"

"Anything."

"Can you blast a message to everyone and tell them we are closed today?"

"Of course I can. Are you sure?" Her voice sounded more composed, likely because she had stopped running.

"I am. It seems silly to open when there's a tragedy so close to us. Also, put in the message that we encourage everyone to join the search party."

"That works for me."

"Would it be possible to leave a similar voice message when guests try to enter? I don't want customers thinking we are turning them away for no reason."

"I can do that. Makes sense. I can even do it remotely. Let me finish my run and I'll get right on it."

"You're the best. Thanks so much."

"No, thank you. This is a great thing you're doing."

He grinned. "Well, it's the least we can do."

After receiving Jessica's confirmatory text, he decided to double-check her work. He rolled down his truck's window and the box in front of the Holland Vineyard announced, "Hello! We are closed today due to the recent AMBER Alert related to a local resident. We encourage anyone who is able to help the Sonoma police force in locating the missing girl. Have a great day, and we will reopen soon."

Perfect, Jacob thought. Jessica surprised him more each day. She would make a nice substitute for Sherri once things settled down.

He pressed the passcode, and the gates opened. He pulled into the parking lot, and as before, he was alone. Jessica had performed her job admirably. Perhaps a raise was in order. He was in a generous mood.

The sun rose as he pulled into the wine cave, empty of any human presence aside from Jacob. A part of him missed Ethan. Jacob had enjoyed having company in his little room away from the butler's house.

He stepped out of his car and surveyed the area. Clean, aside from a few spots of blood. Overall, the area could have looked a lot worse. Still, he needed to tidy up a bit.

From a nearby closet, he grabbed various cleaning supplies and started his work. He swept, mopped, and dried where needed in the wine cave, including places where Ethan didn't touch. Thoroughness was his friend. He had much to gain and everything to lose.

The work was hard and his muscles ached. He was beginning to feel like he was running on steam. Not that he needed much sleep, but everyone needed some. Thankfully, he had all the medicine he would ever need to aid him in that goal.

Once the wine cave was spotless, he walked to the resting area across from the extended dining room table; in it, a large sofa faced a TV above a fireplace. The fireplace was automatic, and though he rarely used it, he loved that feature.

Jacob flicked a switch above the fireplace. In under five seconds, a fire raged within the pit, spilling warmth into the room, warming his bones and staving off any lingering chill from his run.

Jacob opened the grate and pulled out the bag. He tossed in the rag, blood-stained Lysol wipes, all the paper towels he used to clean, and the tracking device. Finally, he threw in the two burner flip phones along with the pieces of Jenna's cell phone. The fire blossomed.

He sat on the couch and watched the fire, enjoying its dance. Fire calmed him, always had. He related to the controlled chaos of the fire. It did not spread without the proper fuel. That was him. He would not take any unnecessary risk unless the rewards were worth it. And today, he would feast from the horn of plenty he had acquired through sheer force of will. Like fire at a certain point, nothing was stopping him. He alone decided when it was time to burn out.

He got back into the truck and drove towards the butler's house. Once inside, he did a last check of the entire cottage, searching for specks of blood, stray hair, fingernails, or any other damning evidence. Everything looked clean, so it was time to put the final touches on his masterpiece.

29

Sensations returned before Ethan opened his eyes. His shoulders ached from the awkward position in which Jacob left him. Many other parts of him hurt. His head, his back, his legs, his wrists. But the pain was bearable. He had experienced worse even that day.

The important thing was he sat next to his daughter, arm's length from her. He listened for her breathing. At first, he detected nothing, causing his heart to race. But then, her breathing quickened a touch, and he recognized it, the most beautiful sound in the world.

Though close to one another, she was too far to touch. He tried to scoot closer, but Jacob had bolted the chairs to the floor. His arms were out of the question as he needed to keep them in the exact position behind him. His legs, though. He could move his legs.

Before he did so, he again shut his eyes and listened. He waited over a minute and only detected his daughter breathing. Then, he heard something else: muffled crying. His daughter didn't cry, though, which was all he cared about. For a while, he just listened. The crying persisted, but otherwise, he detected no other noise, and Jacob did not do anything to cause the hushed weeping to cease.

Taking a calculated risk, he opened his eyes. The world twisted, curved, and blurred. The pain built up behind his temples. He blinked several times and refocused. His vision sharpened, and he saw a lady near him. He did not recognize her, but she looked badly beaten up. He felt bad for her but was also happy. The more people Jacob took, the more people on the outside who would worry.

To distract from the discomfort, his mind focused on Jacob. Specifically, Adam Holland's funeral, the last time Ethan had seen Jacob. Ethan recalled paying respects to Adam's wife, Gretchen, before the readings, and as he did so, he turned to the young, blue-eyed boy holding Gretchen's hand. Ethan tried comforting the boy, who stared through Ethan and sat motionless, unaffected by any well-wishes. At the time, Ethan wrote off the odd behavior to shock. But perhaps there was another explanation.

Maybe his father's death bored young Jacob.

Ethan shut his eyes again and resolved to keep them shut. He wanted one last thing, though. With short, considered movements, he turned his torso slightly towards his daughter and extended his leg outward. Now, they touched. Barely, but he still touched his little girl.

He enjoyed her warmth and awaited his moment.

30

THIRTEEN YEARS PRIOR

Jacob watched his father stumble around like a baby giraffe. He'd take one step, stop, level himself, then repeat the process over and over, making their walk to the hunting grounds take way too long. The problem was that Jacob's father, Adam, was not clumsy. Jacob had watched his father play basketball against his buddies several times, and Adam usually was the best player. So, he didn't stumble because of any lack of coordination. Even at a young age, Jacob realized Adam stumbled because of the effects of the liquid in the flask strapped to his right hip.

As they walked, Jacob remembered how he used to idolize his father. That changed one day—Jacob couldn't remember when—and Jacob's worship morphed into hatred. Jacob hated Adam's deep voice and performative manners. Jacob hated Adam's drinking and his interests, like these dumb hunting trips Adam dragged him on, never once asking if Jacob enjoyed the long days and sleepless nights. But most of all, Jacob hated his father because of the way he looked at Jacob, like a patron may gawk at a monkey in the zoo.

"This looks like a pleasant spot," Adam suddenly announced,

startling Jacob and breaking him from his thoughts. A pleasant spot for what, Jacob did not ask. Instead, he just sat down across from his father and waited for further instruction.

For a while, the two sat in silence. Adam gazed at Jacob with that cold businessman's stare, careful to show just enough emotion without really revealing which emotions he felt. Jacob did not stare back, instead averting his eyes to the ground, studying the grass, watching his father in his periphery.

"Goddamn, son," Adam muttered as he took a long pull from his flask. He flinched, replaced the flask, and asked, "What the hell is wrong with you, anyway?"

This question piqued Jacob's interest. He directed his eyes to his father's, but still sat motionless and soundless.

"Nothing?" Adam asked. "You got nothing to say?"

Jacob did not react, and instead just held his stare.

"I remember the day you were born like it was yesterday," Adam continued as he turned his head away and surveyed the horizon. "I was so damned proud. A son. I finally had a son. And you were perfect. Quiet, beautiful." He shook his head. "But something changed. I noticed it in your eyes."

Jacob remained silent but cocked his head. For the first time in a long time, Jacob was interested in his father's words.

"Yup," Adam intoned before taking a long pull of whiskey. He hiccupped and shook his head before staring off into the distance. "I know the exact day, too. You were seven. You fell off a swing and hit your head hard. You cried for a bit, but we didn't think too much of it. Didn't even take you to see a doctor. But we should've."

Jacob vaguely remembered falling off the swing, but the memory was hazy, the type of memory that is hard to discern from a dream. But, giving it some thought, what his father said made total sense. He didn't know exact dates, but he figured he stopped feeling things around seven years old. At least, feeling things the way he used to, the way normal people feel.

Adam pointed two thick fingers toward Jacob's irises. "After that day, it's like the spark in your eyes disappeared. Haven't seen the spark since. Don't know where it went. I don't know who you are. Hell." He stood and lorded above Jacob. "I don't even know what the hell you are. All that shit you've been getting into. I can only hide the animals' bodies for so long, Jacob."

Adam turned and straightened his back, causing it to crack. He bowed his head and whispered, "All I wanted was a boy to toss a ball with, and I get you."

Adam's words had little impact on Jacob, aside from reinforcing his decision. Adam stepped away, and Jacob yelled, "Hey, Dad."

Adam stopped, paused, and turned on his heels, his eyes wide.

"Catch this," Jacob said with a grin as he pulled the trigger.

The gunshot rung out. Adam's body flung back as the top of his head flew off in a different direction, maroon blood and grey brain exploding in the air like a violent firecracker. The gunshot echoed all around Jacob, and his body trembled from the gun's kick and his adrenaline.

Then, all was still.

Jacob sat for a while and watched his father, ensuring he didn't need to do anything else. While he waited, Jacob detected a sensation he could not immediately place. He first thought he was sweating, but the weather was chilly.

Jacob realized his face was wet with his father's blood.

He licked his lips and savored every drop. He had finally seized the control he so craved. Before that moment, Jacob existed as a meek and weak child. Now, the taste of his father's blood proved he had ascended, giving him a rush he would chase forever. It also didn't hurt that the one man who started to see through Jacob was now dead.

In the distance, Jacob heard someone yell. This snapped him

from exaltation to reality. He had little time to spare. The best he could, he used his shirt to wipe down the gun and placed it next to his father's body, interlacing his fingers with the trigger. He stepped back, reviewed his work, and decided it was acceptable.

He took one final lick, then forced himself to cry.

31

NOW

Before descending, Jacob placed his ear to the trapdoor and listened. Silence. He was in the clear.

He adjusted the trash bag in his hand, opened the trap door, and closed it behind him. As soon as he descended the steps, he saw his prized trophies in the same places he had left them.

From the table, he grabbed the blood pressure monitor. As he did so, he heard movement near him. Debra's stare could kill.

"Good morning, sunshine," he said as he walked towards Ethan and Jenna. "How are you?" She flopped in place but did not lessen the distance between them.

"Well, it seems like you're in a good mood. Give me one sec and we'll chat." He dropped the trash bag before approaching and slapping the blood monitor on both Jenna and Ethan. Both were pumping well.

"Looking good you two," he said in his most doctorly voice. "I'd give you a lollipop if I had one."

He turned to Debra, who had stopped struggling and instead focused on trying to stare him down.

The stare weakened him. He regretted how things ended up. She was just doing her job. Had she never pursued him, he would never have taken her. But here she was, on her belly in his reserve, surrounded by bottles of wine worth more than her annual paycheck.

"I'll tell you what," he said as he approached her while pulling out the gun from the back of his pants. "We can talk, but you have to behave. I'll even untie you a bit so we can have a glass of wine like civilized people. Can you be a good girl?"

Her stern look faded away, replaced by softness. She nodded and placed her head on the floor. Whether this was a police tactic or genuine resignation he did not know. Either way, he craved conversation.

"Okay, I'm going to cut off the duct tape around your mouth. If you scream, I'm giving you more medicine, understand?"

She nodded, her head still on the ground in that defeated position. He cut the tape and ripped it away. She barely flinched. He then untied the rope that bound her feet to her arms, keeping the gun pointed square at her in case she tried to make a move on him.

She did not resist, and once the rope was loose, he helped her to her feet, his gun pressed against her temple, and guided her to the table. She had to take little hops because of the handcuffs around her ankles.

He aided her in taking a seat, her cuffed hands on the table, her cuffed ankles below it. He then used one end of the rope to further bind her legs together and tied the other end to the single, center pole stabilizing the table. He knew this pole was bolted to the ground. She would have enough freedom of movement to drink wine with him, but escape was impossible.

He stepped back and beheld her, slumped over the table, barely able to sit. She was tired and defeated, exactly as he wanted her. She obviously knew that acting out may spell bad news for little Charlotte. The power kids wielded over their parents amazed and baffled him.

"Okay," he said. "That has to feel better. Before we begin, I want to show you something so you know where we stand."

Jacob turned and headed towards the trash bag. After rifling through it for a few seconds, he pulled out and displayed a thick wad of twenty and one-hundred-dollar bills. He reared his arm back and tossed the wad onto the table, which bounced twice before skidding off. With a chuckle, Jacob said, "I've never been much of an athlete. But the point is, I have a lot of cold hard cash at my disposal. More than you could ever imagine. I just got this in case things get heated." He approached and sidled up to Debra. She withdrew as he leaned over and whispered into her ear, "Even if your pig friends figured out where I am, I got enough cash to bolt, hire a hitman to kill little Charlotte, and still never miss a meal on some remote island." Jacob leaned back with a smile and continued: "Just thought you should know."

With this, he walked towards and grabbed a nearby glass. He uncorked a fresh bottle of Burgundy, setting the wine cork near the bottle as he slid her a filled glass. "Now, what do you want to talk about? The weather? The local sports team?"

She studied the wine for almost ten seconds before asking, "Why?"

"You mean, all this?" He drew a big circle around him. "It's kind of hard to explain, so let's play show and tell."

He stood and walked towards the freezer past Jenna and Ethan. From it, he pulled a bag filled with crimson liquid labeled: "JENNA PAXTON, 8/16." He carried the bag like a mother might carry a newborn baby. He sat across from Debra and displayed it for her.

She looked up, took in the bag and its label for a moment, and her eyes grew large. "Is that what I think it is?" she asked.

"Yes ma'am," he said. The bag in his hand was cold, close to freezing, yet the liquid inside still had some give and flow. He swayed the bag to and fro, watching the streaks of purity break from the frozen parts and run, waltzing with the other life-giving components. The essence of man lay in his hands, its purity made true and whole. She would not understand it, no one would. But he did, and that's all that mattered.

He carried the bag back to the freezer and placed it down. After doing so, he kissed his fingers and caressed the bag before closing the top.

Debra sat silent for almost a minute before muttering, "You sick son of a bitch. You sick son of a bitch."

"Eh," he said and waved his hand contemptuously. "That's what they say about many trailblazers. The British called the lightbulb unworthy. Then Edison turned around and said people shouldn't waste time with alternating currents. See? Even geniuses can have difficulty spotting genius, which makes sense. True genius is taking what is in front of you every day and changing it in a way that no one intended, no one expected. People don't react well when their reality is challenged. But that is the only way to achieve true greatness."

"You're not great," she countered. "You're just nuts."

"Hey, look at that! Another common stone cast towards those operating at a higher level. But trust me, you won't knock me down. I'm riding too high for you to reach." In thought, he walked towards the table, sat down, and lifted the glass of burgundy.

"See this wine?" he asked as he displayed it for her. She did not move to look. "If you could somehow buy this wholesale, a single bottle would be worth several thousand dollars, double or triple that at a restaurant." He finished most of the wine and placed it on the table. "And yet," he said, pointing towards the freezer, "it pales in comparison to that. And the best part is that I have a stock that will last forever. The only drawback is I can only harvest every forty-five, maybe fifty days or so."

He stood, glass still in hand, and said, "That's what happened to Jodi. I got too greedy, drained her too quickly." His vision clouded, and he poured out the remaining wine onto the floor. "She was my love, my muse, and I screwed it up."

He placed the glass back on the table and said, "I tried other methods, too. I guess you could call them experiments. For a while, I was convinced that the trick was to keep the bodies cold, as cold as possible without freezing. That would cause the blood to slow and thicken, and—" Jacob cocked his head and considered. "You know, I don't really know why I thought that would work. I'm no scientist. I can only learn by doing."

He stepped towards Debra and said, "See, that's the trick. Not relying on one source. And it's more fun that way anyway. I remember when I first started trying wine, all I wanted to drink was pinot noir. I couldn't believe there could be anything better than that sweet, sweet juice. But then my palate shifted, matured. I still love pinot, but I love many more varietals." He faced he and said, "Does that make sense?"

"Fuck you," she shot back.

He ignored her and continued, "Anyway, with you, I now have more than enough stock. See," he pointed at Jenna, "she'll be my pinot noir. And him," he pointed at Ethan. "He'll be my cabernet. And you?" He looked at her as she glared back. "I don't know. Maybe my merlot? The exact varietal doesn't matter. It'll be fun to experiment."

He grabbed an empty blood donation bag and small foam stick and said, "Hey, want to see how it's done?" He couldn't hide the joy in his voice. Little separated him from a kid heading to the pound to get a new puppy.

"No," Debra said.

"Oh stop," he replied. "You know you're interested."

He walked towards Jenna and pointed at her. "As you saw, I've already harvested her today. So, let's do Ethan." He walked to Ethan and looked him over. Ethan's head bowed, but his breathing sounded normal. "The biggest problem is I need to take off the handcuffs to input the needle and assist with the flow. That's where the medicine comes in. I've got it down to a science. Something between 50 and 75 micrograms per kilogram per minute keeps the stock nice and sleepy." To check, Jacob slapped Ethan, whose head snapped to the side but, otherwise, he did not move. Jacob smiled at Debra and said, "Can never be too careful."

Gingerly, he placed the gun on the ground, knowing he would need both hands free to harvest Ethan. From his pocket, Jacob pulled out a set of several keys. He reviewed a few before finding the right one which he used on Ethan's handcuffs.

Once free, he expected Ethan's arms to fall, but they stayed in place. Jacob leaned in close and realized that Ethan sat on his hands.

Did I place him like that? Jacob wondered but couldn't remember. In thought, he almost didn't notice when Ethan's right hand shifted. Jacob watched the hand move as one may watch a train approach when it was too late to jump away.

Ethan threw a hard punch towards Jacob's head. Jacob tried to sidestep to his left to avoid the blow, but it caught the left side of his face, flinging his head the opposite way of his body.

Stars filled his vision as he stumbled before something struck his midsection, unbalancing him more. He started to tumble to the ground, forcing him to flail his hands out, reaching for anything to stabilize; his hands latched onto something solid, allowing him to catch himself before he fell to the floor. Once steadied, he blinked hard to refocus his sight and saw that he clung to the table where he sat moments before with Debra. In his upper periphery, he saw her face, a smile plastered on it.

He had only a second to also notice that she held something in her hand, something silvery and metallic. Before he could react, she flung her fist forward and struck Jacob in the face.

At first, the impact stunned him. He stood, stepped back, and shook off the blow. Then the pain rushed in, and his left eye noticed the object sticking out of his right one.

32

Jacob's scream reverberated off the bottles in a way that sounded near musical. The pain was unlike any he had ever experienced. Though the injury was localized, agony crept throughout his body, crippling him and his ability to react. Every pore hurt, compromising every sense. He even smelled pain, and it smelled sour. He gripped the handle of the wine opener with both hands, steadied himself, and pulled, the pain surging as the metal exited his body.

Though he understood his new reality, he needed to test. He shut his left eye, hoping the right would maintain some level of sight; instead, blackness enveloped Jacob, which dissolved to red as the rage built inside.

He opened his eye and glimpsed at the corkscrew covered with blood and optical tissue clinging to it like Ramen noodles. The blood rushed from his eye socket, pouring onto the floor, staining his shoes.

He threw the wine opener, tossed his head back, and shrieked, rage flowing out of him like lava.

At that moment, an object smashed against his head, causing him to stumble back against countless wine bottles, each of which stuck into his back like fat bee stings. His body ricocheted and tossed him to his knees, forcing him to brace himself to stop his head from plunging into the floor. Next to him lay the bottle of wine he opened with Debra earlier. She had obviously tossed it, and it had struck him on the head.

"Bitch!" he yelled as he shook his head, warding away this new pain only for it to be soon replaced by the resurgence of the agony from his missing eye. He grabbed the bottle and charged towards her. "Look what you did to me!"

She cocked her head and said, "I like this look on you."

Furiously, he smashed the bottle onto the ground, causing its bottom half to shatter. He raised the remaining half and angled the jagged shards towards her eyes. She recoiled but her eyes stayed locked on his.

"I told you I could make life much worse for you," he said. "Now you're about to find out just how much worse."

To his surprise, she smiled and said, "Oh, I don't know about that."

Realization hit Jacob. He turned and saw Ethan use his foot to scoot the gun towards him. Knowing he had little time, Jacob jumped to his left as Ethan raised the gun; the shot rang out and shattered a wine bottle, the liquid inside exploding throughout the room, some of it splashing on Jacob. Before Ethan readied a second shot, Jacob bolted for the stairs.

A second shot rang out, and Jacob swore it *swooshed* by his eye before striking yet another bottle, tens of thousands of dollars spraying across the room. Jacob was halfway up the stairs before the third gunshot ran out and all the way up for the fourth, neither coming close to hitting him.

The adrenaline pushed aside his pain and propelled him forward as he ran out of the kitchen through the living room and into the beautiful morning. He turned his head to look behind him, but no one followed, which made sense considering he bound Ethan to the chair and Debra to the table.

He darted for the truck as he patted his pocket to ensure the keys remained. Still there. He opened the door and fell in, blood from his hand, body, and eye coating much of the car. He lay for a moment on his seat as the situation washed over him, its implications smashing against his mind.

An hour ago, he thought himself next to a God. Now, he knocked on death's door. He had to do something, and quickly.

He pulled himself into a driving position and hit the ignition. As he drove, he watched the butler's house grow smaller in his rear-view mirror. All his work, his life's passion, dwindling away, all because of some bossy bitch with a badge.

He pulled up to the gate, and the sensors detected him, causing the gate to open in a maddeningly slow turn. As he waited, he counted all his mistakes, all the little screwups, the chief of which was putting Debra in a position to grab a wine opener. Why the hell had he unbound her? He had been arrogant, that was the short and long of it. Had he not been so cock-sure, he would have been able to grab the gun before Ethan plowed into him, and Jacob would still have both eyes.

Ethan's punch was also borne of Jacob's arrogance. In an effort to avoid overdosing, Jacob had obviously underdosed Ethan, figuring an underdose was far preferable to the alternative. Ethan proved that conclusion wrong.

The gate finished its process as Jacob sorted through his few remaining choices. Even the possibility of ending his life was difficult now that Ethan had his gun. But that wasn't Jacob's only piece.

He considered two options. First, he could get his second handgun and end it without thought, exiting into that beautiful darkness where eyes don't matter.

Conversely, he could formulate a final plan. He embraced this approach, embraced it like a father embraces his son. His motivation was no longer mere pleasure. No, his motivation was deeper, stronger.

Revenge now drove him. Not towards Ethan, who was only reacting to a situation Jacob created. A scientist cannot get mad at the rat who solved his puzzle. However, that same scientist can yell at the colleague who smashed all the barriers between the rat and the cheese.

And that's what Debra was, an intrusive pest who had ruined a well-set plan. Multiple plans, in fact. Without her interference, Jacob would have disappeared scot-free. No one would have looked in his direction. He would have left Ethan in the office for much longer and would have had more time to perfect Ethan's dosage. The entire force would have circled Sugarloaf until they got dizzy. Instead, police would soon invade his treasured private reserve, their unworthy hands handling wine —both from grapes and otherwise—that they could never appreciate.

And, if not for Debra, Jacob would still have both eyes and would be able to blend into the background as he continued his experiments. Now, she had deformed him forever, and he would never go unnoticed again.

"Stupid bitch," he screamed and punched the steering wheel. No, he was not driven by lust, greed, or pleasure. Revenge drove him. Revenge was the fuel to his rage, the blood that pumped through his veins, keeping him alive. He would have his revenge, come hell or high water, he would have it.

First things first. He needed the tool to enact his wrath.

33

Jacob fled up the stairs like a coward. Ethan fired two more rounds, but neither came close. He had a knowledge of guns and understood, more or less, the one he held did not have a large chamber. He needed every last shot.

He tried to move, but his waist remained strapped to the chair, so he turned to the side and located the rope binding him. He pressed the gun close to the rope and pulled the trigger. It severed immediately, freeing him.

Next, he turned to face his daughter, who remained unconscious. He was unsure how many bullets he had left and did not want to waste them. He hopped to her and examined her situation, locating the rope that bound her to the chair. As before, he placed the barrel of the gun against the rope and fired; this time, most of the rope disintegrated, but a sliver remained.

He tried pulling but to no avail. Instead, he searched for the wine opener Jacob had thrown, which rested across the room near shattered wine bottle fragments.

With a few hops, Ethan neared the opener. It took much of

his remaining energy to bend over and pick it up, but he did so without passing out. He then hopped back to Jenna and used the foil cutter to cut through the remaining strands.

Once free, Jenna toppled to the ground, still under the effects of Jacob's drugs. Mustering all his energy, he placed his cuffed arms under her limp body and pulled up her dead weight, placing her on his shoulder before hopping to the stairwell.

Ethan stopped and considered the woman chained to the table. She did not factor into his only remaining goal: getting his daughter out of this pit.

Still, she had played a major part in his possible escape. Whoever she was, he owed her a great deal. He could not leave without at least trying to help her.

As he adjusted to slip Jenna from his back, the woman asked, "What are you doing?"

Ethan froze for a moment, unsure how to react. "I'm going to help you."

The woman shook her head furiously before saying, "There's no time." She then beheld him with clear, striking eyes as she instructed, "I need you to listen closely. My name is Detective Debra Foley. As soon as you get out, tell the police I am down here. Ask for Officer McCarthy. He'll know what to do."

"I," Ethan said before quieting. "I don't know."

"Enough, there's no time. Take Jenna away and don't waste any more ammo trying to get me free. What if Jacob comes back?"

This logic made sense. Still, he had to say, "Thank you, Detective Debra. Thank you."

She smiled warmly and said, "You can thank me by getting Jenna the hell out of here and finding help."

Ethan nodded, stood, and looked down upon Debra the detective who looked up at him with kind eyes. Motherly eyes, if he had to guess. Before leaving, he said, "In case I don't see you again, when you get free, check the wine caves. Trust me."

Debra opened her mouth to respond, but instead just silently nodded.

Ethan turned and headed toward salvation. At the stairs, Ethan paused, unsure if he could make it up. He pushed aside doubt and proceeded up the stairs. Hop by hop, he went up one step at a time, each step leaving him feeling as though he had just run a marathon.

Three more hops to the top. Two. One.

He scanned the living room, looking for Jacob. He did not see him but detected the faint sound of a vehicle racing away. The coward was already gone. He refused to own up to the mess he made.

Ethan hopped through the bedroom into the living room and out the front door. In the distance, Jacob peeled off out of the property and onto the highway, the screech of his tires startling birds. The distance between where he stood and the front gate seemed like forever and then some. But, as he concluded, he was all Jenna had left. No distance was too far.

He hopped. And hopped. Down the hill towards the gate. With every hop, he had to rest a moment to regain his composure and energy. These breaks became longer, and halfway through he wondered if he would be able to make it at all.

He took a short break and fell to his knees. Beauty besieged him, encircling them like a halo. Vines to his back, the spectacular tasting room to his left. The tranquility of the surroundings both calmed and energized him. He wondered how someone like Jacob could sprout from such soil.

Jenna's weight pressed against his back, though she did not seem heavy. It was a good weight, like the weight of a marathon medal. He would forever carry her weight, or at least as much as possible. She was his burden, responsibility, passion, and world. He embraced and appreciated every facet of what was to come, good or bad, hard or easy. Until his dying day, he would carry her upon his back. She deserved as much.

Break over, he pushed up to his knees and started hopping again. Before long, he approached the main tasting room. He hoped someone there could help, but it looked deserted, and the parking lot was empty. Instead, he headed towards the road, figuring someone would eventually cross their paths.

He hopped and hopped and hopped until he reached the Holland Vineyards' front gate. He tried jumping in front of it, but he was not big enough to trigger detection. The gate did not open, and he was stuck.

Rather than trying to trigger the gate, he bounded towards the adjacent fence which was, at most, as tall as him. Once there, he started jumping up and down, hoping to draw the attention of commuters.

For almost thirty minutes, he jumped without notice. Cars sped by, unimpressed with his antics. He prayed they missed him as opposed to ignoring him.

Eventually, a small truck slammed its brakes and pulled to the side. A large, bald man stepped out and jogged towards the father and daughter.

"You guys okay?" he asked through the gate.

"No," he replied. "Not at all. Take my daughter, please." With all his might, he maneuvered his daughter into his two joined hands and pressed up. The man on the other side mirrored Ethan's movements, and their reaches eclipsed the fence.

Soon, another man held Jenna. A stranger.

"You got her?" Ethan asked.

"Yeah," the stranger said, sweat pouring down his face. "I got her, no worries."

The stranger lowered her to the ground and looked her over. "She's breathing!" he yelled.

"Yeah," Ethan replied. "Just call the cops, please."

"Got it," the stranger replied before pulling out his phone and dialing three numbers. Ethan stared at his helpless daughter through the fence. So young, so innocent, so defenseless. He would forever protect her.

No matter the cost.

34

J acob pulled into the parking lot of the storage place, likely for the last time. His eye socket still throbbed, but the desire to press on overwhelmed the pain, to damage those who had damaged him. His entire existence had been so juvenile, so thoughtless. Kidnapping people for wine—though the wine was wonderful—paled in comparison to the rush of planning the ousting of his greatest enemy.

Perhaps he needed an enemy. The uppity students in his baloney college classes would describe his life as "privileged." Indeed, he was the privileged among privileged, both from a financial and mental standpoint. He had been blessed with the resources to handle any circumstance, so few phased him. Until then. Someone had pierced his armor, and that someone would pay.

He walked through the hallways, a trail of blood following him. He passed his chilled unit and continued into the back area. There, he also rented a smaller, non-temperature-controlled unit. He made his way to the right side of the unit, pulled out a small gun locker, and opened it. It held two handguns and several rounds, all of which he stuffed into the pockets of his jacket before he placed the gun into the back of his pants.

He recalled the fire he lit earlier in the wine cave. He focused on this memory, mentally watching the flames flicker and flow. The items he threw in were now gone, purified in a flame of his creation. Even deeper, the essence of the fire bore into his soul, igniting his passion. He had been too by-the-book, too cognizant of every possible outcome that he missed the most likely ones.

He needed to emulate the fire. A fire did not care about best intention, well-laid plans. A fire just burned, taking with it anything in its path, decimating all that would oppose it.

The blaze within Jacob grew. He would not bow to his over-analytical side. He would burn, burn all around him and especially those who oppose him. What did he have left? Better to flame out with a bang than a whimper.

Jacob recognized where he needed to go next. Though a fire burned within, human frailty bound him. Blood gushed from his eye, and he needed to stem it, one way or another. A hospital was out of the question. By the time he checked in, Ethan and Debra may have already sounded the alarm. Thankfully, there was an alternative.

He turned onto the street and towards the house built from the crumbs of his family's feast. The neighborhood was wonderful, full of homes owned by the accomplished. Businesspeople, lawyers, doctors. There was but one exception on this street, and Jacob funded that exception. Hopefully, Justin would remember who buttered his bread.

Jacob pulled up to the home—a massive Victorian which stuck out like a sore thumb—and parked. Justin's eyes were always bigger than his wallet.

Jacob exited his vehicle and walked up the steep stone steps to the ridiculously ornate front door. He slammed the doorbell, initiating elongated musical chimes that persisted for nearly ten seconds. He then released the doorbell and rammed his fist against the door so hard his knuckles ached.

"Justin, it's me!" he screamed. "It's Jacob! Open up, Goddammit!"

When nothing changed after a few seconds, Jacob screamed, "Open this Goddamn door now!"

After another five seconds, light shone under the door and through its stained-glass windows. Justin—donned in a full-length burgundy velvet smoking jacket—opened the door and stared at Jacob with wide eyes behind oval lenses.

"Jacob?" he asked. "What is wrong with you?" His expression morphed from anger to panic as he reviewed Jacob's face.

Instead of responding, Jacob pulled the gun from his pants and pointed it at Justin. "That's the last question, got it? From now on, you will follow instructions."

"Justin?" a female voice called from up the steps. "Everything all right?"

"Yes!" Justin screamed back. "Just stay up there!"

She didn't listen. A few seconds later, she was downstairs, a silk nightgown clinging to her tall, thin frame, her dark brown eyes studying him.

"What, what is happening here?" she asked.

"Nothing, babe," Justin yelled back. "Nothing at all."

"Is that true?" Jacob inquired. "Does that broad know you're a fraud, living off the teat of someone far more successful? That you are essentially a high-priced drug dealer specializing in medical products? Tell her, Justin, or should I?"

"Shut up," Justin replied. "Just shut up, okay? What the hell happened to your eye?"

"That's where you come in." Jacob kept the gun pointed at Justin's head as he stepped inside and slammed the door.

"What's happening here?" the woman cried from upstairs. "Why is that man in our house?"

"Our house?" Jacob screamed back as he aimed the gun at her, causing her to duck behind the stair's railing. "This is my house. Got it? I paid for it, every Goddamn gaudy inch. And I'm cashing in today."

"Jacob," Justin began with his most clinical tone. "We had a deal, right? You can't get mad at me for providing a service you asked for. And this was definitely not in our, what's the word, understanding."

"Our understanding, huh?" Jacob chuckled and pressed the gun against Justin's trembling forehead. "Well, I'm adding a little to our understanding. An addendum, if you will. It's not much, just one night's work. If you do it well, there'll be a big bonus in it for you, of that I promise. If you don't, well, there's going to be another type of bonus, one I don't think you will like."

The woman screamed, and Jacob fired a shot in her direction, the blast echoing throughout the mansion's innards. "Tell her to come over here, now!"

"Babe," Justin pleaded. "Please come down. For me. For us."

She looked at Justin, back at the gun, and decided to comply, approaching them without taking her eyes off Jacob.

"The illustrious Alice!" Jacob exclaimed and dropped the gun to his side. "Nice to meet you in the flesh. Well, Alice, here's the skinny. Your boyfriend, or whatever you call him, owes me, owes me a lot. As you can see," he lifted the gun towards his missing eye, "I'm not in great shape. If he can fix me up, you two will never have to worry about money again. You can run off to any damn island you choose, I don't care. Alternatively," he rested the gun on Justin's head, "you can visit another type of paradise. Which will it be, guys?"

"Jacob, please," Justin pleaded. "I'll obviously help you out. Why all the dramatics?"

"Just needed to get my point across, that's all. Do you have everything you need?"

"Yeah, yeah I do. It won't take long, but I'll have to sew your eyelids together. It's called a tarsorrhaphy. I can't help you with a replacement eye."

"That's fine. I may grow to like this look. You got pain meds?"

"Yeah," Justin replied, his tone hopeful. "You need some?"

"Yeah, but not right now, dumbass. Do you think I'm an idiot? Go get them, and everything else you need. For now," he shifted his gun towards Alice, "I'll just talk to your girlfriend here. I'd love to get to know her better."

Alice's mouth opened, and Jacob shoved the gun inside. "Don't scream," he commanded. "It won't get you anything, and it'll just piss me off."

Justin scurried out of the room and soon returned with several bottles of pills and a sewing kit.

"Here," Justin beckoned, "you'll have to come close."

"Great," Jacob replied as he walked towards Justin and placed the gun's barrel to his temple. "Proceed. But any funny stuff may cause an involuntary reaction, and I can't be held responsible in such a circumstance."

Justin nodded, sweat beading on his forehead, and he began the tarsorrhaphy. The pain was terrible, but nothing compared to ripping his eye out with a corkscrew. Justin worked fast, impressively fast. He finished in a few minutes.

"There," Justin said. "There, that should do for now. It'll stop the bleeding and protect the wound. What the hell happened, anyway?"

"Nothing, nothing at all. Thank you so much." Jacob embraced Justin and noticed Alice trying to sneak away.

"No, no," Jacob said. "You get a hug, too." Jacob walked towards Alice, who instinctively took a step back.

Jacob frowned. "What? Why are you afraid of me?" Jacob

gave his best sad puppy dog look. "Is it because of the eye? Do I look that ugly?"

"No, no. It's just—"

"Just what?" Jacob said as he took a step towards her. "Just that I'm not a freak?" He took another step. "I'm about to set you up for life." Another step. "You'll never have to worry about money again." One last step, this one putting him right in front of her. "But, because I lost an eye, I'm so disgusting that you won't even touch me?"

She shook her head but otherwise did not move, her eyes locked on his one.

"Well, then show me." He leaned in, slowly, to avoid startling her. She leaned back at first but didn't take a step away. As he took her in his arms, he noticed her body shook.

"There, there," he whispered in her ear.

He then placed the gun against her temple and pulled the trigger. The gunshot rang out as blood and brain sprayed out over the house, covering the floor in maroon and gray.

"Jacob, no!" Justin screamed what became his last words.

Soon, Jacob stood in silence above the two bodies that lay before him. He sensed a twinge of guilt. Neither Justin nor Alice deserved this fate. Neither intended to mess with Jacob's plans. They were merely collateral damage in a war initiated by Debra. She fired first, knowing others may be hurt in the crossfire. Justin and Alice's blood was on her hands, not his.

Still, he needed to do something. He walked over to Alice's body, wiped the gun with part of his shirt not drenched in blood, and placed it in her hands. This ruse would not stand up to the slightest bit of scrutiny. His fingerprints were everywhere, as was his blood, and he had neither the time nor inclination to clean it all. But maybe the murder-suicide pose would pass initial assessments. It's not like he planned to stick around for much longer.

He parked in front of Sherri's house and drove away in her car, which was safe. When he bought the car for her, he paid a little extra because it was title jumped. If the police checked, they would pull up a name two owners ago. They wouldn't even be able to trace it to Sherri, much less himself.

As he drove, he thought about his next steps. He had a lot of money in an untraceable car and many contacts who would help him out of a jam. He knew professionals who would take care of anyone he wanted for far less than the money he carried.

But he didn't want Debra dead. No, he wanted worse, far worse. He wanted to enact pain on her that dwarfed his. He wanted to inflict everlasting pain, the type that thwarts sleep and wards away any semblance of happiness.

He rolled down the windows and allowed the sweet wine country air to wash over him. His life of privilege was over, the burden of his family's legacy behind him. He drove away from all the chains that bound him, all the impediments to true happiness. His aimless wandering was over. He had a new goal, an admirable one.

Revenge. No more, no less. Revenge.

He put his arm outside the window and tapped along to the beat of the song on the radio, confidence filling his soul. Debra left him with only one eye, but he had other advantages. Money. Intelligence. Connections.

But beyond all that, he also possessed rage. Pure, unadulterated rage. The type that flows through every vein into every limb. His rage burned with a persistent flame that would not quell before he extinguished Debra's candle.

35

Debra lay on the ground, her feet still bound to the table, her thoughts on Ethan. Like him, she would do anything to protect her daughter, no matter what.

Charlotte, she thought, her eyes watery. She would be with Charlotte soon. Because of Ethan's quick thinking, she would again hold Charlotte, stroke her hair, and tell her everything would be all right.

Charlotte was safe, and good parenting or bad, she would remain that way. Debra was concerned with the next kid Jacob would take. She wasn't sure Jacob would evade detection, but a part of her assumed he would not be captured so easily. Jacob was not like the typical criminal. Beyond just being far more intelligent, he thrived on misdirection.

If he was not caught, Debra was sure he would continue his sick conquests. Maybe he would focus instead on adults, but she doubted it. He was weak, if affable, and that combination worked best on children.

No, she concluded, *I will not let him hurt another child.*

She did not hear any additional gunshots or Ethan's steps returning, so she figured she had a long wait ahead of her. She rested her head on the table and let her mind focus on memories of Charlotte, as well as thoughts of the future.

She imagined sitting on the Disney teacups, Charlotte next to her, Bill across from them. They rode in the orange diamond cup, which Debra knew, by reputation, is the fastest. The family would spin carelessly, their hands in the air, the world rotating around them in a constant, safe blur.

Though she had no sense of time, it seemed like an eternity passed before the door raised and a familiar voice yelled, "Police, announce yourself!"

"It's me, McCarthy," she yelled back. "I'm down here alone."

"Let's move!" he screamed, followed by the sound of countless officers descending the steps, a cavalcade of police presence.

A young officer approached her and said, "Ma'am, are you okay?"

"Yes," she replied. "Yes, so please get these damn handcuffs off me."

"Roger that," he said before disappearing up the steps.

McCarthy made his way down the stairs, each step causing an audible crunch. He saddled up next to her and said, "Well hey there, Detective."

"Hey yourself," she replied.

"Yeah," he said as he sat at the table and studied her. "So, you find the Holland private reserve while looking for a missing girl? Next time, leave some fun for the rest of us."

"Aw, yes," Debra said, wiggling the handcuffs. "I've just been having loads of fun."

"Looks like it." McCarthy stood and approached the wine, studying the bottles like they were paintings in a museum. "Just look at all this. Look at it. Could you imagine?"

"No," Debra admitted.

"The whole world, and that bastard takes it for granted. I'll never get crazy, Deb."

"Funny, 'cause I thought that was your forte. Now, where are those dipshit officers?"

"Here," he replied as two young officers approached with a device that looked like a small jaws-of-life.

"Don't let them hurt me," Debra said.

"These guys? They're trained professionals." McCarthy smacked one, who worryingly scanned the device up and down.

"I bet," Debra muttered.

"Hey, Deb," McCarthy said.

"Yeah."

"I don't tell you this enough, but it's an honor working with you."

Debra smiled. "The feeling's mutual."

It did not take long for the officers to free her, and they did so while only causing her a little pain. She came to her knees with McCarthy's help.

"Take it easy now," McCarthy coaxed. "We got an ambulance on the way."

Debra shook her head. "I'm fine. We'll deal with that later. But we got something to do first."

McCarthy looked at her like a puppy dog, his head cocked, his eyes wide and curious. "And what the hell is that?"

Debra smiled. "We gotta check the wine caves."

———

It took the police less than an hour to locate the false barrel. The first clue was the fact that it was empty, though several other barrels were empty. The bigger giveaway was the fact that it rested on small, nearly invisible wheels. Two officers pulled it away from the wall, but one could have easily accomplished the task. Different, lighter materials were used to construct the barrel, yet it looked like the others in the wine cave.

The bigger issue was unlocking the door behind the barrel. The techies took over two hours to accomplish that feat, and in that time, Debra reluctantly consented to receiving on-site medical attention. Bill had also made his way to the scene and waited for her outside the premises. While waiting for the nerds to crack the code, she chatted with him from behind the Holland entrance bars, blowing him a kiss once she learned they had bypassed the lock.

When she returned, she saw McCarthy waiting by the open door. He appeared tired, but also satisfied. "Ready, boss?" he asked.

She nodded. "Ready. Let's roll."

Beyond the door awaited a long hallway, lit only by a few dull lights. The police made their way through, with Debra gingerly leading the charge. Thirty seconds later, they entered Jacob's room.

The most striking aspect of the room was the fact that pictures of Ethan's family covered it from top to bottom. Otherwise, there was a table that rested in the middle along with a television that hung from the ceiling of one corner. A small printer sat on the side of the table.

"Jesus Christ," Debra whispered under her breath.

McCarthy shook his head and replied, "He has no place here."

Filing cabinets lined the walls. She approached one as she slipped on gloves. She gingerly attempted to open it, and it slid open without issue, unlocked. Inside, the cabinet contained many folders. She pulled one out at random and opened it.

The folder contained pictures and notes. At first glance, the pictures appeared similar to the ones that hung on the wall. She grabbed a picture from the folder to compare it to those that Jacob hung. In the picture that hung in front of Debra, Jenna ran through a wooded area, her hands in the air, a smile on her face. The picture in Debra's hand also showed Jenna, but contained Ethan, though the picture caught him with an awkward expression, as if he was in the middle of saying something.

"What's the difference?" McCarthy asked, startling her.

"What do you mean?"

"Difference between what you're holding and what this psycho hung on the wall."

She shrugged. "No idea. If I had to guess, he hung the ones he liked."

She placed the picture back where it had been in the folder and focused on one of Jacob's notes. It contained dates and times, with a header that read "JENNA." This note contained descriptions about her school activities. The details were horrifying. He had jogged down minor details such as where she sat at lunch, where she ate, and her favorite playground activities. Apparently, Jenna loved the monkey bars.

Debra shuddered, replaced the notes, and slipped the folder back into the cabinet. Her attention turned to the desk in the middle of the room, where a single red folder rested.

Debra approached and noticed the name "DEBRA FOLEY" scribbled on the front of the folder in large, fat font. With a gloved hand, she lifted the folder and pulled out the first page, a full-color picture of Charlotte.

36

ONE YEAR LATER

Debra poured through the same data and files for the thousandth time. Every time, she hoped to find something new, realize something she missed before. She once read that the definition of insanity was doing the same thing twice and expecting a different result. She now understood the phrase's meaning and took it to heart.

Over the last year, her faculties faded. It took her longer to remember things. She pushed details like phone numbers and birthdays to the back of her mind. Anything that did not relate to Charlotte or Jacob took a backseat to everything else.

Her addictive personality was no secret. A shrink diagnosed her with such after a few visits during her rambling post-college years. But, what did that even mean? Extreme passion meant addiction? She did not smoke or drink or use drugs. Her addiction was productive, perhaps the most productive passion one could have: stopping a killer.

But, her addiction had victims, even she would admit that. Other cases piled up on her desk until, quietly, someone redistributed them to other officers. With the cases she took, she often caught herself trying to tie them to Jacob. He waited in every file and behind every bush. Jacob remained an omnipresent fixture in her life and would remain so until she busted him.

Her other cases weren't the biggest issue, though. She worked with competent officers who could assist. No, the biggest casualty of her addiction was her marriage. Jacob had dug a Grand Canyon-sized pit in her relationship. In her entire life, she had only loved two men: her father and Bill. Another man lay between Bill and Debra, and she needed to cast him out of their bed.

But perhaps she should refocus on psychologically pushing him out. Jacob was not stupid. He likely fled to another country on the other side of the world. He had the money and resources to make it happen.

Yes, she thought. *It's time.*

She pulled out her phone and dialed Bill, who picked up after one ring.

"Hey," he said in a concerned tone. "Everything okay?"

"Yes, of course it is. Why would you assume things weren't okay?"

"You just never call anymore when you're at work. Not unless something's wrong."

His response floored her. She used to check in with him multiple times a day. Now, she didn't even call and hadn't realized that she stopped?

"Everything's fine, babe," she replied. "I just wanted to hear your voice."

"Oh." He sounded dubious. "Well, it's good to hear yours, too."

"Quick question. Would you mind if I picked up Charlotte today?"

He paused for a beat before saying, "Sure. But I don't mind doing it if you're busy."

"No, I want to. Also, I had an idea. How about you take me out on a date this weekend?"

"That sounds great. Charlotte likes that new place down the street, the one with the good chicken as she calls it. I forget the name. Gordon's or something?"

"I didn't say take *us* out. I said take *me* out. Get a babysitter and let's go have some fun."

The line went quiet for a few seconds before he said, "Just you and me?"

"Yeah, baby," she leaned into the phone. "Just you and me."

"That sounds, well, amazing. But you sure you're ready?"

"Yeah. I'm sure. I'm ready to be a wife again, ready to live again. And I'm so sorry it's taken me this long."

"Baby," his voice cracked. "We've got forever. A year is nothing."

"That's right," she replied, her eyes filling with tears. "We've got forever." In her periphery, she noticed McCarthy, her tears distorting his figure that now carried much less weight.

"I got to go," she told Bill. "Love you."

"I love you, too."

She broke the connection and looked up as she rubbed her eyes, trying to play off her tears as fatigue.

"I can come back," McCarthy said.

"No, no, it's fine," Debra motioned towards the seat by her desk. "What's up?"

He sat and surveyed her with exhausted eyes. "I wish there was something up, but they still ain't pulling up nothing."

"So, just the three bodies, then?"

"Yup. Jodi Johnston and the two others we haven't identified yet due to decomposition. The theory is he picked up homeless folks and brought them there. That may be crap, but it sort of makes sense."

"Yeah," she replied, her eyes on the floor. "He had almost endless money and desperate people will do desperate things."

He sighed. "Guess so. I'll call you if they find anything else."

"No more sightings?"

"Not a one. Guy's a ghost, Deb. Disappeared like a fart in the wind."

She shuddered. "Stop that, I hate that expression."

"Apt, though."

"Apt? Where did you learn that?"

"Eh, I've been takin' some classes. What do they call it? Auditing?"

"Really? Why?"

"Well, I'm just, like, not so good with words. I figured if I got better, I could think more like you. That may not make much sense, but whatever. It seems to be working."

"Good, I'm glad. Because I've been running blind lately."

"That'll change."

"Yeah?"

"Yeah. Great doesn't leave forever. It always comes back." He stood and headed to the door. He then turned and said, "By the way, I chatted with Ethan recently."

Her eyes grew wide. "Yeah? How's he doing?"

"Great. At least he sounds it. Joined the district attorney's office down in San Francisco."

"No shit?" She considered this development. "Wonder why he'd do that."

McCarthy shrugged. "Who knows. Maybe he wanted to be closer to the action, know what's going on. Not like he needs the dough."

"Did he say how Jenna's doing?"

McCarthy nodded slowly. "Yeah. He said she's coming along. Day at a time, you know?"

"I do."

"Anyway," McCarthy said as he adjusted his uniform, obviously uncomfortable with the conversation. "I'm grabbing some lunch from Freddy's. Need anything?"

"No, I'm fine. Thank you."

He left, and she sat in contemplation. She was glad that Ethan seemed to be doing well, but the lack of clarity about Jenna gave her pause. She needed to visit her, and soon.

McCarthy words rung in her mind. Great always comes back. What the hell did that mean? Probably nothing, but sometimes McCarthy's mind worked in mysterious ways, oddly insightful ways.

She considered the situation. So many unnecessary deaths. Scars on countless people. And for what? To fulfill the desires of a creep? It was unfair, all of it. She had dealt with nutbags her entire career—both on the streets and in her place of work—and no one else had even approached Jacob's level of crazy.

And this exact instability gave her pause about her prior conclusions. Yes, a sane person would have fled the country, especially one with Jacob's money. But Jacob? He rarely did things the normal way, the predictable way. He thrived in creating waves and then surfing them.

Either way, it didn't matter. Jacob's impulsiveness and her desire to reconnect with her husband were not competing propositions. She was a far better cop when she had a stable marriage and a bunch of cases dividing her attention.

She glanced at the clock on her phone and saw it was time to pick up Charlotte from school. She stood and smiled. Charlotte beat any Holland hangover. Debra's day was about to get much better.

She arrived and parked near the pickup and drop-off zone, which was a madhouse at the end of the school day. Children twirled and ran, burning off their remaining energy before their parents picked them up and asked endless questions about the day. Debra didn't judge. She was no different. And she figured

Charlotte was like the rest of the kids when she shrugged and said, "It was okay."

She stepped out and studied the mass of kids but did not immediately spot Charlotte. Debra rarely did. Charlotte was small for her age.

Debra walked up and through the crowd, reviewing each child. Bobby, Sandy, Jamie, Gina. All friends of Charlotte, but no Charlotte.

Debra noticed Quinn, Charlotte's best friend, across the lot. Debra flagged down Quinn, who ran over with a skip in her step.

"Hey there, Mrs. Paxton," she greeted Debra with a wide smile. "How are you?"

"I'm great, dear. Have you seen Charlotte?"

"Yeah, she was here a little while ago. She wanders off sometimes to think."

"She does?" Debra hadn't realized this. "Any idea where?"

"She didn't tell me. Just said she'd be back before you got here. She never leaves for more than a few minutes."

"How often does she do this?"

Quinn shrugged. "Not sure. She's just a loner sometimes."

A loner, Debra considered. Perhaps she didn't understand her daughter as well as she imagined. Had Jacob pushed her away as well? It was possible. She had been distracted despite her best efforts to focus on Charlotte.

"Thanks, sweetie. Let me know if you see her. I'm going to go talk to Ms. Buckley."

"Cool. Later, Mrs. Paxton!"

"Later!" Debra sounded way less cool than Quinn saying that.

Debra navigated the labyrinth of middle school hallways, the walls lined with blue lockers and fliers. She liked this school. The kids were friendly, and the teachers were understanding.

Especially Ms. Buckley, a pretty 25-year-old who moved with a pep in her step and a smile on her face.

Debra walked into the classroom and saw Ms. Buckley busily cleaning after the kids. She soon noticed Debra and said, "Hi, Mrs. Paxton! How may I help you?"

"Hi. I can't seem to find Charlotte."

"She's not in the pickup zone?"

"No, unfortunately. Quinn says she sometimes wanders off alone."

"Yeah, I've caught her doing that a few times. I'd check the playground. If she's not there, I'll make an announcement. We'll find her."

"Thanks," Debra replied. "I appreciate it."

She made her way through the hallways and, after two turns, was in front of the entry to the playground. She stepped out and cool air washed over her. The kids looked up when she walked out but went back to playing after confirming Debra wasn't a teacher.

Debra reviewed each kid and finally spotted Charlotte. As Debra approached, Charlotte waved and ran towards Debra.

"Hey, momma!" Charlotte screamed as she ran into Debra's arms.

"Hey, baby." She gave Charlotte a firm squeeze. "Why are you out here? You had me worried."

"Sorry, momma. I was just playing out here and forgot about the time." When Charlotte pulled away, she asked, "Where's Dad?"

"Oh," Debra replied, "I thought I'd try picking you up more often. Is that okay?"

"Yeah!" Charlotte exclaimed.

"Great! Now, what did you learn about today?"

"A bunch of stuff." Charlotte took Debra's hand and they walked towards the car, Debra gripping hard. Charlotte grasped a lollipop with her free hand that she licked as they walked. "We learned a lot about dinosaurs today. See, I always thought there was just a Brontosaurus. But the teacher said there was also a Diplodocus that came before the Brontosaurus. You know, I'm not sure which one came first. Can't remember. They looked kinda similar, ate the same stuff, but I guess the Brontosaurus had a thicker neck. Anyway, I'm just saying there are so many dinosaurs I didn't know about. I always learned about the same ones, T-Rex, Velociraptors. But there's, like, a bunch more. Hundreds more!"

Debra smiled in response to Charlotte's rant and said, "That's wonderful, baby. And super interesting."

"It really is. Hey, Mom," she muttered.

"Yeah?"

"Um, I dunno." Charlotte diverted her eyes from Debra.

Debra lightly placed her hands under Charlotte's chin and shifted her head back so that she looked squarely at Debra. "No, tell me. What's on your mind?"

"Are you sure you can pick me up more? I know you got work."

Debra shrugged and said, "I know I've been working a lot, but I've also been thinking. I figured some things are more important than work. Work will always be there. But you learning about Diplodocuses won't be. Does that make sense?"

"Sort of," Charlotte replied, her neck craned, and her eyes fixed on Debra.

"Don't worry," Debra replied. "It will someday. Now, tell me again. What's the difference between a Diplodocus and Brontosaurus?"

Charlotte beamed a toothy grin with the lollipop stick extending from her teeth and said, "I drew a picture of a Diplodocus! It's in my backpack."

Charlotte continued to talk as they walked, but after she mentioned her backpack, Debra instinctively glanced at it, and something about the pink JanSport bag distracted Debra. Most of it appeared normal. A pink ribbon tied to the top buckle. A coke stain below the JanSport logo and the name CHARLOTTE written out in bold above it.

She noticed something unusual, though: A yellow button with the phrase "LOOK INSIDE!" was pinned to the backpack. Charlotte did not pin any button to her bag.

She pulled Charlotte back, stopping her in her tracks. "Let's take a look at this Brontosaurus picture," Debra said before letting go of Charlotte's hand.

"Diplodocus!" Charlotte chided with a grin as she handed Debra the backpack.

Carefully, Debra unzipped the bag and peered inside. As she rummaged through the bag, her hands sensed something unusual: grainy wood. She pulled out a small object and reviewed it closely, the horror of the situation coming into focus.

Debra held a wine cork stamped with the Holland Vineyard logo. But that wasn't the only stamp on the cork. On the other side, Debra saw another stamp in the shape of a winking face: ";)."

"What is it, momma?" Charlotte asked.

Debra knelt to look Charlotte in the eyes, held up the cork, and asked, "Where did you get this?"

"Oh!" Charlotte said with a smile. "I forgot to tell you. While I was waiting for you, I met a new friend. He was kind of funny looking, but nice. He gave me that pin, the wood thing, and this lollipop!" Charlotte showed Debra the lollipop, and Debra grabbed it from her. She studied the lollipop, its color nauseated her.

Blood-red.

ABOUT THE AUTHOR

Outside of his family, Jason Huebinger has two great loves in his life—the law and writing. Jason is a proud alum and fan of Texas A&M and Notre Dame, and he scares his dog when he roots for either. He has a beautiful wife, Yasmin, whose only flaw is she's an LSU fan. By day, Jason is a lawyer who specializes in labor and employment litigation. Jason's biggest writing influences are John Irving and Stephen King, and he tries to incorporate elements of both into whatever he writes. *The Private Reserve* is Jason's first novel for Winding Road Stories.